The
Duke's
Diary

The Duke's Diary

ashtyn newbold

THREE LEAF
PUBLISHING

CHAPTER 1

Choosing what to wear for my first kidnapping was more difficult than I had expected.

I stared at the contents of my wardrobe, biting the tip of my fingernail. The various fabrics and colors blurred together. Was it best to wear a dull color—perhaps beige, brown, or black? Or was something more vibrant a better choice? I reached for my bright yellow spencer jacket, held it up in front of me, and stood in front of the looking glass.

I grinned at my reflection. A giggle escaped my throat.

Yes. Yellow was the perfect choice. I needed to ensure I was noticed. The yellow spencer with my bright white gown beneath it would be sure to catch my father's eye from the window of his study when my kidnapper swept me away.

My heart raced as I slid my arms into the long sleeves of the jacket and fastened the buttons. Charlie, my elder brother, had already sneaked my trunk to the carriage that would be waiting beyond the treeline—the one that would take me to my hiding place in Northumberland. I had only packed a few items in order to make my disappearance appear accidental. A kidnapper wouldn't allow me to bring all my favorite gowns, now would he? As frightening as the ordeal was, I felt like a ninny with the smile that was plastered on my face. How much time did I have? I checked the pocket watch on my writing desk.

Good.

I still had time to write the beginning of the story.

Nestling into my chair, I dipped my quill, touching the tip to a fresh page in an empty book. I had only written fictional stories up until now, but I had a feeling that my upcoming adventure would be worth documenting. My real life had always been too dull to write about. The novels I had written were full of danger and romance and secrets, and finally my life was about to include at least two of those things.

I rubbed the feather across my lower lip. How should it begin? I couldn't very well write it as a novel if I had no idea how the story was going to end. Perhaps these writings would serve me better as a diary of sorts. If I took notes about all my experiences, then I could draft it all into a novel when the adventure was over.

I gave a swift nod, agreeing with my own logic as I came up with a title. This entire adventure was about the year leading up to my twenty-first birthday, so I titled it:

Nora's Coming of Age Diary
June 27, 1816

Yellow is a rather cheerful color to wear on the day of my kidnapping, but most young ladies, I imagine, do not have the chance to prepare for a kidnapping the way I have. That is a dreadful thought. Speaking of dreadful thoughts, with each day that passes, Father makes further plans for my marriage to Mr. Verwood. I shudder to even write his name.

If there is to be a villain in this story, Mr. Verwood is the only suitable character—besides Father, of course.

Mr. Verwood is more than twice my age and has a thick mustache that is constantly dusted with snuff and particles of his most recent meal. Each time he looks at me, I feel like a horse being appraised. After returning from Bath, I overheard my father and Mr. Verwood in the study, discussing what price my father required for me. I nearly barged inside and informed them that I am not for sale, but the truth of the matter is that I can indeed be forced to marry that revolting man, at least for another year and a week.

It does sound quite dismal, but do not fret. There are two heroes in this story, and an additional heroine as well.

First, my brother, Charlie. He has never agreed with my father's plans for me, so he has made arrangements with his best friend, the Duke of Heywood, to have me secretly transported to a place where I will be kept hidden for the upcoming year. The duke—who I shall refer to as Timothy, is my kidnapper. As my kidnapper, one might think he was the villain. He often has a villainous demeanor to someone who doesn't know him as well as I do. He can certainly be a bit irritable or peevish, but he is actually the second hero. I suspect he will look quite intimidating and handsome in his highwayman disguise.

Could this journey to Northumberland include the danger element of my story?

I laughed under my breath.

In truth, there is nothing dangerous about Timothy. He is the best of men. He and Charlie have always protected me, and they have gone to these great lengths to ensure my father believes I won't be returning. Any search will be in vain by the time I reach the old hunting lodge, Foxwell House, in Northumberland. Timothy will be making frequent visits to help ensure I am safe and comfortable.

Finally, Anne (Lady Daventry), Charlie's new sister-in-law, has been kind enough to accompany me on the journey and live with me at the hunting lodge for the entire year. Anne will be acting as my sister, and I will assume the false identity of 'Miss Jane Flowers.' No one shall know that I am Lady Leonora, or that my father is the Marquess of Swindon.

As you can see, there are many secrets involved in this tale as well.

I paused, stretching my hand as I blew the ink dry. There was still room for a few more lines.

Any good story ought to include elements of romance, but I'm afraid it will have to wait until the end of the year when I come out of hiding and travel to London to find a husband of my own choosing. Once I've reached the age of majority, any union will not require my father's approval, and I shall be free to marry for love.

A thrill raced across my skin. Perhaps the story could include romance after all. I would simply have to be patient. A year was a very long time, and London still seemed like a distant dream. My heart raced as I read over what I had just written. It didn't seem real.

The door creaked behind me, making me jump. I whirled around.

Father stood in the doorway. I snapped my diary closed. His large frame was partially shadowed, dark hair swirled inward around his long side whiskers. His pipe was clamped between his teeth, and a plume of smoke filled my room. The smell had always made my stomach hurt.

"Writing your silly stories again, are you?" His raspy voice made my muscles tense. "You are fortunate Mr. Verwood doesn't care to have an intelligent wife."

I swallowed, standing cautiously from my desk. "I think writing makes me more intelligent."

He walked toward me, and I took a step backward, crashing into my desk. I clenched my jaw.

Father eyed my diary, and my heart plummeted. Why had I been foolish enough to write down the entire plan? If he saw it, everything would be ruined. He reached for it, and I nearly dove in front of him. Despair wrenched at my heart as he examined the leather cover. I counted my heartbeats, each one growing louder in my ears.

His grey eyes met mine, and then he dropped the diary onto the floor with a thud. He kicked it toward the hearth, but it didn't quite reach. I held perfectly still. *Let it be burned.* At least then he wouldn't read it.

He was too lazy to kick it again. Instead, he took another breath from his pipe, exhaling far too close to my face. "Mr. Verwood would like to meet you again in the morning. We will make wedding preparations soon." He started toward the door, then turned around one more time. "He requests that you wear your pink dress tomorrow."

My stomach lurched, but I nodded.

Father clamped his pipe between his teeth again and

marched out of my room. The tension in my body released, and I hurried to retrieve my diary from the floor. I smoothed the soot from the cover, holding it close to my chest. I took several deep breaths, trying to calm my shaking legs. Father rarely barged into my room in such a manner, and it had completely unnerved me. The thought of complying with Mr. Verwood's request for which dress to wear when he came calling the next day was enough to make me vomit.

My kidnapping could not have come at a more welcome time.

I returned to my desk, putting my face in my hands as I willed myself to relax. Just when my breathing began to slow, my door opened a second time.

I jumped all the way out of my chair, relieved to see my brother, and not Father, slipping into the room. "Charlie! You frightened me." My nerves were tight, my heart racing in my chest. I couldn't deny that there was much that could go wrong with the kidnapping plan. As daring and adventurous as it all sounded, it could end in disaster. What if we were caught? What if my father organized a search more extensive than what Charlie anticipated? What if I was eventually found?

"Father is in his study. It's almost time," Charlie said, releasing a nervous breath of his own. His dark curls stuck out all over his head the same way my blonde ones did.

I crossed the room, an anxious bounce in my step. "Is Timothy here?"

Charlie nodded.

I swallowed, rubbing the palms of my hands over my skirts. I knew the rest of the plan. I had been rehearsing it in my mind for days.

Taking a long glance around the room, a pang of grief

raked over my skin. Was this the last time I would see my bedchamber? My childhood had been one of strange independence, having never known my mother and having a father who was indifferent to me. I had roamed the woods and grounds with Charlie and Timothy, rarely associating with other young ladies, or being accepted by them. I had never had a governess, and my knowledge of dancing and other talents was severely lacking. My behaviors were too wild, my disposition too exuberant, Father had told me. Even my hair could not be tamed. Nor could my imagination. I had spent many hours at my writing desk, hunched over countless sheets of foolscap. Leaving behind the place all those memories had been made brought up more emotions than I had expected.

Going into the unknown was as thrilling as it was terrifying. My future was unwritten, and the possibilities were overwhelming. I had always been able to plan what the next day of my life would look like. I would awake, call my maid to help me dress, eat, read, write, embroider, practice the pianoforte, eat again, drink tea, walk outside, and sleep. Rarely was there any variation or unpredictability.

Today, however, I was standing on the edge of a precipice. I no longer knew what came next. All I knew was that if we succeeded, what came next *wouldn't* be Mr. Verwood and his snuff-and-breadcrumb-coated mustache. That reason alone was enough to make me jump off the edge.

"Will you visit me?" I asked Charlie for what must have been the tenth time. I needed reassurance more than I cared to admit.

"Staying at the estate will be the best way to avoid suspicion, but Timothy will visit you at least every three months." He walked closer and wrapped his arms around me. I sniffed as I buried my face in his shoulder. Charlie was taking a bold risk by hiding me from my father, and I was forever grateful. "I promise I will try to visit. Henrietta will come too."

I pulled back to offer a teasing smile. "I would hope so. I wouldn't dare ask you to be parted from your new wife so soon."

He smirked. He didn't like when I accused him of having such romantic inclinations, but he could no longer deny his change of character. He was madly in love with his wife, and it inspired me. I wanted to love someone just as much one day.

"Henrietta would be happy to visit you and Anne at Foxwell House," Charlie said.

I nodded. Even Henrietta was making sacrifices to enable my escape. She was very close with her sister, Anne, who she was willing to be parted with for so long to ensure I was safe and in good company. Tears stung my eyes. I had never been one to easily contain my emotions.

Charlie groaned, a soft smile on his lips. "Don't turn into a watering pot now, Leonora."

I sniffed as a tear slid down my cheek. "Perhaps 'Miss Jane Flowers' has a weaker constitution."

"A watering pot named Miss Flowers? That is quite fitting."

I snorted, wiping beneath my eyes. "I can do this," I said around a deep breath.

"You can. It will be an adventure, and I would trust Timothy with my life—and yours. No harm will come to you. I will keep Father in the dark. He will be none the wiser."

That was the part that made me hesitate. Father wasn't a

fool. How could I ensure he didn't suspect Charlie or even Timothy for creating such an elaborate ruse? How could we make the kidnapping appear realistic from Father's view in his study? How could we escape before we were caught? Dozens of questions flitted through my mind, making me lightheaded.

I dried my tears and lifted my chin, looking Charlie straight in the eye. "Very well, then. I'm ready to be kidnapped."

My feet sank into the soggy grass as I walked along the outskirts of the lawn. I usually took a walk around the same time of day, following the same route. The sun was beginning to set, sucking away the last of the daylight from the sky. As I walked along the edge of the woods, a chill ran over my spine. I knew it wasn't a real kidnapping, but I still didn't know when Timothy would run out from the trees. I jumped when I heard a twig snap, but it was under my own foot. A nervous laugh burst out of my chest.

I glanced at the house—at the window of Father's study. He was so far away. I could see the outline of his head and shoulders, and Charlie's as well. I was within their sight. If I screamed loud enough, Father would hear me. He would see Timothy tug me backward into the trees, and he would have every reason to believe that I had been abducted.

I walked slower, squinting into the woods. Why hadn't I heard Timothy yet? Not even a rustle. My pulse raced as I searched for him between the trees. I needed to stay out in the open, but my curiosity burned. Where was he?

Just as the thought crossed my mind, a set of strong arms wrapped around me from behind.

A scream burst out of my mouth, and I instinctively thrashed my arms.

"Stand and deliver," Timothy's voice whispered in my ear.

I instantly relaxed, though my heart still hammered. I laughed. "I am already standing."

"What are you doing?" his gruff whisper carried a hint of panic. "Don't stop moving."

It took me a moment to realize what he meant. If I were actually being kidnapped, I would still be thrashing and screaming. I let out another scream, this one louder than the first, thrashing back and forth and kicking my legs when Timothy lifted me off the ground.

"That's better," he muttered. My heels dragged in the wet grass as he pulled me slowly into the trees, making the struggle last long enough to give Charlie time to point it out to our father. At least I hoped so.

I didn't dare look up at the window. There wasn't time.

The very moment we were behind the cover of the trees, Timothy released me, taking my hand as we ran toward the waiting carriage.

"Why did you sneak up on me like that?" I asked, breathless, taking my first glance at him.

"Your scream needed to be authentic," he said, offering his hand again to help me into the carriage. "I didn't trust your acting abilities."

He wore a venetian mask over his eyes with a cloak draped over his shoulders and the top of his head. He looked just like a highwayman. If I hadn't known it was Timothy, I wouldn't have recognized him. A laugh burst out of my mouth, a broad smile tugging on my lips. "You look ridiculous."

He didn't say a word as I lunged into the carriage and sat on the available cushion across from Anne. Timothy slammed the door closed and jumped into the coach box. The horses jolted into motion. My legs and hands shook as the interior of the carriage filled with silence.

Anne sat across from me, and we exchanged a nervous glance in greeting. Her pale skin contrasted with her hazel eyes and dark hair in the fading daylight. We both braced ourselves against the walls of the carriage as we moved over the bumpy ground. Charlie's plan had been to witness the kidnapping with our father, and then run out to the stables with his pistol and a horse, chasing after us himself. He would return to Father with the 'horrible news' that he had not caught up to us. I could only hope Charlie was a better actor than I was. I already knew Henrietta was not, so I prayed she would remain distant from my father during the ordeal.

"Anne, it is so good to see you again." I gave her a bright smile, one that seemed to surprise her. "I cannot thank you enough for accompanying me. I shall never be able to repay you."

The corners of her eyes pinched in a slight smile, but she still watched the windows anxiously. "I told you. I have come for selfish reasons as well. I longed for an escape and adventure of my own."

She had never struck me as a woman who would crave adventure. At twenty-seven, she was completely grown up, always regal and elegant, even as we bounced uncontrollably in the wild carriage. Why was Timothy driving so recklessly anyway? My stomach lurched with every bump.

From behind the coach, I thought I heard another set of

hooves. Just as the thought crossed my mind, our carriage slowly came to a halt. I sat up straighter, my breath lodging in my throat. "Why have we stopped?" I whispered, meeting Anne's wide eyes.

We both stared at the carriage door.

I shrieked when it opened, slapping a hand over my mouth.

"*Lud*—Nora, it's me." Timothy tore his venetian mask off his eyes, revealing his face. He lowered the hood of his cloak, raking a hand over his sandstone hair. His eyes were usually light brown, almost golden, but tonight they looked darker, especially now that the sun had fully set. A hint of amusement crossed his expression.

"Sorry," I said, forgetting to move my hand from my mouth. The word was muffled. "Why did we stop?"

In answer to my question, Charlie stepped up behind Timothy, leading his horse by the reins as he walked closer to the door. "Father witnessed the entire thing. I assured him I would try to catch you. When I return home I'll tell him your captor took you on horseback, and I'll provide an inaccurate description of both the horse and the man perchance Father does choose to begin a search."

A question burned on my tongue, my heart pounding. "Was Father...upset? Is he worried?"

Charlie's jaw tightened. "Yes, but not for the right reasons."

The truth settled over my shoulders. If I wasn't found, Father wouldn't be upset to have lost his daughter. He would be upset to have lost the sum Mr. Verwood would have paid to marry me. The pain that blossomed around my heart was not new—but moments like this served to water it, keeping it ever present and alive.

"I will not delay you," Charlie said. "Tomorrow I will leave the fake ransom note at the doorstep. The price will be beyond what Father can afford."

I frowned. "Do you suppose he will ask a friend for assistance? Or obtain a loan?"

Charlie shook his head with a grim expression. "Father does not have many friends, and none who would loan him money considering his debts. Mr. Verwood is the only one who might offer to pay the ransom, but then Father wouldn't be the one to receive the money he hoped to acquire from Mr. Verwood's marriage to you. It is my guess that Father will choose to wait—to keep the ordeal quiet in the hopes that your kidnapper will surrender when he doesn't obtain the money and bring you home. It will be interesting to see what lies Father tells Mr. Verwood about your whereabouts."

I exchanged a glance with Timothy. My 'kidnapper' had plenty of money of his own, but he didn't want to match Mr. Verwood's sum in order to appease my father. Timothy hated my father and refused to see him rewarded for trying to profit from my misery. Once the year was passed, Timothy would show his generosity in yet another way by funding my season which would enable me to find a husband that could keep me far from my father's reach forever. The stakes were high enough to make my head spin.

"You are safe to resume your journey at a comfortable pace," Charlie said, giving my hand a squeeze. "Timothy has made all the preparations. You will be safe with him."

I nodded, biting back my tears. "Thank you, Charlie." My gaze slid to Timothy, those dark eyes connecting with mine. "And thank you, Timothy. I didn't mean it when I said you looked ridiculous. You looked nefarious and...dangerous." I gave a bright smile.

He scoffed, half his mouth twitching upward. "Coming from you, I will take that as a compliment." He turned and walked away, presumably back to the coach box.

With one last encouraging smile, Charlie closed the door, leaving me alone with Anne once again. She was still looking in the direction of the door, and for a fleeting moment, I wondered if she was regretting coming with me. Guilt drove a blade into my chest. What was going through her mind?

Finally she spoke, her voice gentle and quiet. "He must care for you a great deal."

I smiled, blinking away my tears. "There is nothing Charlie wouldn't do for those he loves."

Anne gave a light laugh. "I do agree, but I meant the duke."

"Timothy?" I gave a swift nod. "Oh, yes. He has always protected me as a brother would. I am forever grateful."

Anne gave a slow nod as if she understood, but it wasn't entirely convincing.

Perhaps it wasn't necessary, but my words rambled out before I could stop them. "There is nothing else between us if that is what you are wondering. I suppose I should make that entirely clear, perchance you had any interest in Timothy yourself. I should hate for you to think that I am an obstacle of any sort. He views me as a sister, I am certain of it, and there will be plenty of proof of that if you pay attention to our interactions." I punctuated my words with a wide smile. Yes, Timothy was handsome. Very handsome. I had always tried my best not to notice.

It never seemed to work.

I glanced out the window, catching sight of his face as he exchanged a few more words with Charlie.

Anne's eyes widened. "Oh—no, Leonora, I am not interested in the duke." She laughed.

"Your heart is otherwise engaged," I said with a nod. "Henrietta did mention that."

The lightness in Anne's expression faded. "She does like to speak of Miles."

"Miles Holland, is it? He went away to India?"

"Yes." Anne wrung her fingers together in her lap. "I may never see him again." She shrugged. "So I couldn't resist the opportunity to travel and explore a new place."

Though her mouth was smiling, I noted the sad, downward tilt at the corner of her eyes. How would it feel to love someone who was so unreachable? I could only imagine how torturous it would be to carry such feelings without knowing if they were returned…or if they *ever* would be.

I jerked forward as the carriage set off to our destination.

CHAPTER 2

According to the plan, we would travel for as long as the current team of horses could manage before stopping to rest for the night. It had been hours, and my back ached. After seeing miles of open country, we came into the nearest town, stopping at our first inn. The windows were flooded with candlelight, and an iron sign hung above the door.

The Lion's Crown.

There were few travelers and townsfolk on the street, and I was desperate to jump out and stretch my legs. I took a deep breath and rapped on the roof of the carriage three times, grinning as I waited for Timothy to notice.

We stopped moving when we entered the courtyard, and Timothy tugged the door open. His eyes were wide, reflecting the moonlight. One eyebrow lifted. "What was that for?"

"I wanted to see if you were paying attention. I saw the inn from the window."

He leaned one hand against the carriage door frame. "If anyone was likely to not be paying attention, it's you. I was certain you would be sleeping in here by now."

I laughed. "I couldn't dream of it, not with the wild nature of your driving. You've made Anne ill." I nodded toward Anne, who appeared paler than usual.

"I'm perfectly well," Anne said in a tight voice, though she looked on the brink of vomiting.

"I'm afraid your new coachman is even more wild with the reins," Timothy said.

"Truly?" My stomach sank. I caught sight of a chaise across the courtyard where our new coachman, John, had left it. Timothy would travel separately for the rest of the journey to ensure he was not seen with Anne or me should we be recognized. John was employed by Timothy, so I knew I could trust him.

"You'll discover whether or not I'm jesting when you resume the journey in the morning."

My eyes narrowed. Timothy's smile was difficult to read.

"You two go inside first," he said, changing the subject. "I'll come shortly." He glanced in all directions as he helped Anne and me out of the carriage and transferred his own trunk to the chaise across the courtyard.

I glanced at him from over my shoulder as I followed Anne around the front of the inn. I wrung my fingers together, tipping my head up to look at the iron sign. Lions did not wear crowns. That was my first thought as I followed Anne inside. The floor creaked under my feet, the scent of ale and meat flooding my nostrils from down the hall. I grimaced when I smelled something else.

Fish. Perhaps mildew.

I had never traveled far enough to require the use of an inn, so I didn't have anything to compare the Lion's Crown to. From the wrinkle on Anne's nose, I suspected this was not the most enticing establishment she had ever seen. Dust coated all the sconces on the walls, and the rug beneath my feet had a dark stain along one side. I stared at it, swallowing hard. I didn't dare guess what it could be.

Several servants stepped into position as an older woman with an apron bustled forward. I assumed she was the innkeeper's wife. A man who appeared to be similar in age to her was sleeping in a nearby chair, mouth agape, chin resting on his chest. The woman threw a scowl in his direction before she addressed us.

"Evening, mistresses. How may we be of service?" Her bushy eyebrows were made up of dark brown and gray hairs, each sticking in a different direction. "Food? Beds?"

"Both, please," Anne said.

My stomach grumbled. From down the corridor, I could hear the voices of the other guests. It seemed we weren't the only travelers to stop at the Lion's Crown so late at night.

The woman eyed Anne from the top of her head down to her toes, then did the same to me. I shifted backward a step, a jolt of nervousness entering my stomach. I didn't know what measures my father would take to locate me, but I didn't want to leave any traces at the inns we stayed at. If this woman remembered any details of my appearance, my father could know the direction in which my journey had begun.

The woman's thick eyebrows contracted as she observed my skittish reaction to her appraisal. She was obviously taking note of our manner of dress to determine which room to offer and what price she might fetch for it. I should have been accustomed to such appraisal, given the manner my father and Mr. Verwood looked upon me at every interaction.

"I've two rooms available," she said. "I can offer ye the finest one. Ye might find the other to be beneath yer tastes." She eyed me again, and I began regretting my choice of the yellow spencer jacket. It was fine, and this woman could clearly see that. "Room number six just up the stairs." She handed Anne a key. "Ye may take a seat over there. If ye be wantin' food, I can fetch ye a meal of beef or fish."

I glanced at Anne, intent to follow her lead. "I would like fish, please," she said.

The woman nodded, turning her gaze to me.

"Beef, please," I said with a smile.

The woman scowled, as if my cheerfulness was offensive. "When it suits ye, I'll show ye to yer room." She glanced at a nearby servant, who sprung into action down the corridor toward the kitchen.

"Thank you," Anne said, offering a gracious nod and starting toward the scant furnishings to the left. She chose the least dirty of the chairs, and I selected a red settee with sunken cushions. When I sat down, I noticed what appeared to be grey cat hair clinging to the arm rest. I stared at the trail of fur that led down to the cushion I was sitting on. Blast it all. Now it would be on my skirts too.

My gaze roamed around the room, at the various animal heads mounted on the walls, the dust-coated artwork, and the walnut bookcase beside me. My gaze traveled up and up.

I jumped.

A grey cat perched on top of the bookcase, bright green eyes fixed on me. Its tail swayed back and forth, its back arched slightly.

"Heavens, I'm hungry," Anne said in a quiet voice. "I wonder how the fish here tastes."

"Anne," I hissed under by breath, not daring to take my eyes off the cat, who seemed to be wondering how *I* would taste. Its paws were spread, eyes wide and menacing. I gulped. Had I stolen its favorite seat? It was clear that the fur I was sitting on belonged to the cat, and it seemed that he assumed the entire settee belonged to him as well.

Perhaps the entire inn.

Anne followed my gaze to the top of the bookcase, a smile spreading across her lips. "What an adorable little creature." She laughed. "And quite talented to have found himself atop the bookcase. He's looking at you. Perhaps he wants to be your friend."

Adorable was not the word I had in mind. I was usually quite optimistic, and quite inclined to love every creature, but I also considered myself an excellent judge of character. I could easily see that this cat did not have friendship on its mind.

It likely didn't even know the meaning of the word.

I kept my gaze fixed on the cat until the inn door swung open. Timothy strode inside. He had removed the ridiculous cloak, revealing his black jacket, blue waistcoat, and perfectly tied cravat. As tall and broad-shouldered as he was, with that constant stoic expression, it didn't surprise me that so many people found him intimidating. I didn't, of course. I knew him too well. But tonight, his hair, the color of wet sand, was falling out of place in an unfamiliar way. I stared at the wayward strand, struggling to make it suit him. He was always composed. It was strange to see even a hair out of place. His eyes met mine from my place on the settee before they shifted away to focus on the approaching innkeeper's wife.

I sat forward, eager to observe their interaction. Timothy was humble, as the nobility went, but there was no question that the woman would gather a sense for his station. His dukedom dripped from every aspect of his appearance, whether he liked it or not.

Well, besides that wayward strand of hair. Today, it was making him more human. More approachable.

"'ow may I be of service?" the woman asked.

I watched as her eyes slid over his entire person, much as they had with Anne and me. A scowl marked her brow, and when she looked at his face again, her throat bobbed with a swallow. Her eyes darted in her husband's direction. He was still sleeping with his mouth wide open, a whistling snore accompanying each inhale.

Timothy's reply was too quiet to hear. All I caught were a few deep intonations before the woman spoke again.

"I've one more room available. And will it be beef or fish?"

"Beef."

The woman bustled off toward the kitchen, kicking her husband's foot as she passed. He snorted, sitting up straight and rubbing his eyes. His gaze settled on Timothy, and he immediately stood.

Less than a minute after her departure, the innkeeper's wife hurried back to her station in front of Timothy. "Yer food'll be served shortly. If ye'd like to take a seat in the foyer, ye may. If ye'd rather eat in the kitchen, it is just down this corridor."

Just as she said the words, a sultry female voice came from the direction of the kitchen. "Your grace!"

Why did that voice sound so familiar?

I craned my neck to get a better look as a woman and her daughter came into view.

Drat. Drat, drat, *drat.*

I immediately rotated my body toward Anne, hiding my face. Perhaps we had chosen an inn too close to home after all. It was the baroness, Lady Shaftesbury, and her daughter,

Miss Portia Grant. While I didn't see them often, they were fully aware of who I was and would certainly recall seeing me at that inn if any inquiries were publicized concerning my whereabouts. If they noticed me, casually sitting in the foyer of the inn, the kidnapping tale would be entirely discredited.

My heart thudded fast, panic seizing my muscles.

"What is the matter?" Anne whispered.

"I know them," I mouthed, too afraid to speak.

Anne's dark eyes flitted over my shoulder, a hint of panic entering her expression. "Keep your back turned and do not draw any attention to yourself."

I nodded. At least they were distracted by Timothy at the moment. With any luck, the ladies would be enamored enough by him not to glance in my direction. If only my hair weren't so recognizable. The tight, natural curl that covered my entire head was difficult to tame, and Miss Grant had even commented once on how it resembled a bird's nest.

I had never been fond of that comparison.

Or of Miss Grant.

As if she had read my mind, Anne slipped me the bonnet she had removed from her own head and had been holding on her lap. I put it on my head, tying the ribbons tight under my chin. The deep burgundy was a horrendous match for my yellow spencer jacket, but at least it would keep me unrecognizable from behind.

I listened to their conversation, the sound of my own pulse mingling with the voices.

"I would not have expected to find the Duke of Heywood at an inn such as this," Lady Shaftesbury said in an alluring voice. I could envision the coy upturn of her lips. Timothy tended to attract women of all ages, even if they were at least twenty years his senior like the baroness. It was disturbing. "Where are you traveling?" she asked.

Timothy didn't hesitate. "Gloucestershire to visit my uncle."

"D-duke?" the innkeeper's wife stammered, interrupting the conversation. She drew an audible breath. "Y-your grace, forgive we, 'tisn't often we 'ave a duke on our doorstep. I thought you'd 'ave sent a servant to reserve a room for yer stay. Allow me to remedy the arrangements." Her voice lowered, but I still caught the words. "I'll ensure you 'ave the best room The Lion's Crown 'as to offer."

"There is no need for special arrangements, ma'am," Timothy said, his voice kind, yet inarguable.

The woman must not have listened, because soon she was right behind me, her clamoring footfalls unmistakable. I didn't dare turn around as she addressed Anne. "There's been a mistake. Ye'll be in room four." She extended a new key to Anne before snatching the key to the previous room out of her palm.

I listened to her footfalls again as she returned to Timothy's side. Did he recognize my plight? Lady Shaftesbury and Miss Grant lived in an estate that neighbored both Timothy's and my family's. He must have known their presence at the inn could ruin our entire plan.

"Ye'll be in room six, yer grace." The innkeeper's wife's voice was candied now, sweet and sickly, much like the tone Lady Shaftesbury had presented.

I wanted to shoot a scowl in the woman's direction, but I refrained, choosing to keep my face hidden. I couldn't blame the innkeeper's wife for wanting to display her best room to a duke, but it did make me feel like a pile of fish bones in comparison. As a marquess's daughter, I wasn't anything to be scoffed at. Well, except for the times that I didn't present myself properly…which was most of the time. A duke trumped a marquess's daughter any day, and Anne—a widowed baroness, had little to boast of when compared to a duke.

Lady Shaftesbury's voice came again. "It was a pleasure to cross your path at such an unlikely place. I wish we could visit longer, but my daughter and I must retire. Goodnight, your grace." I imagined the flourishing curtsies of both women. Then I heard their footfalls as they moved toward the foyer. The staircase was near where Anne and I were sitting. I needed only to hide my face a few moments longer as they passed.

"I'll walk with you to your room," Timothy said, his voice a little quicker than usual.

I practically sighed in relief. If he was walking with them, they would have no reason to even glance in my direction. Timothy was a living, breathing distraction. Lady Shaftesbury and Miss Grant wouldn't be able to take their eyes off of him, no matter what. In fact, Miss Grant was likely hoping that she might catch his eye as a potential wife. Unfortunately, she didn't know what I knew about Timothy.

He didn't plan to marry, at least not anytime soon.

He had tried to make that very clear to society, at least in recent years since his father had died and he had become a duke. I had never understood his reasoning, but perhaps it was because I had never asked. Miss Grant was like many other young ladies of the *ton* who thought they might be the one to change his mind.

But there was another thing she didn't know about Timothy. He never changed his mind.

"Oh, that is so very gracious of you," Lady Shaftesbury said as they started toward the stairs.

Anne's eyes followed their movements as they passed, and I finally released the breath in my lungs. I was safe.

Well, not quite.

A wild hissing sound came from somewhere above me, and not a second later, something heavy landed on my back and shoulders with a thud.

CHAPTER 3

I gasped as a set of claws scraped against my skin, a streak of grey fur scrambling up and around the front of my neck, clawing and hissing as it went.

I shrieked, attempting to throw the blasted cat off of me, but his claws were stuck to my yellow jacket, which only made him thrash more wildly. The hissing turned into a feline scream of sorts. His green eyes were round, teeth bared as if he blamed me for embedding his claws in my jacket when he had been the one plotting his attack from atop the bookcase.

I grabbed at his front paw, attempting to detach it from me, but he sunk his teeth into my hand in response. Pain shot through my skin. I jerked back with a gasp. "I'm trying to help you!" I hissed back.

From the corner of my eye, I saw Anne jump to her feet.

Not a second later, Timothy was there, rushing forward to pry the cat off of me. He gripped it with one hand while using the other to unhook the claws from my jacket. With that wayward strand of hair hanging over his brow, he looked like some sort of rugged explorer detaining a wild beast. He managed to avoid being bitten himself as he set the cat on the floor. It hissed at me one more time before skittering away.

My heart was tapping against my breastbone so forcefully I was afraid it would burst. Timothy stood between me and Lady Shaftesbury and Miss Grant, both of whom had undoubtedly witnessed my struggle.

That *blasted* cat.

I locked eyes with Timothy. The same panic I felt was evident in his expression. If he moved, the baroness and her daughter would see me. If they hadn't already recognized me, they would certainly take a prolonged look at the crazed young woman who had just provoked such a violent creature.

Not knowing what else to do, I put my face in my hands, lowering it to my lap. I sniffled, pretending to sob.

I peeked at Timothy. He was still standing there. His brow was creased, mouth and jaw set with worry. He crouched down. Did he not realize I was pretending?

I shook my head fast. "Go," I urged.

His eyes rounded and he gave a nod, turning on his heel as I covered my face again.

"Good heavens," I heard Lady Shaftesbury mutter. "Do you know that woman?" She and her daughter had never been discreet when speaking about other people.

"I believe that is Miss Jane Flowers. I met her brother once in London." Timothy spoke without flinching.

"Is she…all right?"

"She appears to be distressed with any attention at the moment. Once we take our leave I'm certain she will be in better spirits."

"How mortifying." Miss Grant's voice faded as they walked away.

I held back my laughter, which made my shoulders shake.

I hoped it looked like a sob. I sniffled again, keeping my hands pressed firmly against my face as I hunched over my lap. In truth, the scratches on my neck and shoulders stung. A burning sensation spread across my skin where the welts were surely forming. The part of my hand that the cat had bitten also throbbed with pain, but thankfully my gloves had protected them from any wounds.

Anne leaned toward me. "They are gone."

I peeked out from behind my hands, only then noticing that I was shaking.

The innkeeper's wife had been busy calming the wicked grey cat, hugging it close to her chest as she walked toward me. "Did he 'urt ye, mistress?"

"Only a little." I cast a sidelong glance at the cat, who now purred contentedly in the woman's arms. I might have been mistaken, but I thought I saw a gleam of pride in its eyes.

" Forgive me, I thought I'd taught 'im not to attack guests," the woman continued. "Lion can be quite ferocious around strangers."

My ears perked. "Lion?"

The woman nodded, and the cat's pride gleamed even brighter. It was no wonder the blasted creature thought he owned the entire inn.

As tired and hungry and shaken as I was, I was impressed with my ability to keep a polite smile on my face.

"Yer food'll be served shortly, I thank ye for yer patience." She marched back to the corridor, thankfully taking the cat with her. It stared at me from over her shoulder. I held its gaze as I vengefully settled into his fur-covered cushions.

"I suppose not all cats are as sweet as they appear," Anne said, dark brows drawing together.

I stared at the empty staircase. "Or people."

Was Timothy fooled by Miss Grant as so many others had been? She was charming in public, pretty, and her voice was far more grating to my ears than it was to anyone else's. I could already imagine Lady Shaftesbury and Miss Grant's conversation in their room that night. They would be considering every word and glance from Timothy as encouragement, exaggerating his attention and plotting how they might ensnare him that evening. He would have to sleep with his door locked, to be sure.

I absently rubbed at the scratches on my shoulder until Timothy came back down the stairs. He glanced once to the right to ensure the innkeeper wasn't watching as he walked toward Anne and me. "You should take your meals in your room to avoid any further incident." His brow furrowed. "I'll ensure the food is brought up to you." His gaze landed on mine. "Are you certain you're all right?"

"Yes." I smirked before letting out a laugh. "I expect you'll never accuse me of having incompetent acting skills ever again. You really thought I was weeping, didn't you?"

A ghost of a smile passed over his lips, and I tried to freeze the image in my mind. I counted it a victory whenever I pulled such an expression from him. When Timothy smiled, it always looked like he was trying not to. I couldn't imagine why. Smiles weren't anything to be ashamed of.

He tipped his head to one side. "Perhaps you *were* weeping and you're trying to hide the fact."

"I wasn't!"

There was that faint smile again, but it didn't last long. He passed Anne a candle and she ushered me forward and up the stairs.

"That was almost a disaster," I mumbled when we reached

the top of the narrow stairwell. It would certainly make for an interesting addition to my novel. I never would have guessed the most danger I would encounter on the first day of my journey would come from an angry cat named Lion. A laugh bubbled out of my chest. Anne stared at me with just as much concern as she would have if I'd burst into tears instead.

She took our key to room four and unlocked it. The scent of mildew and dust immediately flooded my nose. The cramped room had one large bed in the corner, the center of which was drooping as if it had been slept on by one very large man for decades.

Even centuries.

A solitary painting hung on the opposite wall. The subject was a rather pale man with dark eyes and black hair, his sixteenth century fashion giving him strange proportions. His eyes seemed to follow me as I walked into the room and onto the rug that had tufts of grey fur similar to the ones on the settee. If this was the lion's den, I didn't want anything to do with it. An assortment of suspicious stains marked the rug every few inches. I nearly gagged when I noticed three, then four, then *five* spiders in their webs dotting the slanted ceiling.

Anne took a deep breath, as if steeling herself. Her hands twisted together in front of her. We exchanged a glance.

"Well, then."

I gulped as she walked directly beneath a spider to reach her trunk. Both our trunks had already been brought inside. I must have missed that during the cat incident. I squared my shoulders and followed her into the room. I wasn't a coward. I had just survived a fight with a cat that believed itself to be a lion, after all, and I hadn't even cried. Not real tears anyway. I took a deep breath, exercising all my strength not to look up at the ceiling.

A young maid cleared her throat in the corridor behind us, a tray on each arm. She stepped inside and set the trays on the edge of the bed before taking her swift leave of the room. At least it was finally time to eat. My stomach had begun cramping with hunger, and it was not helping my optimism about the five days still ahead in the journey.

Anne and I both hurried over to inspect the trays. My stomach turned, and the gag I had been holding back returned with vigor.

Fish.

Both plates were filled with the same, even though I had asked for beef. My heart sank a little. I despised fish—and any creature that came from the sea. I could not eat it without gagging. Even the smell had begun making my stomach writhe with discomfort, as if it were trying to remind me not to dare fill it with anything that had once breathed under water.

I hid my disappointment as Anne picked up her tray and set it on her lap. I couldn't believe that she had chosen to eat that vile substance, but she appeared happy with her selection. I considered hurrying down the stairs to chase after the maid who had brought me the wrong food, but I was meant to be hiding. I didn't want to inconvenience Anne any further by asking her to do the same. There was a slice of bread on the tray—At least I could still eat that.

I sat down, sliding the tray onto my lap, my nose wrinkling as I swallowed hard to fight the urge to wretch. *If I were starving, truly starving, I would eat it,* I told myself.

It was a lie. I would much rather starve.

I jumped at the soft knock on the door. As uninterested as I was in my food, it was a pleasure to set down my tray and open the door. Timothy stood on the other side of it.

"What are you doing?" I whispered, casting my gaze into the corridor behind him.

His eyes glowed the color of molasses sugar in the candlelight, matching his hair almost perfectly. He towered over me, that ever-present look of concern on his face as he examined the room behind me.

He held out his hand, where a key rested in his palm. "I've spoken with the innkeeper about my desire to be placed in room four instead. I insisted on making the arrangements myself."

I shook my head fast. "You mustn't sleep in this room. It's horrendous."

"Precisely." He nodded toward the corridor. "Out you go, both of you."

"Timothy," I protested, but he was already inside. He deposited his own trunk, and then took our trunks as if they were filled with feathers instead of heavy books, fabrics, and shoes.

There was no arguing with him when his mind was made up. He was behaving as a gentleman should, but at times I wished he would simply enjoy his privileges of being a duke. He deserved it. He didn't deserve to spend the night covered in spiders. But then, neither did Anne. I could see the gratitude and relief in her gaze, and perhaps I should have had more of that. Instead I bit my lip with worry as we followed him down the corridor with our trays.

Timothy opened the door to room six and set our trunks inside. The room was actually clean. And it only smelled slightly of mildew. There was no cat fur in sight, and no paintings of strange, possibly possessed men hanging on the walls. I examined the ceiling. No spiders.

"Timothy." I groaned, frowning up at him. "You should have this room. This isn't fair."

"How is it not fair?" He crossed his arms over his chest.

"Well—" I sputtered. "You drove us all the way here, so you must be the most tired. The innkeeper wanted you to have this room. *And* you're a duke." Why did I prefer the idea of myself sleeping under a canopy of spiders than Timothy enduring the same fate? Guilt tightened my chest.

"I disagree." Timothy's eyes gleamed with amusement. "It is entirely fair."

"All is fair in love and war," Anne said in a quiet voice, a slight quirk to her lips.

I couldn't tell if she had wanted me to hear her or not, but I had very powerful ears when it came to eavesdropping. "Well, this isn't love *or* war." I looked Timothy straight in the eye.

"Are you certain? That cat waged a war on you tonight, did it not?" He studied my face for a moment before his gaze lowered to my shoulders. His brow furrowed, and he softly touched one of the welts near the edge of my collarbone. My next inhale faltered a little, a shiver racing across my skin. What the devil was that about?

It tickled. That was what.

"Does it hurt?" he asked.

"No," I lied.

Timothy's fingers moved away as quickly as they had come. There was a weariness in his eyes that made them appear softer, his eyelids heavier as he looked down at me. It gave more weight to his gaze, and it covered me like a blanket. The reality of my situation had yet to fully sink in, but at least I knew I was safe. Mr. Verwood would not be my husband. Father would no longer control me. Timothy was here. Those three things comforted me, despite the scent of fish wafting up to my nostrils.

Timothy's attention shifted to my tray. "Why did you ask for fish?"

"What?" I shook myself of my distractions, following his gaze to the scaly mass on my plate. "Oh, yes." I sighed. I almost told him that I had meant to order beef, but I knew for a fact he would go straight to the kitchen to have a new assortment made for me. He needed to sleep and eat his own meal in peace. "I—I thought to try something new." I swallowed.

"You hate fish."

"How do you know?" I challenged.

Timothy held my gaze for several seconds. I kept my chin up, hoping he couldn't see the revulsion in my eyes.

"You've never liked it. Any time it's been served to you, you've picked at it with your fork rather than eaten it."

"Well—" I was at a loss. "That is very…observant of you." I frowned. How was it that I could never hide anything from him? It was infuriating.

"As it turns out, I regretted ordering beef," Timothy said with a shrug. "If you'd like to repay me for giving you the more comfortable room, I propose a trade."

"You want my fish?" I asked with surprise. My stomach grumbled, and it sounded like a desperate cry of assent.

"Well, my first choice would be cat." A flash of anger crossed his face as he glanced at my scratches again.

A laugh burst out of me, bringing a smile to his face. "Mine too."

He took the tray of fish from my hands. "Do we have an accord?"

"Y-yes." I beamed, unable to hide my smile. "Although I am slightly appalled at you for liking such a revolting food."

Anne looked up from her tray, her mouth partially full. "I beg your pardon."

I laughed, covering my mouth with my palm when the sound came out far too loud. It was amazing what the prospect of a better meal had done to my spirits. Anne smirked and went on eating the vile creature on her plate while I picked up the tray of beef, bread, and vegetables. I twirled, then sat on the edge of the bed with the tray on my lap. I beamed, nearly grabbing my food with my hands. "I have never been so grateful for a meal in my life," I said with a content sigh. "Thank you, Timothy. Truly."

He smiled—really smiled. I stared at that rare expression for a long moment. He must have been happier at the prospect of having the meal he favored as well. At any rate, I was glad he was in good spirits.

"Goodnight," he said.

He turned to leave, but I stopped him. "Timothy, wait."

He pivoted at the door.

"Thank you for giving us this room. It is too kind."

"I told you. The debt is repaid." He nodded toward his tray of fish, that wayward strand of hair shifting on his forehead as he smiled.

I sighed. "Very well. But please try not to be eaten alive by spiders."

"I will try my best. Be sure to lock the door behind me. John will have your coach prepared by dawn, and I will see you out. My route and inns will be the same as yours, but I'll be an hour behind you. We won't be seen traveling together from this point forward until we arrive at Foxwell House."

I nodded, still fighting the guilt in my stomach as I imagined Timothy's large frame trying to be comfortable on that sloping bed.

At least he was smiling as he disappeared into the corridor. Perhaps he liked spiders. Anne liked cats. At the moment, the two creatures were equal in the lowest trenches of my affections.

Along with fish, of course.

I smiled as I took a bite of beef and stood to lock the door.

CHAPTER 4

A s it turned out, I still didn't sleep well in room six.
Anne thrashed her arms out when she slept, and I
was struck by her elbow multiple times throughout the night.
By the time I drifted off, it was almost dawn, and the coaches
in the courtyard had begun leaving. The sound traveled easily
through my window. I stared at the dark ceiling, wide awake,
until light began creeping through the clouds.

Anne and I readied ourselves quickly before tugging the
bell pull for a servant to bring our trunks down to the coach.
We crept down the stairs, and despite my weariness, I kept
myself alert enough to watch for any sign of Lady Shaftesbury
or the lion. Thankfully, both were nowhere to be seen.

We ate breakfast quickly before making our way to the
courtyard. Timothy was waiting there, arms crossed, with his
back leaned against the coach we had arrived in the night
before. The tension in my shoulders relaxed as we approached.

I studied the puffiness around his eyes. They drooped
slightly. Did he always look this way so early in the morning? Or had he hardly slept at all? Concern bloomed in my

chest. I examined what I could see of him for any red bumps that might have been caused by spider bites. He wore a jacket and cravat, so there wasn't much to examine besides his face, and it was clear of any evidence. He looked endearing and surprisingly childish with such a tired expression. I wanted to tease him about it, but I couldn't find the words.

The truth was that Timothy wasn't a child. Not at all. He was twenty-four, though his position in society made me imagine him older, and it likely made *him* imagine *me* younger. There was a space between us that had been created by his closeness to my elder brother and the differing maturity with which Timothy and I approached life. He looked after me as if I were a child in need of constant supervision and coaching, and perhaps he was right. I would be quite lost without his help.

"Did you sleep well?" Timothy asked, brown eyes taking me in.

"Yes," I lied again to ease his worry. "Did you?"

"Yes."

At least I felt better about lying when he had lied to me too. A slow smile crept over my face. I couldn't help it.

He raised his eyebrows in question.

"I don't believe you."

He pressed his lips together as if to suppress a smile. He didn't reply, dismissing the accusation by changing the subject. "John will be your coachman from this point forward. I will be close behind, but I should arrive at each inn after the two of you have already gone to bed. We will make it our goal not to be seen interacting in public from this point forward. If not for the cat we would have succeeded last night."

I twisted my fingers together. "Do you think Lady Shaftesbury recognized me? Or Miss Grant?"

"It didn't appear so."

I smirked. "You were a sufficient distraction for both ladies. Neither one could take their eyes off of you. I daresay they *both* would like to court you."

Timothy cringed, shifting uncomfortably. "Lady Shaftesbury is the same age as my mother."

"Well, she *is* a widow. Perhaps she wishes to marry again." I laughed, and it came out as a snort. Why was it so amusing to tease him? The terror on his face was perhaps my favorite of his expressions, and even more rewarding when my words were shocking enough to be the cause.

Timothy shook his head at me. "I think her ambitions were related to her daughter."

I studied his face. Why had his grimace disappeared? Was he interested in Miss Grant? As his friend, of course I wanted Timothy to fall in love and be happy, but I would never, ever choose Miss Grant for him. She was too…

My thoughts trailed off into a dark abyss. There was actually nothing wrong with her, at least as far as Timothy was concerned. She was pretty—unfairly so—refined, and came from a respectable family. Yes, she had called my hair a bird's nest, but that didn't mean she was not occasionally kind and agreeable. I hadn't witnessed one of those occasions yet, but if Timothy had any interest in her I would have to be optimistic about her character.

I wanted to ask Timothy if he was indeed interested in Miss Grant, but I stopped myself. He had always said he wouldn't marry, so I didn't expect his mind to have changed. It would be better to allow the subject to die for now and return to the business of the morning.

Timothy's eyes settled on me, a distant look still hovering in them.

I cleared my throat. "Shall we be on our way, then?"

He nodded, his brow falling back into its stern line. "We shall speak again when we arrive at my hunting lodge. Should you need anything along the journey, you may send John to fetch me."

A burst of nervousness entered my stomach. It would be strange to have Timothy traveling apart from us, but it was wiser to do so. He helped Anne into the coach first, then turned to me. I rested my hand in his, noting how very small it appeared in the palm of his leather glove. His fingers wrapped around mine as I stepped into the coach.

"What happened to your glove?" he asked as he released my hand.

I settled into my seat, glancing down at the kid leather gloves I wore. They had been my favorite, and I hadn't failed to notice the damage they had sustained the night before. "The cat scratched them." The soft leather had been smooth before, but now it had shallow tears on the front in three different places, as well as several snagged stitches. "They were my favorite pair of gloves until now." I sighed.

"I'm glad the gloves protected your hands, at least." Timothy took hold of the coach door, leaning slightly inside. "Let us hope we don't encounter any more disagreeable creatures on our journey."

My mind went straight to Lady Shaftesbury and Miss Grant, though I was certain he hadn't been referring to them. "If we do, I will be prepared for battle." I cast him a broad smile.

He seemed hesitant to close the door, glancing over his shoulder and back at me again. "I will see you soon."

I nodded, a pang of nervousness stabbing my stomach again. I was so grateful that Anne was with me. She had a confident independence that rivaled Timothy's. "Thank you, Timothy." It seemed such an insufficient way to express my gratitude for all he had done to arrange my escape, but I didn't know what else to say or do. "Thank you for everything."

His dark gaze captured mine. "It's nothing."

I wanted to argue with that statement, but I held my tongue. If this elaborate scheme to help secure my future was 'nothing' to Timothy, I could hardly imagine what 'something' would be.

With a brief nod in farewell, Timothy closed the carriage door.

I very nearly kissed the dirt and gravel drive when the coach stopped for the final time in front of Foxwell House. Tripping over my hem, I stumbled out of the carriage without waiting for assistance. I heard Anne sigh behind me. I couldn't tell if it was a disappointed sigh in my unladylike behavior, or a sigh of relief to have arrived at our destination.

At the moment, I didn't care.

All I wanted was fresh air, a comfortable bed, and to sit on a cushion that wasn't situated above four wheels. After five days of travel, my mind was a little muddled. I had awoken several times each night at the various inns we had stayed at, burdened by nightmares that Father had found me. In each nightmare, he hovered over my bed with a set of chains and shackles. I had never been able to stop the nightmare before he secured one around my wrist. Each night, I followed the chain out of the room and down a dark corridor. At the end of it was always Mr. Verwood, a matching shackle on his own wrist with the chain binding us together.

The accuracy of the metaphor was chilling, and as I looked up at the hunting lodge in front of me, a surge of emotion gripped my throat.

This was my home now. Foxwell House. The facade of the old manor was perfectly square, with three rows of symmetrical windows and a white-columned porch. The red brick was weathered and dark, shadowed by the stormy sky. It hadn't rained yet that day, but the clouds were moving, dark and quick. Timothy had sent a few trusted servants to attend to us at the hunting lodge over the next year, and they had already stepped out from inside to assist us with our trunks.

The cries of birds met my ears. I couldn't tell if the moisture in the air was from the sea or the pending rain. "Are we near the coast?" I asked Anne as we started toward the front door.

"I think so." Her dark eyes glittered with delight. "I hope the views are beautiful."

"How could they not be?" I grinned, a new burst of energy entering my steps. "I don't believe there is such a thing as an ugly sea."

"Can the same be said for the sky?" she asked, glancing up at the dark clouds. They were directly above us now. A fat rain droplet landed on my arm, then on my cheek. We hurried inside, reaching the shelter just seconds before the light rain turned into a heavy downpour.

My stomach formed a knot. "I hope the storm ends before Timothy is caught in it." He was at least an hour behind us. As promised, we hadn't interacted at any of the inns along the way, but I had watched for his arrival from my window each night. Our coachman had always met him in the courtyard to confirm that we had arrived. Thankfully, I hadn't encountered any other acquaintances, possessive felines, or spiders at the other inns. The only real difficulty I had experienced on the journey was a lack of patience with the duration of it.

I stared at the intensifying rain for a few seconds, biting my lower lip with worry. I tore my gaze away from the drive for long enough to examine the interior of my new home.

The light was dim, a few weak candles burning on a table in the corner of the entryway. The grey and white checkered floor was slightly wet, as if it had just been cleaned. The air smelled of dust, yet the furnishings didn't appear to be neglected. The new maids must have been working hard to make it presentable for Anne and me.

I cast a smile in the direction of the row of servants who all stood at attention. There were two maids, a housekeeper, cook, butler, and two footmen. I would have to become better acquainted with each of them. Timothy would be paying their wages for now, but Charlie had promised to repay the debt once Father was no longer keeping watch on the estate's finances. I could hardly believe Timothy's generosity as I cast my gaze around the room. I couldn't wait to explore every floor and room of the quaint manor. The dark, mysterious furnishings had already intrigued me. With a few vases of flowers and smelling salts, the scent of mildew could be masked well enough.

One of the maids, Julia, led me out of the vestibule and up the staircase to my bedchamber. Anne followed and was directed to hers as well.

The wooden floors creaked as I stepped inside the room

that Timothy had chosen to be prepared for me. A dark rug covered the spacious floor. A writing desk, wardrobe, vanity, navy velvet chairs, and several additional cabinets and book-cases lined the walls. My jaw lowered as I took in the four-poster bed with a gold tasseled canopy. The bed covering was a soft blue, with more gold threads creating a stunning design. I walked closer, running my fingers over the soft fabric. There was no question this was the most grand room in the small manor.

It was the room of a duke.

Had it been the room Timothy had used when he lived here?

Had this been his bed?

The thought made my cheeks hot. Why did that feel too personal? Too much of an invasion of his privacy? Timothy had once called this manor home, and now I would be sleeping in his bed.

Not his *current* bed, I clarified in my mind.

My face burned even hotter. I didn't even know how long he had lived here, or why, but now I was excruciatingly curi-ous. Why could I envision him so well in this space? He was always dressed so elegantly, holding himself with a dignity and grace that intimidated most people he met. This room matched him with its elegance and apparent perfection. If anything was ever amiss in Timothy's mind or heart, I wouldn't know it.

I was realizing that there was a great deal I didn't know about him. He had never allowed me to know more than what existed on the surface.

The rain distracted me. I looked out the window, peering at the unrelenting dark clouds through the glass. I couldn't remain in my room and worry about Timothy's travels. He would be here soon. The last thing I wanted to do was sit, so I strode out of my room to the corridor. The room directly beside mine was Anne's, and the door was partially open. She was likely tired of my company after so many days together without any separation, but that was something both of us would have to grow accustomed to. I liked Anne, and I truly admired her, so I had high hopes that we would become dear friends over the course of the next year.

An entire year.

I gulped, letting the truth of that sink into my bones. A thrill quickly followed the dreadful sensation. Considering how mysterious this abandoned manor was, the rainstorm added perfectly to the atmosphere. Perhaps the story I planned to write would become a gothic one.

"Anne?" I pushed on the door until it moved a few inches.

"Come in." Her friendly voice encouraged me. She might not have been cursing her decision to be my companion yet.

Her bedchamber was similar to mine, but slightly smaller, with far less grandeur in the furnishings. My heart sank with guilt. It was still a lovely room, with a floral bed covering, writing desk, wardrobe, and modest decorations, but why had Timothy given me the grandest room? Anne was a baroness, and though she had insisted on coming, she was still sacrificing time that she might have spent elsewhere in order to protect me. She deserved more comfort than I did. I tapped my fingertips together in front of me as I paced the room. At least there weren't any cobwebs on the ceiling—or their inhabitants.

"I confess I was expecting worse," Anne said with a light laugh. "At the words, 'abandoned hunting lodge,' I never would have imagined such a beautiful manor."

The tension in my chest loosened as I laughed. "I thought

the same." I paused. "Why on earth do you suppose Timothy purchased a manor like this if he didn't plan to live here? Or find tenants for it at the very least."

"He did live here for a time, did he not?"

I frowned. "That is what he said." Why hadn't I asked him more questions? I was suddenly eager to know the reasoning for his purchase, his moving here, and how long he had been in such a secluded home by himself. He must have been so lonely. My mind refused to let go of my curiosity.

"Shall we explore the other floors?" I asked. If Anne's legs were as stiff as mine from sitting in the carriage, she would be glad for the opportunity to walk. If the weather had been better I would have suggested an outdoor exploration, but that would have to wait. I needed something to distract me from the storm and Timothy's absence. Worrying now would be premature. If he didn't arrive within an hour, then I could be concerned.

Anne gave an eager nod, her dark curls bouncing against her forehead. She stood with a groan. "My legs may never be the same again."

"Nor mine." Both our laughs were slightly delirious, and I noted the redness of Anne's eyes. She must have been as sleep deprived as I was. She followed me out the door to the corridor. The dark walls were undecorated besides a few fading tapestries. We took the stairs to the second floor, which mostly consisted of a long corridor with more empty walls and rooms. Deep in my heart, I had been hoping for secret passageways and mysterious paintings, but whoever had inhabited this house before Timothy must have stripped away most of the furnishings and taken them to their new destination. The darkness on the second floor of the house was unsettling, especially with the storm still raging outside the windows. I followed Anne quickly down the staircase until we reached the ground floor again. We had already seen the vestibule, so we turned left toward the drawing room.

It was nearly as magnificent as my bedchamber. I gasped in awe as my gaze swept over the ornate hearth, chairs, settees, and tables. Had it always been so lovely? Or had Timothy arranged to have the furniture moved there prior to my arrival? If I asked him, he likely wouldn't tell me the answer. I didn't even dare imagine the expense of such measures being taken for my comfort. If Anne and I weren't allowed to entertain guests, then what was the purpose of such grandeur? My throat was dry as I tried to swallow.

"This is…" Anne's voice faded. She shot her gaze to me.

"Elaborate." I made a sound that was half laughter, half astonishment.

After taking a turn around the drawing room, I crossed the corridor to the dining room, and then to what appeared to be a library. Shelves partially filled with books lined the walls, as well as a writing desk and a set of two armchairs near the hearth. If there were any secret passageways in this old house, the library would be the first place I would look. A smile crept over my face, but it was quickly wiped away by the worsening rain. I stopped by the window. The sun had almost gone down for the day.

"Do you think Timothy is all right?" I asked, tracing a droplet of water as it rolled down the other side of the glass.

Anne stepped up beside me. "I don't think the Duke of Heywood could be harmed by a simple storm."

I didn't answer, my chest tightening with worry. The Duke of Heywood couldn't, but perhaps *Timothy* could. Contrary to how he appeared to everyone else, I knew he wasn't immune to all danger. I had seen him climb onto the stable rooftop at the age of thirteen, and I had seen him slip as he tried to climb down. He had broken his leg. He wasn't indestructible.

Anne touched my arm, drawing my attention away from the window. "I suspect the storm has slowed him down, but no harm will come to him. I'm certain he will be here soon."

I nodded and smiled, but her words hadn't actually put me at ease. My stomach twisted as we finished our tour, and the clock hands completed a full circle.

Then another.

Our new cook planned to wait to serve our dinner until after Timothy arrived, so Anne and I sat in the dining room in silence. I tapped my foot on the rug, wringing my hands beneath the table. Two hours. That was an entire hour beyond the time I told myself I could begin worrying. The storm had not ceased, and it seemed like it never would. Even Anne's brow had creased at the center as she looked out the window into the blackness of the night.

In one swift motion, I stood from the table. Anne jumped. The candlelight flickered shadows over her dark features.

"I'm no longer hungry. I shall retire early."

Anne's eyes widened, but she nodded. "Very well."

I had never been skilled at hiding my intentions, especially when I knew they would be disapproved of, so I hurried from the room before she could notice anything unusual about my behavior.

I bounded up the stairs, keeping my footfalls as light as possible. I found my pelisse, gloves, and most sturdy bonnet. Dressing quickly, I made my way back down the stairs and slipped through the front door. Heavy raindrops fell over every inch of me, but my choice of attire kept me somewhat dry. My boots squelched in the soaked grass as I made my way toward the road. I didn't plan to venture far, but the dread in my stomach was tugging me forward, urging me to investigate as far as I could for what might be delaying Timothy. The sense of foreboding in my chest wouldn't be subdued. I could no longer ignore it.

My eyes adjusted to the darkness after a few minutes, and it became easier to avoid the puddles in my path. My pace slowed as my wits returned to me. What did I plan to accomplish? Timothy had likely stopped at an inn to avoid the storm, and I was only proving my ridiculous dependence on him. He wouldn't always be beside me; in fact, he would rarely be there. I needed to learn to rely on Anne instead. Most of all, I needed to learn to rely on myself.

I stopped in my tracks, glancing back at the house that now appeared as nothing more than a few floating rectangles of light in the distance. The back of my neck was soaked, and the rain had even penetrated the layers of fabric I wore. I shivered, scolding myself for attempting such an ill-planned rescue. I could still claim the benefits of the exercise, at least. My legs felt much better now that I had walked such a distance, and the cold air was refreshing in my lungs. Once I returned to the house, dripping from head to toe, I could explain to Anne that I had just been on an evening stroll. Not a heroic rescue.

I released a frustrated sigh. There were times my imagination and creativity made me a fool. How many of my actions were motivated by my fantasies for the novel I planned to write? This was not a novel. I was not a heroine. This was my life, and I was now soaking wet and alone in the dark. My skin tingled with fear as I looked out at the desolate landscape. Besides Anne and the household staff back at the manor, there wasn't another person for miles.

At least I hoped not.

I almost turned back toward the house, but the sound of hoofbeats caught my attention. The sound was distant, but growing in volume. I squinted toward the place where the path forked and connected with the woods. My heart picked up speed as I caught sight of a horse leaving the cover of the trees and starting in my direction. As it came closer, its pace slowed. Its distressed whinny made my insides lurch.

I stepped aside, attempting to calm it vocally until it stopped a few feet away. Its brown hair was soaked, hanging over its eyes, ribs expanding rapidly as it recovered from whatever spook it had just endured. My heart sank as I noticed the saddle on its back, reins dangling to one side. This wasn't a lost or wild horse.

Someone had been riding it.

CHAPTER 5

My legs rooted me to the ground as I stared at the soaking wet horse. Timothy had come in a chaise, not on horseback, I reminded myself. I inched closer to the animal, careful not to spook it again. I touched its neck, stroking softly against the cold, matted hair. From one look, I could see that the saddle was expensive. It could have belonged to a distant neighboring estate, but the dread in my stomach told me otherwise. Was this Timothy's horse? If his chaise had been broken in the storm, there was a chance he would have taken a horse the rest of the way.

Could I ride it? I examined the creature straight-on, meeting its eyes in the dark. I had ridden horses with Charlie on many occasions growing up, but never like this. "Are you sufficiently calm?" I asked, as if it could answer me.

I examined the stirrups in relation to my own height. The width of my skirts was also something to consider. This certainly wasn't a side saddle, and if I were to straddle the horse, the fabric of my dress might be too restricting. I had no qualms about riding in such a manner after dark, when I likely wouldn't be seen. Riding an unfamiliar horse that had possibly just dismounted its rider was not wise, however. Neither was walking into the woods alone. The horse watched me, waiting for instruction. He must have been well-trained. He no longer seemed distressed.

I bit my lip, a sense of urgency rising in my chest. Before I could change my mind, I took hold of the saddle and hoisted my foot into the stirrup. Pulling as hard as I could, I stood and swung my leg to the other side of the saddle. My skirts slid up my calves, settling around my knees, but thankfully they didn't tear. I took the reins, urging the horse back toward the trees. He followed my lead without any resistance. The rain continued to fall, soaking through my exposed stockings and obscuring my sight. When we entered the trees, the leaves rustled with a slight breeze. The branches stretched out like the arms of a monster, slender and long, ready to coil around me. I could hear every step the horse took on the sodden ground.

"Timothy?" I called. My voice shook. "Timothy!" I tried again, louder.

Nothing.

What was I doing? Timothy was a skilled rider. He never would have lost his seat, and if he had, how would I find him in the dark? The reality of my position sank through my skin like the rain soaking through my dress. I was improperly astride a strange horse, alone in an unfamiliar place after dark. If I was concerned for Timothy, I needed to inform the staff at the house. That would be the best way to remedy the situation. Perhaps one of them would be able to identify if the horse was his or not.

With my mind made up, I turned the reins, but the horse remained still.

"Come now, Geoffrey." It was the name I had spontaneously given the creature. Not surprisingly, he didn't respond to it. His attention was fixed straight ahead. What I had assumed to be a log or rock of some sort moved in the distance. It shifted, then became still again.

My heart leaped. What the devil was that? My hands shook as I held tight to the reins. "Timothy?"

Geoffrey wouldn't move. I dug in my heels but he only took a few steps before stopping again, ears twitching as he stared at the lump on the ground.

Was it an animal? A person?

Was it Timothy? The thought sent a fresh wave of dread through my stomach. Left with little choice in the matter, I dismounted, holding the front of the saddle and swinging both legs to the left side of the horse. The ground was much farther away than I had anticipated, and a jolt of pain shot through my lower legs. I gritted my teeth as I limped away from Geoffrey.

It only took a few steps before I recognized the shape as a person. I saw the back of his head, broad shoulders, and long, outstretched legs. I ran forward, heart in my throat. It was Timothy. I recognized his hair, his shape, his jacket. His hat was a few feet away from him, strewn on its side. My pulse thrummed wildly, my breath trapped in my lungs as I fell to my knees behind him. I gripped his shoulder, hovering above him until I could see his face. His eyes were closed, half his face covered in mud. His wet hair was matted to his forehead, and part of it was darkened with blood. Tears sprung to my eyes. "Timothy?"

I gasped with relief when I saw his chest rise and fall with a slow breath. He was alive, but he was not well.

"Timothy, what the devil happened?" I muttered, cupping one side of his face. It was so cold.

His eyes remained closed, but his brow furrowed. Did he know I was there? Was he entirely unconscious?

My gaze darted in every direction, a new fear scratching over my skin.

Had someone done this to him?

Had Father somehow found us? My eyes frantically searched the trees. Where was Timothy's chaise? Why had he ended up on horseback and then...not on horseback? The questions raced through my head faster than I could comprehend them. If he had been attacked, where was the attacker now? Would it be safe to leave him alone to go fetch help from the house?

Did I have any other choice?

I aimlessly caressed his face, pressing back his wet hair on the uninjured side. I turned in three different directions, my indecision impossible to please. I whined in my throat, a frustrated sound that was unfamiliar and raw. "I will bring help," I said, though I was certain Timothy couldn't hear me. Hot tears cascaded down my face like the raindrops on his. He looked so helpless, an image I had never seen, and it shook me to my core. "Please do not die while I am away. Do. not. die." I leaned over him, holding his face in my hands as my panicked tears dripped onto his face. Without thinking, I pressed a kiss to his lips and leaped to my feet. I hardly had time to comprehend what I had just done before I ran. I stumbled over my muddy skirts on my way back to the horse. My heart pounded as I mounted quite ungracefully and raced back to the house.

I burst through the front door, the sudden warmth and light making me dizzy.

"Leonora!" Anne came from somewhere to my left, and it took a moment for my gaze to focus on her. She gripped my upper arms. "Where have you been?"

I swallowed hard, my breath burning in my throat. "Timothy is hurt. We must fetch John and the footmen."

Anne's eyes flew open wide. "Hurt? How? Where is he?"

"There's no time." I started moving past her, tugging my arms away, but the servants had already begun gathering in the vestibule, apparently having heard the commotion.

I led them outside, where the rain still fell steadily. "The duke is just beyond the trees. He seems to have f-fallen from his horse. He isn't conscious." I gulped, my words stumbling out. "He will need to be moved inside at once."

Thankfully, the coachman didn't require further instruction. He sprung into action, bringing the staff with him to the small stables. They returned a few minutes later with a team of horses, once again pulling the carriage that had conveyed us to Foxwell House earlier that evening. I tried to follow them, but Anne pulled me back.

"We shall wait here," she said in a stern voice. "There is nothing more that you can do for him. Come." She pulled me gently to the shelter of the vestibule, but I stared through the open door until the carriage eventually came back through the trees. The rain had finally stopped. It took all my energy not to run out to meet their approach.

The footmen exited the carriage first, then hoisted Timothy out together. Dread crept through my stomach, tying it in knots. He seemed to have come to his senses a little, and a flame of hope ignited in my chest. His eyes drifted open and closed in confusion, a deep crease in his forehead as the two footmen helped him begin his slow walk to the front door of the house. I took several steps back, clearing the way. A puddle remained where I had been standing, rippling with the vibrations of loud voices.

"To the drawing room!" The housekeeper, Mrs. Taylor, had taken control of the situation. I followed the group to the sofa, where a blanket and pillow had already been spread. Timothy collapsed onto the cushions with a groan, squeezing his eyes shut again. The candlelight was dim, but it gave enough light to display the blood in his hairline and the mud streaked down his face.

"Call for the physician!" The housekeeper demanded to a nearby servant.

"No." Timothy's eyes opened for a moment, but his brow tightened, closing them again.

The room fell silent.

"No—don't call any physician."

My heart thudded in my chest as I walked forward, stopping in front of him. His eyes were still closed, so I gently touched his forearm.

His eyes opened slowly, settling on my face.

For a moment, I felt inexplicably vulnerable with his gaze on mine, and it took a few seconds for me to realize why. I had kissed him. I had kissed him, right on the lips. Shock vibrated through my body. That was not something that was generally considered appropriate between friends—especially when one of those friends was a very important, respectable duke. My face flamed, cutting through the cold.

He didn't remember, did he? He had been unconscious. Whether or not he remembered that I had kissed him was not the most troubling part, but why I had done so in the first place. I shook the fogginess from my head, grasping onto my words. "Tim—er—" I glanced around at the servants. I didn't know how many of them were aware of my close friendship with Timothy, so it would be best to address him properly. "Your grace. You struck your head quite hard. It would be dangerous and neglectful not to have it examined."

"What happened to you?" Timothy's eyes traced over me and my wet gown, dripping hair, and what must have been cold-flushed cheeks. There might have even been some mud splattered throughout.

I gave an astonished sigh, planting my hands on my hips. "You cannot possibly be concerned for me at this moment."

His alertness seemed to grow by the second, and he struggled to sit up. "You look freezing."

"Well, you look dead." I leaned forward to gently push his shoulder back until he was lying down. "I thought you *were* dead. We really must call for a physician."

"No." Timothy shook his head, but the movement made him wince. "No physician will be called tonight." He looked up at Mrs. Taylor. "You are all dismissed."

The housekeeper hesitated for a brief moment before giving a silent curtsy and ushering all the staff from the drawing room.

I gaped at him as the door swung shut, leaving Timothy alone with Anne and me. "You are so stubborn! What if— what if your brain has…burst? Or your skull has cracked? Perhaps you have lost your mind entirely, and that is why you are making such poor decisions." My voice broke.

"Nora…" his voice trailed off as one corner of his mouth lifted.

"This is not humorous. Not at all." I blinked hard against a tear in the corner of my eye. It escaped anyway, rolling down my cheek. All of these emotions were as shocking as they were potent, and I didn't know why I felt tempted to throw my fist into Timothy's smug smile. He could have died, and it would have been my fault. He had come here for *me*.

Anne stepped closer, and I heard her voice from behind. "His grace is right to prevent a physician from coming, Leonora. Your connection to him cannot be known. It is safer for all of us if he is not seen here with you."

I groaned in the back of my throat, addressing Timothy again. "Well then, if you will not allow a physician to tend to you, then you must allow me to."

I didn't pause to check for Timothy's approval. I turned toward the door. "Please ensure he doesn't move," I said to Anne as I passed. Her features twinged with discomfort, likely because she had never played nanny to a duke before, but I gave her arm a reassuring squeeze as I marched from the room.

I wiped the tear from my cheek when I stepped into the corridor, taking a deep breath. After finding Julia to assist me, we heated a bowl of water, gathered a few rags, and prepared a tea tray. She helped me carry it all back to the drawing room before taking her leave.

Timothy was still awake when I returned. Anne sprung up from her chair, apparently eager to escape the awkward situation I had left her in. I cast her an apologetic look as I dipped a rag in the bowl of warm water and wrung it out. Kneeling down in front of the sofa, I touched it gently to Timothy's forehead, wiping away the first layer of dirt and blood. With careful strokes, I cleaned around his hairline, not daring to look into his eyes. I could feel him watching my face, aware of every move I made. He didn't protest as I had expected him to. When I reached the mud near his mouth, I paused, studying his lips. Had I really kissed them? It felt like a blur—a dream—and it would be best if I pretended it was. I scrubbed away the mud near his lower lip in one swift swipe. I could already feel my face heating up, and his intent gaze only made matters worse.

Silence hung between us. It was terrifying to think of what might have caused Timothy to fall off his horse, but I was tired of guessing.

"What happened?" I asked, wringing out the rag a second time. When I looked at his eyes, they were already fixed on mine.

He seemed to struggle to gather his words. "The wheel of my chaise broke a few miles back. I lacked the tools to repair it. Fortunately I had a saddle, so I left the chaise and rode the horse in this direction. He was spooked in the woods and threw me. Obviously, I hit my head."

Relief plunged through my chest. So he hadn't been attacked after all. Father hadn't somehow managed to catch up to him. I should have known such a thing was impossible, but my imagination had run away with me. I released a tense breath. "I've never known you to lose your seat on a horse."

"That horse was not well-trained for riding. I never would have attempted it if I'd had any other choice."

"He seemed well-trained to me." I immediately regretted the words. I bit my lip, avoiding his gaze.

"You rode him?" Timothy's voice was heavy with dread. He must have already anticipated my answer.

"Yes, but I assure you, I felt perfectly safe with Geoffrey." I continued dabbing at his wound.

"Geoffrey?"

I shrugged. "That's what I named him."

With a groan, Timothy took hold of my wrist, lowering my hand and the rag so he could see my face.

I frowned. I had been blocking it for a reason.

"That was reckless," he said in a gruff voice.

My neck grew hot with frustration. Why did he always treat me like a child? Anything he did was heroic, but if I did the same, it was considered *reckless*. "If I hadn't gone looking for you, then you would still be lying in the mud. I was worried for you. You're fortunate that I found you when I did."

He cringed as I dabbed at the wound on his scalp. It was hidden by his hair, but I could still see where he had been cut. It must have been quite bruised as well.

He rubbed one side of his face, closing his eyes. "You could have been thrown or injured even worse than I was."

"But I wasn't."

His voice hardened. "It is not your place to protect me."

Anger rose in my chest. "Yet you have made it your duty to protect *me*. It is only fair that I took an opportunity to repay the debt."

"You are not indebted to me."

I scoffed. "Of course I am! You have sacrificed time, money, comfort, and taken countless risks to save me from an unhappy marriage. There is nothing I could ever do to repay you. Please, accept my actions tonight as a token of gratitude and not a death wish of some sort. I am not a fool."

I hated that we were speaking in terms of debts and repayments, because I knew that my actions that evening hadn't truthfully been led by any feelings of indebtedness. Not at all. I swallowed, my throat dry, anger still pulsing in my veins.

Timothy's gaze traced over my face, his dark brows drawn together. "You have never been in debt to me, Nora, and you never will be. Nevertheless, I surrender for now." He closed his eyes. "Please go change into dry clothing and warm yourself by the fire so I can sleep soundly. You're shivering like a wet dog."

I gaped at him, wishing his eyes were open to witness my vexation. "Very well. If it will help you sleep, then I will leave you in peace." I dropped the rag on his chest and stood, turning away with a huffed breath. If he was going to be so ungrateful, then he could finish cleaning his own face.

I didn't wait for his reply, walking straight out the door.

My throat was raw as I wandered into the corridor. Anne followed behind me, leaving Timothy alone in the drawing room. My eyes stung, my muscles still on edge. And Timothy had been right—I was shivering.

"He is far too stubborn," I muttered through gritted teeth.

Anne caught up to me, casting me a sidelong glance. "He cares for you. This is how he shows it."

My heart gave a strange squeeze before picking up speed. "Yes. My brother would have done the same thing, I suppose." I didn't know why I felt the need to instill that comparison in Anne, but perhaps it was because of the gleam of suspicion in her eyes. I would die with the secret that I had kissed Timothy that night. It had been completely unexpected and uncalled for.

We reached the top of the staircase, and I stopped outside Anne's bedchamber. "Forgive me, Anne. I have been out of sorts tonight. I am not usually so…waspish."

She smiled, taking my hands. The genuine, comforting gesture made tears spring to my eyes. I had been without my mother for my entire life. And without any sisters, I wasn't accustomed to any sense of sisterhood either. "*Anyone* would be waspish after the evening you have endured. Go to sleep. You may contend with the duke in the morning."

I suspected I would be contending with him in my mind all night, attempting to explain to myself the strange emotions I had been feeling. But I nodded, slipping into my room and tugging the bell pull. A maid came to assist me, and within a few minutes, I had tucked myself deep inside that oversized bed. The blankets were soft and warm, and I might have been imagining it, but they seemed to smell like him.

I rolled over, staring at the canopy above me. At least Timothy didn't have any recollection of when I had found him on the ground in the woods—and most importantly when I had kissed him squarely on the mouth.

Good heavens.

I squeezed my eyes shut. In general, I did consider myself a friendly and compassionate person, so that must have been why I had committed such a wayward display of affection.

Regardless of what had caused the strange impulse, Timothy could never, ever know of it. I would do well to forget it myself.

In the morning, I found a letter awaiting me outside my door.

Nora,

I regret not thanking you properly for saving my life. Should you need anything, do not hesitate to write to me.

As for the gloves, I found them in a shop on my way to

Foxwell House. They are a birthday gift. Let us hope you do not encounter any more cats.

Sincerely,
Timothy

The address of his estate was scrawled below his name.

I lowered the letter with a frown. He had already left? Without a proper farewell? What had happened to his broken chaise or his head that was in obvious need of stitches? Perhaps he felt uncomfortable with our argument from the night before. Or he knew I would protest to his departure so soon, especially with his injuries. I shouldn't have been surprised. This was always how Timothy behaved. He never stayed anywhere longer than necessary, and if he ever found himself in a vulnerable position, he ran away and hid where he couldn't be seen.

I read the short note from the start once again. I snatched up the gloves, turning them over in my palm. They were exactly like the pair that had been scratched, but these were new and pristine. The soft leather was flawless, and not a stitch was out of place. My heart softened, and I struggled to release the air in my lungs.

It was my twentieth birthday.

In the chaos of arriving at the manor the night before, I had completely forgotten. But Timothy hadn't.

I frowned, tugging one glove onto my hand, flexing my fingers until they settled into their perfect fit. My throat tightened. I sniffed, rubbing my nose with the back of my opposite hand. How thoughtful. How observant. How…Timothy. Was he ever anything else?

I blinked fast as I folded the note. As grateful as I was for Timothy's help, he was gone now. I needed to stop fretting over him when he obviously didn't wish to be fretted over.

My twentieth birthday was also the start of my last year in my father's control.

In three hundred and sixty-five days, I would come of age. I would be free. Between now and then, I had the opportunity to learn all I could about what to do with that freedom when it was finally mine.

I hurried back to my desk and opened my diary. I would need to document all my thoughts and feelings and adventures if I wished to compile a riveting story. I couldn't waste a moment.

Nora's Coming of Age Diary

July 3, 1816

Beauty, clothing, accomplishments, manners, and even posture will make up my worth in the eyes of society. In the eyes of Mr. Verwood, I'm worth a total of eight thousand pounds, though my father was hoping for ten.

It is an impressive number, I cannot deny that. I might have been flattered that anyone thought I was worth so much money, but I have no wish to be sold or bargained away. I don't care to be wanted for my outward appearance or social standing as a marquess's daughter. My heart aches to be seen. Truly seen. The good things, the bad things, the silly and quirky things that make me who I am, and to still be wanted and loved for it. The difficulty is that I will never have the opportunity. As I eventually seek a husband in London, I will have to repress those peculiarities of my character in order to be liked and respected. I need a kind man who will marry me and keep me safe from my father, and to obtain that, I will need to become what society wants. To be loved, truly loved, will be impossible.

Perhaps my romantic notions are childish, but perhaps they aren't. They might be an indication that I am mature enough to know my own mind—to know what I truly want:

Love.

Happiness.

A husband who will protect me and who does not repulse me like Mr. Verwood.

I picked up my quill, staring at those three things.

Love.

Happiness.

A husband who will protect me and who does not repulse me like Mr. Verwood.

It felt good to write it down, to admit my dreams on paper. It was not folly or a sign of ingratitude to acknowledge what I wanted. I stared at those words for a long moment before lowering my quill again and slashing a line through the first one and replacing the second.

~~Love.~~

~~Happiness.~~ Comfort.

A husband who will protect me and who does not repulse me like Mr. Verwood.

A mature woman could acknowledge what she wanted,

but she could also *change* what she wanted. I knew what it meant to have realistic expectations. I knew what it would take to prevent my hopes from being dashed to pieces: I had to remove the hope entirely.

I inhaled deeply, a sense of grief accompanying the air I exhaled from my lungs. It would be difficult to say goodbye to my dearest childhood dream, but it was necessary. I could no longer afford to rely on hope. I needed to begin relying on strategy. Love was not to be part of my ambition any longer.

To prepare for London, I needed to be charming, polite, well-mannered, accomplished, vibrant, and unforgettable. I bit the nail of my forefinger. Twelve months was a very short time to become all of those things. I immediately spit my finger out of my mouth.

No longer biting my nail would be a good place to start.

CHAPTER 6

N ora's *Coming of Age Diary*
August 7, 1816

The days have been long, but productive. I have been practicing all my talents for London, and I am improving little by little. I go for a daily walk with Anne. We have both come to love the seaside winds and sand, especially during these summer months when the air isn't so cold. It has been a delight to explore the setting of my future novel. We found our favorite route along the cliffs and we even found castle ruins. I wonder what could have happened there so many centuries ago, but most of all, I wonder what could have happened here at Foxwell House.

It is strange to me that Timothy purchased this manor and yet occupies it so infrequently. When he comes to visit again, I will have so many questions to ask him, he won't have time to answer them all. He assures me in his letters that his head has healed and that he is well, but I still worry for him. I miss him.

I have been thinking about when I kissed him and how

embarrassing it would be if he knew. I can hardly bear to think of it myself. Even now my face is blushing darker than a sunburn. I'm grateful to confide that secret in anything—even if it's just a page in my diary. I have been positively bursting with it.

In other news, I regret to say that Anne and I have not managed to remain completely hidden. Two men from town have learned our address, and

I dropped my quill when Anne burst through the drawing room door with windblown hair and a recently developed smatter of freckles over her cheekbones. "Drat it all," she said through a sigh.

"What is it?" I turned away from my diary, snapping it closed as my eyes adjusted to the bright light that came from the window beside her. In her white dress, with her pale skin and dark hair, she matched the keys on the nearby pianoforte.

She set down the empty basket on her arm, pacing in a circle. "Mr. Ball saw me on my return from delivering bread to the Gilberts and asked if he could call. He is on his way now."

"Blast and botheration," I muttered through clenched teeth, jumping from the bench. Would that man not leave us be? In the month that had passed since we first moved to Foxwell House, we had discovered that besides a few lowly cottages, there was only one estate within three miles. It belonged to a young man by the name of Mr. Christopher Ball. He had passed us on a walk our first week, and he had taken it upon himself to further our acquaintance with frequent, unwarranted visits. Thankfully, he hadn't questioned my identity as Miss Jane Flowers, nor our story that Anne was my widowed sister named Mrs. Benson who had purchased the property from the previous owner with her modest inheritance.

"I wrote a poem about him," I said as Anne fluffed pillows. "I'm practicing for parlor games."

Anne raised her eyebrows. "Parlor games?"

"In London. I have heard people play a great deal of parlor games there, and many of those games include rhymes and wit. Also kissing."

Anne blanched. "I would advise you not to participate in parlor games that involve kissing. That is a sure way to damage your reputation."

"Perhaps. *Or* secure a husband." I chuckled. Her expression was shocked at first, but it slowly melted into a smirk. She shook her head at me as she joined my laughter. What would she think if she knew I had kissed Timothy without his knowledge? Would she still be laughing? I gulped.

In the short time we had been at the hunting lodge, Anne had slowly been loosening her corset, figuratively. The fierce winds and seaside air seemed to be untethering the bounds of her propriety. She no longer sat perfectly straight all of the time, and she laughed a great deal more than she had before we arrived. She had wanted an adventure, and that she had found. She was finally embracing all the unexpected joys that came with it.

I couldn't give Mr. Ball credit for any of it. His visits were becoming progressively less unexpected, and they had never once been joyful.

"Let us hear the poem, then." Anne said, placing her hands on her hips. Her eyes sparked with mirth. "Unless you wish to share it with the man himself?"

I chuckled. "Oh, that may be wise, actually. I have no

doubt Mr. Ball would cease his visits if he heard what I've written about him." I picked up a book from the shelf beside the pianoforte and opened to the pages I had wedged my poem between. I smoothed the paper and read in a strong voice.

"Let us speak of a man named Mr. Ball
Who makes a great deal of social calls
He considers himself quite handsome and tall
But the ladies he visits don't think so at all."

Anne snorted, covering her mouth. "Leonora!"

I composed my laughter for long enough to continue.

"He passes his days with games of chess
Hoping his skills will serve to impress
But the ladies he visits will sooner confess
How they lament the day he learned their address."

Anne shook her head as her body vibrated with laughter. "You are cruel."

I folded the paper with a stab of guilt in my chest. "But is it any crueler than when Mr. Ball stayed in our drawing room for six hours in order to school us in chess when we did not ask for such a lesson?"

"I suppose not." Anne grimaced. "Although, he did have a shocking amount of knowledge of the game. You must admit that our skills have benefited from his guidance."

I hated to admit it, but Anne was right. Since Mr. Ball had given us that prolonged chess lesson, Anne and I had passed many hours that might have been boring and unoccupied in a tournament of sorts with the board we had found in the library. Anne was far more skilled than I was, and she seemed to be improving by the day. Soon she would be even better than Mr. Ball.

"That is true, but I would rather not endure another of his lessons. Perhaps we should make a plan for how we might encourage him to leave sooner."

"Besides suggesting a certain poetry reading?" Anne raised her brows.

"That shall be our last resort." I peeked out the window. "You might feign illness?"

"I fear that will only make him stay until I am well again." Anne gave a hard laugh. "Or he might offer unwanted remedies."

I grimaced. "Yes, we should avoid that." My eyes shifted to the window again. Mr. Ball was approaching on horseback, but he wasn't alone. I gasped. "Mr. Elmore is with him!"

Anne's eyes rounded. She followed me to the window, taking a discreet glance before ducking out of sight. Mr. Elmore had visited once before with Mr. Ball, and he had an unconcealed fondness for Anne—one that was actually quite similar to Mr. Ball's unconcealed fondness for Mr. Elmore. Besides chess, Mr. Ball's other favorite subject was Mr. Aiden Elmore and his many horses, skills, possessions, and even his strength and stature. Mr. Ball aspired to *be* Mr. Elmore, it seemed. Even as they approached the house, Mr. Ball seemed to be overstretching his stride to match Mr. Elmore's, and his deep burgundy jacket was nearly identical to his friend's. I didn't have any doubt that Mr. Elmore had been first to purchase it. As master of a distant estate, Mr. Elmore was only in town to visit Mr. Ball for the summer, which would soon draw to a close.

Anne let out an anguished sigh, planting her hands on her hips. "I had been looking forward to a quiet afternoon."

"Mr. Ball is anything but quiet." I gulped as an aggressive knock sounded on the front door.

We waited as the two men were welcomed inside by the butler, announced in the corridor, and then revealed in the doorway.

Mr. Ball's dark curls spilled over his forehead, curtaining his expressive hazel eyes. His smile stretched wide, large teeth bared as he puffed out his chest. It was a habit of his, it seemed, to attempt to make his stature larger while standing beside Mr. Elmore.

He bowed toward Anne. "Mrs. Benson," then to me, "Miss Flowers." He gripped the front of his jacket, shifting his weight to one hip. "How are you this fine afternoon?"

"Very well," Anne muttered.

"Indeed," I added.

Mr. Ball walked farther into the room and made himself comfortable on the sofa. Mr. Elmore remained standing near the door, eyes fixed unabashedly on Anne.

Mr. Ball released a cackle that made me jump. "Aiden, you are in the presence of friends, there is no need for such formalities." He patted the cushion beside him.

It was clear that Mr. Elmore didn't consider Anne as a mere friend. He couldn't seem to remove his gaze from her as he joined Mr. Ball on the sofa. Anne's jaw was tight as she chose the chair farthest from Mr. Elmore. I sat beside her, crossing my ankles beneath my skirts. Yes, Mr. Elmore's gaze *was* a bit too amorous, but I didn't understand why Anne was so opposed. He was far more handsome than Mr. Ball, more polite, less obnoxious, and he was rich. Any courtship would be complicated given her false identity, but there appeared to be more than just that deterring her.

"How have you occupied your time this week? More chess?" Mr. Ball grinned.

"Far *too* much chess, I'm afraid," I said. Playing chess with Anne was becoming less enjoyable each day. She was smart, and her skills were improving much faster than mine. I had been focusing more of my attention on my preparations for London. I read, practiced the pianoforte, embroidered, danced, and practiced my French, which was quite horrendous. I had also been writing in my diary and writing letters to Charlie and Timothy. My father had never hired a dancing instructor for me, caring little for my future success in society, so most of my attention had been on learning to dance properly. The only dance I knew was the quadrille, but it was still horrendous.

"There is no such thing as too much chess." Mr. Ball rubbed his hands together. "In fact, I am tempted to challenge one of you ladies to a match at this very moment. Miss Flowers?"

I blinked for a moment. I doubted I would ever grow accustomed to being addressed by my fictitious name. "I'm afraid I must decline."

Mr. Ball's face contorted in disappointment. His lower lip pouted dramatically. "You mustn't."

"I must." I sat up straighter. "I must also inform you that our visit with you can only be brief, as my sister and I have a prior engagement this afternoon."

He shook his head, slapping his knee in protest. "That is

unacceptable. I will not allow it." He flashed a wide grin. "Simply cancel your previous engagement."

"I'm afraid that cannot be done."

Mr. Ball's brow contracted as he tore at his fingernail with his teeth. "What is your previous engagement, may I ask?"

"It is of a personal nature. I don't wish to discuss it."

He groaned. "What could possibly be more important than entertaining us? Or more enjoyable?" He threw a smile toward Mr. Elmore, who still hadn't broken his stare in Anne's direction.

Exasperation built in my chest until it was close to bursting. "Many things." The words slipped out before I could stop them.

Mr. Ball's eyes rounded, and he choked on a breath. "Well, if you are so certain, then name five activities that you would prefer to be doing at this moment rather than conversing with Mr. Elmore and myself." His eyes sparked with a challenge. "I would very much like to know what in life excites a young lady more than stimulating conversation with two handsome gentlemen."

His pompous grin made my stomach turn. The objective was to rid ourselves of their frequent visits, was it not? I gave a sugar-sweet laugh. "Only five?"

"Leonora." Anne's scolding whisper barely reached my ears; I was too focused on Mr. Ball's calculative expression.

Feigning illness would have been a gentler way to drive Mr. Ball and Mr. Elmore from our house, but I couldn't help myself from bruising Mr. Ball's pride just a little. The frequent visits from the two men needed to be put to an end. They were all too aware of our circumstances and seemed far too interested in how we spent our time. If this was to be our home for the next eleven months, I couldn't have them slowly uncovering our secrets. No. Most certainly not.

"Name the *first* five that come to mind," Mr. Ball clarified.

I gave a slow exhale. "Very well." Glancing upward in thought, I sprung my fingers out to count my preferred activities. "Puncturing myself with my embroidery needle, having my meals served in a chamber pot, walking barefoot in the snow, mucking out stalls, and...biting into the flesh of a freshly caught fish." I shuddered at the thought, but maintained eye contact with Mr. Ball.

He blinked in surprise for a long moment. Then he laughed. His head tipped backward and a bellow unlike anything I had ever heard burst out of him. Mr. Elmore was rather pale, eyes darting between Mr. Ball and me. Was Mr. Ball not the least bit offended? Or appalled? Drat, he seemed only to be entertained.

"You are a clever one, Miss Flowers." Mr. Ball's eyes gleamed as they raked over me. I despised the feeling. "If you so insist, Mr. Elmore and I shall be on our way. I expect to hear more about how your dinner tastes when served from a chamber pot upon our next visit."

Mr. Elmore stood abruptly, offering a bow to Anne, then to me before striding toward the door. Mr. Ball bowed in a similar fashion, though his declination in my direction was more prolonged, a wry grin on his lips. When the door closed behind them, I jumped to my feet, wiping my palms on my skirts. "Why did Mr. Ball seem...pleased with my insults?"

Anne was still frozen in shock, eyes round. "He seemed to appreciate your wit. A man as prideful as Mr. Ball would never believe you to be in earnest. He might think that you're flirting with him."

"With insults?"

"In order to hide your true feelings."

I paced in a circle, releasing a flustered sigh. "I ought to never read him my poem then! He will fall in love with me."

"It may be too late for that. Why do you suppose he insists on visiting so often?"

I groaned. "Let us not dwell on Mr. Ball. It is Mr. Elmore who is enamored with *you*."

Anne closed her eyes, the dark lashes creating a crescent shape. She shook her head fast. "I wish he would stop."

I laughed. "I cannot fault him for seeing what is so obvious. You are beautiful, kind, and elegant. What is so wrong with Mr. Elmore? He is far better looking than Mr. Ball, far more well-behaved, and he owns an estate."

Anne picked at a loose thread on her gown. "He is not Miles." She exhaled a heavy breath.

I eyed her downcast expression with a frown. Mr. Miles Holland seemed to do little but upset her. Anne's sister, Henrietta, had been encouraging the match, and she had gone to great lengths to try to ensure they could be together. Anne had loved Miles before she had married her late husband, who she had only married to save her sister's reputation. When the baron died, Anne was given another chance to marry for love. But now, Miles was in India with no promise of returning for her. It didn't seem fair. I had always been a romantic, but I had also recently accepted that reality needed to be faced.

"Miles is very far away," I said in a gentle voice. "He might never return."

"I know." Anne's voice was defensive. "But to stop loving someone…it isn't simple. No matter how much you wish to stop, and no matter how much your mind fights against it—

the heart wins. A heart like mine loves and never forgets. It has an indomitable will, yet it is fragile enough to be broken with the slightest disappointment. I have never understood how something can be so strong, yet so weak at the same time."

Her words settled into my skin, sending a chill across my arms. Did a love like that really have no expiration? Even if it was unrequited? There was a great deal I didn't understand about love, disappointments, and even my own heart. My childhood was dotted with memories of being ignored and abandoned by my father. Charlie had tried to explain that our father was bitter about our mother's death, and that because her life was lost during my birth, he blamed me. My father had never even tried to forgive me. He hadn't given me the opportunities other young ladies of the *ton* were given. He had never influenced me for good. I had never been loved by him.

Only by Charlie and Timothy.

The moment that I had kissed Timothy burst back into my mind without permission. Was that the sort of mad behavior that love caused? A sense of panic washed over me, and I had to shake my head to clear it. To entertain any romantic notions when it came to Timothy would only hurt me. This was a discussion I had had with myself many times over the years. Surely Timothy didn't *love* me. He cared for me though. I knew that. Perhaps he loved me the way I loved Anne—as a dear friend. The love of a brother, and of a friend, were the only loves I had ever known. I imagined I would recognize a romantic love if I ever experienced it, but my lack of experience was daunting. Was it thrilling and sudden? Did it build over time? Or did it come when one least expected it? Perhaps the circumstances were different for everyone.

A thought struck me hard. What if I never knew what it felt like to fall madly in love? The truth was that I might not have time or the opportunity. My heart protested the thought, but I shushed it. *We have already had this discussion, too.*

"Well, then," I said, pulling myself out of my thoughts. "If it will make you happy, then it is my dearest wish that you are reunited with Miles one day." I smiled, hoping to somehow apologize for my attempts at discouraging her. "But only if he sees you for how wonderful you truly are. I find it difficult to believe that any man could deserve you."

"Or you." Anne smiled, and then her brow furrowed. "Has the duke mentioned any plans to visit you soon?"

The change of subject surprised me. At least I *hoped* she had meant it as a change of subject. I cast her a brief look of suspicion. "Well—er—I did mention in my last letter that we have been receiving frequent visits from two gentlemen. I suppose he might make plans to visit if he sees that as any reason for concern."

I hadn't meant to alarm Timothy. Admittedly though, I *had* mentioned Mr. Ball with the hope that Timothy would have a purpose in coming back to Foxwell House sooner than planned. I had far too many questions about the house and why he had lived there at all. I also needed his advice on how I might better prepare for London. Of course I could have written to him asking those questions, but I also couldn't deny that I missed him.

It would be a break from the monotony to tease him, talk with him, and see a familiar face. I felt guilty asking him directly to visit after all he had done for me, so I had used Mr. Ball as bait instead.

The line had been cast. All I could do was hope for a bite.

CHAPTER 7

"Stand up straighter, Chesley." Anne circled around the footman and me as we practiced the steps to the cotillion I had been learning that week. Anne was a much better partner than Chesley. He had obviously never danced a cotillion in his life. I laughed at his dazed expression as he struggled to follow each of Anne's instructions.

I threw him an apologetic look. "I know this is not what the duke hired you for, but please entertain us a little longer."

Chesley's pale blue eyes flickered to mine before drifting back down to his feet. His wig shifted on his head, and he hurried to adjust it. He looked quite overwhelmed.

And equally mortified.

I hardly knew what was proper and what wasn't anymore. The rules didn't seem to apply to Anne and me, being so far removed from our old lives. Who was going to accuse me of impropriety if no one was here to witness it? Dancing with a footman was entertaining and insightful, so there was nothing to stop me from continuing. Practicing the dance with a man was much different than what I had grown accustomed to.

Chesley was a great deal taller than Anne, with longer arms and larger hands. He gave me a better idea of what it would be like to dance with the gentlemen of London.

By the time the hour was through, I beamed with pride and excused a very relieved Chesley from his responsibilities. I collapsed on the sofa. My feet ached, but my smile stretched wide. "Am I improving?"

Anne's nose twitched. "Er—I suppose."

"You suppose?" I sat up straight. "I only stepped on his boots twice. And I turned in the correct direction...most of the time."

She sighed. "Yes, but in London, it has to be *every* time. And there is no allowance for stepping on boots."

I pursed my lips. "Well, at least I have plenty of time to practice."

Anne gave an encouraging smile. "You do. Remember, it has only been two months."

A very long two months. I had been doing all I could to keep a positive attitude, but the prospect of the rest of the year was daunting. I missed Charlie. I missed Timothy. I didn't miss home though. It had been nothing more than a cage. The air in Northumberland was different. It was cold and refreshing, filled with mist and salt from the sea. I awoke each day *without* a feeling of dread in my stomach. I hadn't known that dread had ever been there until it was gone.

Still though, each night as I fell asleep, my mind spun with questions about what my future would hold. I often wondered what my father was thinking. Charlie had written and assured me that our father had made minimal efforts to locate me, leaving the task in Charlie's hands.

Timothy hadn't responded to my letter about Mr. Ball yet. It surprised me, but it also sent a spiral of worries through my mind. Had his injuries been more severe than we thought? Was he unwell? How would I know if he was actually safe or not?

I was completely helpless.

"Who is that?" Anne squinted out the window. "A coach is approaching the house."

I put my face in my hands. "If it's Mr. Ball again, please excuse me. I am going to hide beneath my bed."

"It's not Mr. Ball." She gasped. "It's the duke!"

My heart leaped. I jumped to my feet, hurrying to the window. I tripped on the corner of the rug, stumbling forward. My cheeks burned as I caught my balance. Too self-conscious to look at Anne, I fixed my gaze beyond the glass to where the carriage had stopped. Timothy was already on his way to the front door. I only caught a quick glimpse of him before a knock sounded, echoing from the vestibule to the drawing room.

"What makes Timothy think he has to knock?" I said in a breathless voice. "This is his house after all. He is ridiculous." My smile tugged so hard that my cheeks ached. I had never been so eager to see anyone. My feet carried me to the drawing room door and out to the vestibule within seconds. I thought Anne had followed me, but when I looked back, I found the space empty. When I turned around again, the butler had opened the door, and Timothy was stepping inside.

His eyes connected with mine, warm and brown and familiar. I felt ridiculous, bouncing on my toes and rushing toward him, but I couldn't help it. "You came!"

I didn't know what I intended to do by rushing at him like that. Certainly not kiss him again. Or hug him. Or even lay a finger on him. Thankfully I found my senses quickly enough to come to an abrupt halt five feet away. I took a deep breath, laughing at his amused expression. Traveling in the heat, he must have intentionally done without his jacket. His shirtsleeves were rolled to the elbows, and he wore a tan waist-coat with a slightly loose cravat. There were times he looked like a duke, and times he looked like a farmer. Sometimes I wondered which one he would rather be. He had never flaunted his dukedom like others of the nobility did.

Personally, I preferred his farmer look.

His smile reached all the way to the corners of his eyes. It seemed we had both long forgotten our argument that had occurred before our previous parting. "Good afternoon, Nora."

I shook my head in bewilderment. "Good afternoon?"

Half his mouth tilted in a sideways smile. "Did I surprise you?"

I raised both eyebrows. "What do you think?"

He laughed in response, crossing his arms over his chest. His gaze was warm, blanketing me in a comforting sense of security. His eyes didn't leave my face, lingering there for several seconds. That warmth spread over me until it curled and spiraled in my stomach in a strange, unfamiliar sensation.

"I didn't expect you to visit so soon." Of their own voli-tion, my eyes were also performing a rapid examination of Timothy's face. Thankfully, I couldn't detect any scars from his accident the night before he left Foxwell House. The terror of seeing him so helpless and hurt was still vivid in my mind. "You said every three months."

"Unless I had reason for concern."

"Concern?" I feigned ignorance to the best of my ability. Was it about Mr. Ball? Or something else? A jolt of nervousness passed through me. Had my father discovered my location?

His mouth settled into a straight line. "That Mr. Ball sounds like a disagreeable creature."

A smile threatened to spring to my face, but I stopped it. So my bait had worked. I released a sigh. "Yes. I had hoped the journey wouldn't involve any more disagreeable creatures."

Timothy's brow furrowed. He didn't seem to see any humor in the situation. "Has he still been pestering you?"

I hesitated, a thread of guilt stitching my throat closed. I swallowed. Perhaps I shouldn't have mentioned Mr. Ball to Timothy. He had come all this way to investigate. Even if Mr. Ball was just as disagreeable as that cat at the inn, he differed because he truly meant no harm. "Well…he does come calling at least once every week. But he believes our story fully. To him, I am Miss Jane Flowers and Anne is my widowed elder sister, Mrs. Benson." I shrugged. "He is vexing, but rather harmless."

Timothy didn't seem appeased. He walked farther into the house, his strides confident and slow as he examined his surroundings. Was this how a man walked through a house that he owned and took pride in? When he turned to face me again, he gestured at a pot of white roses on the round table in the corner of the vestibule. "I see you have added a feminine touch to the house."

I pressed my lips together. "Mmm, yes?" I cleared my throat. "Yes, they are lovely, are they not?"

Timothy's brow lifted in suspicion. I had started wringing my hands. I stopped myself, but not before he noticed.

"Where did they come from?" He glanced at the roses again.

I exhaled heavily through my lips. "Mr. Ball brought them two days ago."

"For you? Or Lady Daventry?"

I looked down at toes, tapping them just outside my hem. "For me." I looked up, suddenly desperate to acquit myself. "I assure you, I have done absolutely nothing to encourage him. In fact, I have tried very hard to do the opposite, but he continues to call and bring me roses and invite me on walks, which I decline."

Timothy rubbed one side of his face. "A man wouldn't need encouragement to become attached to you. I knew it wasn't wise to leave you without a man's protection. He might see you as vulnerable." He continued rambling about the downfalls of leaving me without a proper guardian, but his words were muffled in my ears. I was still processing his first sentence.

A man wouldn't need encouragement to become attached to you.

Did he really have such confidence in me and my charms? It was humorous. But it also…wasn't. My ears and neck tingled with sudden heat. I rubbed one of my ears, hiding it from Timothy's sight.

"I'm glad I came earlier than planned," he grumbled, his frustration obvious as he took another glance at the pot of roses. He seemed to want nothing more than to throw them off the roof.

"Do not blame the roses," I said with a chuckle. "They are innocent. Truly, so is Mr. Ball. He has done nothing to make Anne or me feel unsafe."

"Not yet." Timothy scowled.

"Come now, Timothy." I laughed. "If you met him, I don't think you would perceive him as a threat at all." I walked closer to him, drawing his gaze back to me. "He is a gentleman who has recently inherited an estate nearby. He tries to be respectable."

Timothy's shoulders relaxed, but he was still scowling. "Do you…like him? Do you welcome his attention?"

"Oh, no, most certainly not," I stammered. "Not in the slightest."

He gave a stiff nod.

"I shall wait until London to attempt to catch a husband." I smiled, hoping to change the subject away from Mr. Ball. "I have been doing all I can to train for the season. I practice my dancing every day."

Timothy's expression lightened. "How can you do that without a partner?"

"Anne dances with me most of the time. And the footman is surprisingly adept as well." I clamped my mouth shut.

"The footman?" Timothy's eyes rounded, then shifted to the two men who stood in their livery against the wall. Chesley's nose twitched, and his Adam's apple bobbed with a swallow.

"Chesley is a very patient and amiable partner."

Timothy stared at me with lingering surprise.

I sighed. "You cannot blame me for asking for his help. If I am going to be dancing with men in London, I need to have a man as a partner when I practice. Of course I could have asked Mr. Ball, but that might have been perceived as too much encouragement."

Timothy was silent for a long moment. Then he cleared his throat, half his mouth quirking upward. "I think you ought to leave Chesley to his assigned duties from now on."

I frowned. "But then how am I to improve upon my dancing?"

He seemed thoroughly amused, eyes bouncing between the flustered footman and me. "We will think of something. Focus on your other skills for now. What else have you been studying?"

I relaxed at his reassurance, taking a deep breath. "I've been practicing the pianoforte, reading, poetry, wit, cards, French, Italian, painting, drawing, embroidery, and anything else that passes the time."

"An impressive list." He gave a soft smile. The light from the front windows reflected off his irises, giving them a golden hue. I lost my words for a long moment, enjoying the familiarity of his eyes and every lash that framed them. To my surprise, a surge of emotion gripped my throat. I hadn't realized how lonely it would be living in this spacious manor with only Anne as company. I had been longing for something that felt like home. Foxwell House had begun to feel like my home, but I was now realizing that brick walls and furnishings could never fulfill that. A friend could. A dear friend.

"What's the matter?" Timothy's expression changed to concern.

I rushed to correct it. I wanted that smile back. "Nothing. I'm simply happy." I took a deep breath. "I'm glad you came. I missed you." I blinked fast, clearing the moisture from my eyes with an embarrassed laugh.

A hint of surprise entered his gaze. It faded slowly, and he stared at me in silence for several seconds before he seemed to find his words. "Well—perhaps I'll stay a while. You'll soon grow weary of my company."

"Not me. I am accustomed to it." I pursed my lips. "Anne might though. You *are* rather boorish at times."

Timothy grinned. He seemed to be in good spirits, so that was a relief. My expression matched his as I stared up at him.

I would never grow weary of teasing him, that much was certain.

"Your grace, what a pleasant surprise." Anne's voice came from behind, tugging my gaze away from Timothy's. Instinctively, I took a step away from him. Anne seemed to have a wayward imagination when it came to my friendship with Timothy, and I couldn't allow her to see anything that might support her ideas.

"Lady Daventry." Timothy gave a bow in answer to Anne's curtsy.

"Pay no heed to what Leonora says. I don't find you boorish at all." She shot me a glance. "This is your home, so of course I could have no objection to you staying as long as you wish to."

Drat. I hadn't known Anne had overheard our conversation. Timothy pressed his lips together to suppress a smile.

"I trust your stay has been comfortable thus far?" Timothy asked.

Anne nodded. "Exceedingly."

"Aside from your unwanted visitor," Timothy added.

Anne's brows rose. "Mr. Elmore?"

"Elmore?"

I pinched my lips together, closing my eyes. When I opened them, Timothy was looking at me expectantly.

"Mr. Ball has a friend," I said through a sigh.

"Is he just as bothersome?" The vexation in Timothy's gaze did not bode well for Mr. Ball *or* Mr. Elmore.

"No, he is rather quiet and well-mannered. He is quite fond of Anne." I slipped her a smile.

Timothy exhaled through his nostrils. "It hasn't been two months, yet you have both managed to acquire a suitor in this nearly lifeless town?"

"It seems you have underestimated our charms, your grace." I grinned up at him, presenting an intentionally wobbly curtsy.

Anne laughed, covering her mouth with the back of her hand to stop it.

Timothy blinked at me, apparently determined not to make light of the situation. I surrendered with a sigh. "As I said before, we have tried to discourage them. I do think the absence of a male guardian in this house has made them less receptive to our efforts though." I scowled.

"So they *are* taking advantage of your vulnerability." Timothy's jaw tightened. "I will have to stay longer than planned."

I shot him a curious look. "How long?"

"A week, perhaps more. Long enough to ensure Mr. Ball doesn't come calling ever again." He turned to face me with a half-smile. "And long enough to relieve Chesley of his duties as your dancing partner."

CHAPTER 8

Why on earth could I not decide on a dress?

I held up my lavender next to my peach, criticizing each one beside my complexion in the mirror. With a frustrated breath, I returned to my wardrobe and chose the light pink instead. I hadn't taken great care with my appearance in weeks, but tonight at dinner I wanted to look pretty. Timothy had seen me at my worst, but he didn't often see me at my best. It shouldn't have mattered so much to me, but I wanted him to see that I could succeed in London. I wanted to impress him.

My heart picked up speed as I selected my jewelry and called for the maid, Julia to assist with my hair and dress. Why was I nervous? I was rarely nervous. I bit my lower lip, aimlessly pacing the room, taking in the now familiar furnishings. If Timothy was staying longer than anticipated, he would surely want to take this room back. It had clearly been his. I couldn't trespass on his hospitality so easily if he would be staying for a full week.

It had come as a relief to hear that Timothy would be

staying, but it had tied my stomach in knots at the same time. I had never experienced such distinct knots before, and it was rather alarming. It wasn't a feeling of dread, nor was it fear or worry. Anticipation? Excitement? Pressure to prove myself? I stopped by the mirror again, scowling at my refection in confusion. Timothy had never judged or criticized me. So why did I suddenly feel like I had something to prove?

As I tried to identify the emotions spinning in my chest, Julia knocked on the door, entering with a curtsy. Her expression was serious, her shoulders tight. Even Julia seemed to be more tense with the presence of a duke in the house. From the dusting of flour on her apron, it seemed she had been busy helping in the kitchen between making Anne and me presentable.

She arranged my hair quickly, taming the wild blonde curls as she pinned them up to the crown of my head, threading a light pink ribbon through them. The curls that had always framed my face, sticking out every which way, were also pinned into the arrangement, leaving my features completely exposed. She applied a soft layer of rouge to my lips and cheeks. I winced as she pinched my skin for added color.

I turned toward the mirror again, and a broad smile tugged on my flushed cheeks. I looked like a lady. A true lady. Much of my fate was connected with my twenty-first birthday, so in my mind, I had assumed that I wouldn't be a real lady until then. But with a little work from Julia, I had been transformed.

"Thank you, Julia," I said with a gasp. "You are so very talented."

"Thank you, my lady." Her face lit up for a moment before settling into the nervous scowl again.

I leaned toward her and lowered my voice. "Don't worry yourself over the duke. He may seem intimidating like a lion, but in truth he is a soft, wooly lamb." I chuckled to myself. "He doesn't believe himself to be as high and mighty as he appears."

A soft smile touched her lips. I couldn't tell if she was amused or relieved. She left the room with a curtsy, and I took one more deep breath before following her out into the corridor. It would only be the three of us—Anne, Timothy, and me—so it wasn't a formal occasion, but it would be good practice if I treated it as such. I straightened my spine as I entered the drawing room.

Timothy was the only one there. I spotted him sitting near the pianoforte, a brown leather book in hand. He looked up as I entered, and I met his gaze with a wide smile. He immediately stood, closing the book he had been holding. His eyes lingered on me for a long moment, and I couldn't quite decipher his reaction. Timothy being difficult to read wasn't a new discovery. He always had been.

He didn't look away as I walked farther into the room, and despite my previous determination to remain prim and proper, I gave a twirl and splayed my hands out to my sides. "I must insist that Julia come with me when I go to London." I grinned. "She made me look like an elegant lady, did she not?"

I held my breath, the knots returning to my stomach when Timothy didn't reply. His eyes connected with mine, and my heart gave a strange thump. Did he disagree?

"She did." He cleared his throat, and a smile finally touched his lips, even if it seemed forced. He swallowed, setting down the book he was holding. He seemed eager to look away from me now, when just seconds before he had been staring with what could have only been scrutiny.

Disappointment settled in my stomach, but I pushed it away. What did I expect? Had I thought Timothy would praise me to the heavens? I was being ridiculous and childish. *I* knew I looked my best, and that was all that mattered. A woman who was truly confident did not require any praise or approval, especially from men. Since living with Anne, I had tried to learn from her confident demeanor. She was not prideful, but sure of herself. If I wanted to be respected in London, I would have to develop the same attribute.

Timothy turned toward me again. He wore a black jacket, white cravat, and a rust red waistcoat. At the sight of his neatly combed hair, I remembered that one strand that had perpetually fallen over his forehead on our journey to Northumberland, and how I had pushed his wet hair off his forehead and held his face in my hands when he was unconscious in the rain. I chose not to dwell on what had come next, especially not when he was looking at me like he had a secret—like he knew how to read my mind.

In our letters, he had assured me that his recovery from his head injury had been easy, but there was still a great deal I didn't know about how he had spent his time since leaving Foxwell House. "I have told you in great detail how I have been spending my days." I smiled up at him. "But what have you been doing these two months?"

"Much."

I raised my eyebrows with a laugh. "Much of what?"

He laughed. "The details will likely bore you."

"It can't possibly be more boring than how I spend my days here."

He looked down at the floor, a soft smile on his face. "I

went back to my estate, met with my steward, managed my finances and tenants, and spent many hours in my mother's company." He looked up. "Much of my time was also spent worrying over you."

Guilt swept through my chest. I never should have mentioned Mr. Ball in my letters. "How is your mother's health?" His father had died years before, when Timothy had become the duke. The last news I had heard of his mother was that she was unwell, but I didn't know the extent of her illness.

Timothy sighed. "She is declining. She has bad days and better days. Her pain is minimal, but she lacks the appetite and energy that she once had."

My heart ached. "I'm so very sorry, Timothy. You should be there with her! I promise Anne and I can fare well on our own." My guilt intensified. "I'm grateful that you came to visit, but Mr. Ball is not worth the trouble of staying longer than you planned."

Timothy shook his head, eyes soft with gratitude. "I appreciate your concern, but my mother is living the comfortable life of a dowager duchess. She is waited on by her maid day and night. I suspect she was growing weary of my company and was eager for the solitude."

I groaned. "You must do away with the notion that people grow weary of you. You are delightful, and I am certain your mother would agree."

He laughed under his breath. "She would find me more delightful if I would marry." The mirth faded from his expression.

"Marry?" It was all I could manage to choke out. All I had ever heard Timothy say in regard to his own marriage was that he had no desire for it, and even then, he rarely spoke of the subject.

"It is her dying wish." He crossed his arms over his chest. "I love her too much to ignore it."

I stared at him in silence, hoping he would elaborate. He didn't. He was not one to share more than absolutely necessary, but my curiosity demanded that I pry. "Is there a particular lady she wants you to marry?"

"No." He shook his head, staring at his boots. "But she refuses to leave this earth without knowing that I have set into motion the possibility of producing an heir." He looked up. "It is my responsibility to fulfill her wishes. After the effort and hardship it required of her to have me, I cannot continue to claim that I will never marry or continue the dukedom."

My head spun. It was strange to hear Timothy speak of marriage without dismissal. He had always rejected the idea, at least for the past few years. But with no siblings, the dukedom would indeed die if Timothy didn't have children of his own, particularly a son.

"Effort and hardship?" I swallowed, suddenly nervous to be inquiring about the personal matters of his family. I never had. It hadn't ever seemed prudent to do so. But tonight he seemed more open, as if there was a lot on his mind and he wanted to find relief by sharing it with someone. I knew the feeling.

Timothy hesitated for a long moment before speaking again. "She was forced to endure a multitude of treatments in the hopes that she could conceive, some of which I cannot help but blame for the steady decline of her health. My father criticized her for being unable to bear his children. He did not respect her, nor was he ever loyal to her." His jaw tightened. "I'm certain I have illegitimate siblings running about England somewhere."

Growing up near Timothy, I had heard him speak of his father with little fondness. When his father died four years before, it had surprised me how greatly it upset him. I went months without seeing him, and I had never dared to ask where he had gone. When he returned to his estate, he had been different. More withdrawn and reserved as he was now. He had gone from being a duke's son, to being a duke, and the burden had seemed far too heavy to bear at his young age.

Timothy continued with a deep breath. "When I was finally born, my mother's duty had been completed in the eyes of my father. He hardly allowed me to spend time with her. I was always in the nursery with nannies, and later with my governess. I was being raised as a *future duke*, not as a boy." A faint smile crossed his features. "I was often envious of you and Charlie. As you know, I sneaked out of the house as often as I could to play with you both."

I smiled, but it hurt. My heart stung. I had always admired his mother, but I admired her even more now. I had never known how much she had suffered. She carried herself well, much like Timothy did—never showing the pain that festered on the inside. Was it more admirable to bear pain alone, or to find the bravery to share it with others? I studied his downcast expression and the smile he had forced to cover it up.

"And *I* sneaked out of my house as often as I could to avoid my father." I smiled despite the dismal words I had just spoken. I was just as guilty of hiding my pain. I buried it with positivity and smiles, trying to forget all the nights I had cried in my room. Never knowing my mother and being so disregarded by my father had beaten me down more than I had ever admitted. Watching as Charlie was given so many opportunities and revered by our father had never made sense, and it had never felt fair as I had remained home and hidden away in my bedchamber. Being resented for something I couldn't control had been endlessly frustrating.

Timothy's sad eyes nearly brought tears to mine. "It must be liberating to be so far away from him now."

I nodded, a lump forming in my throat. I hadn't meant to change the subject to myself. I quickly redirected it. "So…" I tried to gather my thoughts, "…you must find a wife as soon as possible."

"I will wait until we go to London next year."

I could hardly imagine Timothy courting a lady, or doing anything romantic. But I could envision how protective and attentive he would be over his wife and his children. He would be nothing like his father. The idea of him choosing between all the young ladies eager to marry a duke was vexing, prickling at my skin with discontent. "Why not sooner?" I asked. Surely he could find ways to meet other ladies before London.

He paused, eyes settling on my face. "I have other duties in the meantime."

My brows flew upward and I shook my head. "You cannot allow *me* to stop you. You could easily court a lady and still visit Anne and me here on occasion."

"I would rather not."

I placed one hand on my hip. "Do you think I will disapprove of your lady of choice? I suppose I *will* have to scrutinize her to ensure she is worthy of you, but that should take no time at all." I cast him a teasing look, but he didn't appear amused.

He sighed. "Let us put this subject to rest." His mood seemed to have changed drastically in a matter of seconds.

I gave him a pointed look. "You cannot deny that you will be performing the same judgment on the man I choose to marry. It is only fair that you allow me a chance to declare whether or not I think your lady of choice is worthy of you."

Exasperation crept through his expression. "I already know I will never be able to say a man is worthy of you."

A wave of unexpected heat flooded my cheeks. "It would seem that Mr. Ball is destined to be judged unfairly, then."

Timothy gave a faint smile. "There is nothing he can do to stop it."

Our attention was drawn to the doorway as Anne walked through it. A fleeting thought crossed my mind as I looked at her perfect dark hair, beautiful complexion and kind eyes: *Perhaps Anne would make a good match for Timothy.*

Did he realize it too? I checked his face in search of any indication that he was admiring her, but he was already looking at me again. "I thought you might like to know there will be no fish on the menu at dinner tonight."

"As it should always be," I said with a firm nod.

Anne gave a light laugh. "We are living just outside a fishing village. I'm missing far too many opportunities for good fish because Leonora cannot bear the smell."

I whirled to face her, eager to defend myself. "I said you could buy fish as often as you like! You and Timothy are far too similar, always opposed to causing me any discomfort. I am capable of bearing the scent of fish so long as I don't have to eat it."

Anne's lips twisted. "Yes, but I also do it for my own comfort. If I were to have fish prepared, you would complain the entire evening and throw open all the windows."

Timothy laughed.

I shot him a glare. "To prove you both wrong, I am going to the market tomorrow to buy fish for Anne if you would like to join me."

"I would love to," he said, obviously struggling to keep a neutral expression.

"Oh, yes. I forgot that you enjoy the vile creatures too." The memory of him switching his beef for my fish at the inn flooded back to my mind. That seemed like so long ago. It was still the most delicious beef I had ever eaten. And the most revolting fish I had ever smelled.

Timothy laughed again as we made our way to the dining room.

CHAPTER 9

I had grown so accustomed to the table being just Anne and me, so my heart lifted at the sight of Timothy sitting at the head of the table. He belonged in the house just as I had envisioned. I had spent weeks navigating my new surroundings, and now the puzzle was finally complete. Timothy had been the missing piece.

We were served white soup, then beef, potatoes, and carrots. I watched as Timothy took a sip from his glass. There had been so many questions I wanted to ask him, but after all that he had shared about his mother, I was nervous to ask anything else that might be deemed too personal. There seemed to be a significance to the time Timothy had once spent at Foxwell House and why he had purchased it. He hadn't indicated as much, but I felt it in my bones.

"I've been curious about something," I said in a quick voice.

Timothy glanced at me from over his glass.

"I haven't ever heard stories about your hunting, yet I was

told that you purchased this house as a hunting lodge. What is there to hunt in this area?"

He lifted his knife and fork, cutting the beef on his plate and taking a bite in an apparent attempt to delay his answer. He swallowed. "There are plenty of deer and grouse in the woods nearby."

"Did you ever invite any friends to accompany you on your hunts?"

"No. I enjoyed the solitude."

"For a hunting lodge, there is an astonishing lack of taxidermy on the walls." I lifted my glass as casually as I could and took a sip.

Timothy's gaze locked with mine. "My intention for purchasing this manor was not only to hunt." He paused, but only for a short moment. "This house was built more than a century ago. The previous owner made many repairs, and I was very impressed with its condition. The previous owner hunted the land for decades, and he told me many tales of his days here, one of which might intrigue you." The rapid change of subject eliminated my opportunity to inquire further. Had it been intentional? He had just confessed that his reason for acquiring the manor hadn't *only* been for hunting, but now he was dodging further explanation.

"What is this tale?" Anne asked. Her eyes flitted to me. She must have sensed my objective and found it too impertinent. Her constant awareness of manners made my life quite difficult at times.

I lowered my glass in defeat.

Timothy sat forward. "He had a hunting dog. A hound by the name of Jeremy. This hound was his dearest companion and friend, until it was killed in a hunting accident."

My jaw lowered. "You said I would enjoy this tale."

He held up a finger. "It isn't over. He buried the dog on the property, but years later, he dug up the bones."

I gasped. "Why on earth would he do that?"

Timothy's smile grew. "He was a strange man, and quite advanced in years. I'm certain he was senile." He stopped the story to take a long swig of water and another bite from his plate.

I tapped my foot, impatient with the suspense Timothy was attempting to create. He seemed far too entertained by my rapture. "So the old man dug up the bones, and then what happened?"

"He took Jeremy's skull and hid it somewhere inside Foxwell House. He wanted his dog to live on within these walls."

I gaped at him, exchanging a horrified glance with Anne. "Did he tell you where he hid it?"

Timothy chuckled, shaking his head. "He claimed that he didn't remember. I did search for it, but not as thoroughly as I might have if I truly wanted to find it. If you are bored during your time here, I would suggest searching for the skull. It could provide a bit of entertainment."

"I'm not certain I want to find a dog's skull." I shuddered, which only made Timothy laugh again.

"How fascinating." Anne's eyes rounded. "But I agree, I would rather pretend the story is nothing more than a sham."

I threw Timothy a suspicious look. "*Is* it a sham?"

He held up his hands in defense. "I am not responsible if it is. I am simply repeating what I was told by the old man."

"The old *senile* man. If he didn't remember where he hid the skull, then he could have easily imagined the entire story."

"Perhaps. But perhaps not." He smirked.

"You are being far too mysterious." I laughed, and was suddenly tempted to throw my water at him. What if it was true? It would be a very interesting addition to the novel I planned to write about my adventure. How many people were given the opportunity to hunt for an old dog's skull? I grimaced. Once again, the idea didn't seen very pleasant.

"Well, if one of us finds the skull, how are you going to reward us?" I batted my eyelashes with a smile.

Timothy scoffed. "You would already have the dog's skull. What further reward could you possibly require?"

"I'm sure I could think of something."

Timothy cast his gaze heavenward with a sigh. "Very well. There shall be a *reward* for the one who finds the dog's skull. Your wish shall be my command."

I sat back in my chair with a satisfied grin. "That will serve as proper motivation." Even without a reward, I would have been far too curious not to search for the skull. I could transform the house into not only a hunting lodge, but a *treasure* hunting lodge of sorts. What other strange treasures might that old man have hidden around the manor? A thrill of excitement cascaded over my skin.

After eating trifle for dessert, we gathered together in the drawing room. I played some of the songs I had been practicing on the pianoforte, and I even read Timothy the poem I had written about Mr. Ball.

"You should read it to him," Timothy said, crossing one leg over his knee. "My interference might not be needed at all." The candlelight flickered on his smiling features, and I couldn't stop the silly grin on my face. I liked this relaxed version of him much better than the anxious, serious one who had brought me to Northumberland. Perhaps it had been the glass of port he had drank after dinner that was causing him to smile so much, but regardless, I was happy to see him in good spirits.

Anne held a hand to her stomach, leaning over in her chair as she laughed at my poem. "No, your grace, the man will not be stopped. Would you like to know what Leonora already said to him?"

I leaped from my seat, giving a furious shake of my head. "Don't you dare tell him."

Anne could hardly speak with how heartily she was laughing. I stopped beside her, fully prepared to cover her mouth with my hands if I had to.

"I would very much like to know," Timothy said.

I pivoted, shaking my head at him. "No, no, it is really nothing of consequence. It is boring, so very boring. Let us talk of something else."

Anne's shaky voice came before I could stop her. "She told him she would rather have her meals served in a chamber pot or bite into the flesh of a freshly caught fish than endure his company."

I squeezed my eyes shut. Anne had not been quite so amused in the moment as she was now. I checked Timothy's expression. He looked just as shocked as I had expected. "Did you really say that?"

I clasped my hands together, returning to my seat with surrender. "Yes…among other things."

He rubbed his jaw, shaking his head. "And the man proceeded to bring you roses."

"It is entirely perplexing," I said. "Is there something I should know about the ways of men in order to be prepared for London? Do all men take harsh words as encouragement?"

"Only the odd ones."

That did make sense. Mr. Ball was certainly odd.

After a few more minutes of uncontrollable laugher, Anne excused herself for the evening. It was wonderful to see her developing a lighter mood, much like Timothy had. Was this an effect of living at Foxwell House? Was there something in the air? I too felt lighter ever since arriving there.

Now that Anne was gone, I became more aware of the fact that I was sharing the settee with Timothy. My knee was touching the side of his thigh, but I didn't dare move it. I stared at all the other empty seats, and they seemed to stare back at me. The longcase clock ticked and ticked. I maintained eye contact with a silk chair near the door until Timothy broke the silence.

"Have you been comfortable in your quarters?"

I rotated toward him, catching the genuine curiosity in his gaze. "Yes." I swallowed. "But I have been thinking about something. It seems that the room I have been occupying was once occupied by you?" I cringed at how awkward and nervous I sounded.

"It was."

I had known, but hearing him confirm it sent a wave of embarrassment through me. I cleared my throat. "I would like to be moved to a different room while you are here. It is your house, after all, and…I think it would be most appropriate if you stayed in that room." I held my chin high. This could not be another situation like the inn, when he had insisted on taking the lesser of the two rooms. I needed to hold my ground.

He blinked. "Absolutely not."

"It is *your* room."

"It *was* my room. It is now yours. I did not come here to uproot you and claim all the finest things of the manor. I came to ensure you were safe and comfortable."

Frustration rose in my chest. "I must insist. You have traveled far to be here, and you deserve the most comfortable bed."

"Nora."

"Goodnight." I stood, starting toward the door as quickly as I could. It was unlikely that Timothy would follow me. Even so, my footsteps picked up speed as I made my way through the corridor and toward the staircase. All I had to do was make it to one of the other guest bedchambers and lock the door. I could wait until Timothy surrendered to call for my maid.

My heart thudded in my ears. Mingled with the sound of my hurried footfalls, I hadn't heard Timothy's footfalls until I reached the top of the stairs. I turned around, a shriek escaping my throat. I pressed a hand to my chest. "Timothy!"

Each of his paces was likely equivalent to two of mine, so I shouldn't have been so surprised he had caught up to me. He crossed his arms over his chest, raising one eyebrow. "Where are you going?"

"To my new room." I whirled around again, walking faster this time. The door was at the end of the corridor, and I had been inside many times. It seemed to be an extra room that Timothy had prepared specifically for his use or Charlie's during their visits to Foxwell House during the year. It was much smaller and plainer—the bed, the furnishings, the room itself. It didn't make sense for Timothy, who stood at least a foot taller and much broader than me, to sleep in a smaller bed. Not this time.

"Nora, stop." His voice was half amusement, half exasperation.

I didn't stop.

The door was only a few paces away. I reached for the

brass handle, but Timothy caught me by the arm. He was laughing, but that didn't make it any less shocking when he bent down and lifted me off the floor.

I gasped, my body limp as he cradled me like some sort of infant, one hand behind my knees and the other around my back, tucking me against his chest. He turned around, starting back toward the grand bedchamber. As soon as I gathered my wits again, I squirmed against his strong arms. "What are you doing?" My voice was louder than I intended.

"Taking you to your room."

I prayed that Anne was asleep. If she heard the commotion in the corridor, I would have much to explain the next day.

I wasn't often vexed by Timothy, but in the moment, my nerves buzzed with frustration. I considered asking him to set me down, but I was too weak to form the words. I stopped squirming, studying the creases in his cheeks from his unreserved smile. "You should not drink port," I blurted in an irritated voice. "It makes you do strange things."

He laughed, crossing the threshold of *his* room. "I am doing what needs to be done."

"No. A *duke* should have the finest things!"

He dropped me down on the bed, and my head sank into the pillow. He hovered over me. "But a gentleman will always ensure a lady has the finest things."

I froze, my tense muscles relaxing into the mattress.

Lady.

He had called me a lady.

A gleeful sensation enrobed my body, but then the realization of my position crashed over me. Timothy still leaned over me, one hand pressed firmly into the mattress on either side of my shoulders. I was caged in by his arms, and his eyes draped over me like a blanket. No, it was heavier and warmer than an ordinary blanket. It kept me captive, stoking a flame in my chest. I couldn't move even if I wanted to.

And I didn't.

My heart picked up speed, sending a strange burst of energy through my veins. Then the butterflies began flapping their wings in my stomach, fluttering around in there until my lungs forgot how to breathe. The worst part of it all was that a strand of his hair had come loose from the rest, falling over his forehead. I stared up at him, at a loss for words.

"Goodnight, Nora," he said in a quiet voice.

I would have continued to fight him, but my voice was still inoperative. He removed his hands from the bed and stood up straight again. He started to walk away, a scowl marking his brow.

"Wait, Timothy."

He turned, a muscle jumping in his jaw. "Yes?"

"Thank you," I grumbled.

One side of his mouth fought against the other, rising in a half-smile. "You have an odd way of showing your gratitude."

I shifted to sit up on the bed. I could feel one of my curls springing loose from the rest. "It's not gratitude. It's acceptance."

He chuckled. "Sleep well."

I watched him go, but the butterflies in my stomach didn't vanish with him. What on earth had been the cause of that?

I fell back into the pillows, wringing my fingers together as I stared at the ceiling. My conversation with Timothy from that night replayed in my mind. He now planned to marry— and soon. It was difficult to imagine him falling in love or proposing to a woman.

It was vexing to imagine, actually.

There were countless women in society who would marry him solely based on the fact that he was a duke. They wouldn't even care to know that he was noble, kind, witty, and loyal. To see him undervalued or valued for the wrong reasons would drive me mad.

I scowled as I rolled to one side, burying my cheek in my pillow. But did it matter? He wasn't mine to keep, nor to give away. My pulse sounded in my ear, thrumming fast and hard. *He wasn't mine.* He never had been, and he never would be.

But did I want him to be?

I pulled my pillow over my head in panic. *No.* No, no, no. These wayward thoughts needed to be stopped at once. My heart was far too imaginative and romantic, and simply because a handsome man had carried me to my room, I was now creating notions that would bring me nothing but harm and disappointment. If he knew I had kissed him, I would die of mortification, I was sure of it. Timothy was doing his duty as my protector, that was all. He was my friend, and I was like a sister to him. That was how it had always been. It could never be anything else.

I scolded myself for my unruly thoughts as I fell asleep.

CHAPTER 10

I arose late the next morning. I only had a few minutes to write my thoughts in my diary before heading to the breakfast room.

Nora's Coming of Age Diary
September 17, 1816

Timothy surprised me with a visit to Foxwell House. He told me that he now has plans to marry when we go to London. Who could ever deserve him? I couldn't sleep last night because of it. Also because he carried me to my bed. I know it sounds quite scandalous, but ~~unfortunately~~ it wasn't. I must confess though that I had butterflies in my stomach, which is entirely unacceptable. I spent the late hours of the night thinking of the best way to banish my strange feelings for Timothy. My conclusion is that I need to help find him a wife—someone I approve of.

• • •

I stopped outside the breakfast room, peeking through the crack in the door. Anne and Timothy were already inside, and I watched their interaction. Was there any potential connection? If Timothy was going to marry anyone, it would have to be Anne. Unfortunately, she was in love with Miles, but surely an offer from Timothy could change her previous feelings. I had no doubt Timothy could succeed in marrying anyone he desired.

Did he desire Anne?

I studied his expression as they carried on a polite conversation across the table. Neither of them appeared to be flirting, but I had also never seen Timothy or Anne flirt with anyone. It was difficult to envision.

"Good morning," I said in a cheerful voice as I walked into the room. I had chosen a yellow dress, hoping to bring a little more sunshine to the cloudy sky. I had a mission to achieve that day, so my steps carried more enthusiasm than usual. I stopped near the table, planting both hands on my hips. "Today I should like to venture into town to buy Anne a fish. Who would like to join me?"

Anne seemed to choke a little on her tea.

I held my chin high as Timothy's eyes lit up with amusement.

"There's a fishing village farther north with the best selection of fish," Timothy said. "The journey would be nearly an hour, but it would be worth the time."

"That sounds perfect." I began filling my plate with eggs and fruit at the sideboard, then took a seat at the table. "Anne, will you be joining us?"

She gave a light laugh, dark brows lifting. "You really mustn't go to the trouble of the journey simply to bring me a fish."

"I want to." I smiled. "But if you come, you might be able to select the fish yourself."

She exchanged a glance with Timothy. "Very well. I will come."

Excellent. The journey would not only allow me to buy a fish, but it would also allow me to witness more of Timothy's interactions with Anne. Perhaps I could make an attempt at matchmaking. If I could manage to attach Timothy to Anne in a timely manner, I could shush my feelings before they developed to a dangerous level and replace them with joy for the union of my two friends.

"Will you be recognized in the village?" I asked Timothy.

"Most likely. I have been there many times during my visits to Foxwell House. I consider some of the residents my friends. I don't imagine you or Anne will be recognized, but we will maintain your false identities regardless."

I frowned. Timothy having so many friends in a fishing village was odd, but I shrugged it off.

After finishing breakfast, I fetched my bonnet and shawl and the three of us set off in the carriage. The sun was covered with clouds, painting the sky a pale grey. The passing landscape was lush green and purple, the heather in full bloom on the prickly moors. I could understand why Timothy had chosen to purchase a manor in the area. It was beautiful.

We arrived in the fishing village just before the hour, and my nose wrinkled with distaste the moment my feet touched the cobblestones. The air was filled with the scent of all sorts of sea creatures. I swallowed, hiding my grimace when Anne stepped out of the carriage behind me. I took a deep breath, releasing it with a content sigh. "It smells delightful, does it not?"

"It does indeed." Timothy looked down at me with a

knowing smile. I didn't expect to fool him. I had never been able to do that.

"Where shall we start?" The streets were filled with shouting costermongers with crates of fish, hot fish pies, and other goods. Most of the shop doorways were crowded with people. Small cottages were packed close together in the distance, situated close to the edge of the cliffs.

Despite the dreary sky, the people on the streets greeted one another with smiles and friendly nods, carrying baskets of food on their arms. These were not servants shopping for their employers. These were mothers and fathers shopping for their own families. I hadn't been raised in such an environment, and for the first time, I felt ashamed of my vibrant yellow embroidered dress, fine leather gloves, and trimmed bonnet. We had already attracted many gazes from the street. Timothy was likely to receive most of the attention though, so I allowed my shoulders to relax.

"I would like to introduce you to my friend, Mr. Prout," Timothy said. "He's a fisherman. If we're going to buy fish, it should be from him."

The idea of Timothy being friends with a fisherman was far too puzzling. I nearly laughed, but after studying his profile, I realized he was serious. How had Timothy become friends with this *Mr. Prout?* During his visits to Foxwell House had he come to this village often? It seemed a strange place to come frequently, especially when he had servants who could make the journey for him. If he enjoyed the fish from that town so much, then he certainly wouldn't have to fetch it himself. It was all so peculiar.

As we walked down the street, I linked my arm through Anne's. At least four people curtsied or bowed with a 'your grace,' as Timothy passed, offering smiles in greeting. He greeted them all by name, which only intensified my shock.

"How do you know these people so well?" I walked faster, keeping my arm looped through Anne's.

"I am not one to forget names or faces."

I frowned. That was not an adequate explanation.

He continued walking with his confident stride, greeting at least three others before we reached the steep walk down to a bay. Small fishing boats sat on the shore, each one filled with piles of fish. Several men worked near the boats, and I nearly lost my breakfast at the gruesome sight of discarded fish parts.

My steps slowed. If I hadn't been so insistent on bringing home a fish for Anne, I would never have ventured down to that bay. Was this some sort of test? There had been hundreds of fish for sale on the village streets, yet Timothy was bringing me down to this secluded bay in order to choose a fish?

He cast a glance over his shoulder, offering his hand to Anne to help her down the first steep step. I focused on her face, searching for any sign that she enjoyed holding his hand, or that he enjoyed holding hers. They were both focused on the ground, so there was no evidence to be collected.

When Anne was safely down the steepest part of the cliff, Timothy came back for me.

I shifted my basket to one arm. "Are you not going to carry me as you did yesterday?" I asked in a flippant voice.

He smiled. "I would offer, but I would sooner expect you to refuse my help and make the venture down the cliff on your own."

I took his hand with a relenting sigh. "I would rather not tumble to my death."

His fingers wrapped firmly around mine, and I followed

where his feet went. "I must apologize for my behavior last night," Timothy said after a moment of silence. "I was not myself."

My heart leaped, and I took a careful step over a rock. "I already know it was the port."

"Perhaps." He scowled at the rocks.

I glanced at our hands, tightly woven together. "I know I thanked you in a letter, but I want to thank you again for the gloves."

Timothy's eyes met mine before focusing on his footwork again. "I was glad to see you wearing them."

"I didn't even remember that it was my birthday that day. But you did." It was still astonishing how attentive and observant Timothy was. In the midst of the lofty task of transporting me safely to Northumberland, he had managed to remember my birthday of all days.

He shook his head. "It was a trivial thing."

"Not to me."

We reached level ground and he released my hand instantly, brushing his against the side of his trousers. His chest rose and fell with a deep breath, and he turned toward the upcoming path. Had he felt the need to rid himself of residue from touching me? He hadn't done that when he released Anne's hand. I kept my confusion from showing on my face, ignoring the dropping sensation in my stomach. The rest of the path down the cliff was smooth, switching back and forth until we ended on the sand.

Besides brushing his hand on his trousers, Timothy showed other signs of nervousness as we walked across the sand. He scanned the area, his gait more hesitant than it had been on the cobblestone street. I walked beside him, watching the side of his face as we came closer to the hollering men and their smelly boats of dead fish.

"Stay close to me," he said, eyes shifting in my direction.

I nodded. My stomach twisted. If Timothy was nervous, that was a sure sign that I should be too. Were these men dangerous? Why on earth would he bring us to a dangerous bay if it wasn't necessary?

My worries faded as a smile broke over Timothy's face. He waved, and I followed his gaze to a man who was pulling in a fishing boat by a rope. His clothing was soaked through to the middle of his chest, his pale hair wild in the wind. A wave hit the back of his knees, making him stumble.

"That is Mr. Prout," Timothy said, meeting my gaze expectantly. Did he want my opinion? My first impression? I stared at the man, confused that Timothy had ever made such an unlikely acquaintance.

"He seems to have no fear of the sea," I muttered, observing as Mr. Prout tugged that old boat to shore. He walked closer, the smile fading from his face as he noticed my presence as well as Anne's. It couldn't have been often that young ladies came down to that rugged fishing bay. Mr. Prout was broad and seemingly strong, but as he approached, I noticed grey hairs mingled with the blond. His sun-weathered skin showed many wrinkles, but his set of sharp blue eyes made him appear more youthful. With the contradictory nature of his features, no age between forty and sixty would have surprised me.

"Your grace." Mr. Prout had an accent that was less refined than the ones I was accustomed to in Somerset. His eyes darted from Timothy to me, settling on my face. I smiled.

"Allow me to introduce Mrs. Benson and Miss Flowers."

The man was silent for a long moment before speaking in that rugged voice again. "'Tis a pleasure to meet you both."

He was still staring at me. I inched closer to Timothy, forcing another polite smile in Mr. Prout's direction.

"I am told you have fish for sale?" I asked in a quick voice. It would be best to get the fish quickly and take our leave.

"Not for sale," Mr. Prout said. "Today 'tis free of charge." He wrung some water from his wet sleeves, his movements flustered as he hurried to the nearest boat.

When his back was turned, I raised my eyebrows at Timothy. Were dukes and their friends often offered free things? It made no sense at all considering that dukes were rich. I had pin money of my own from Charlie as well. "No, sir, I must insist on paying you for—" I gulped as he staggered over with the largest fish I had ever seen. The veins in his neck swelled as he hefted it up to show us. He beamed with pride. Now I could see why Timothy found him endearing. He seemed eager to please, and his smile was one of the most genuine I had encountered.

I laughed. It was the perfect fish to gift to Anne. I turned toward her with a grin. "Will that fish suffice?"

She covered her mouth with one hand, eyes round.

I eyed the basket on my arm. It was far too small for that particular fish. "Do you happen to have anything smaller?"

Mr. Prout followed my gaze to the basket before letting out a hoot of laughter. "Of course."

Timothy chuckled beside me as Mr. Prout returned with a fish of a much more manageable size. When he placed it in my basket, it flopped down to the bottom with a squelching sound that made my stomach turn.

"I thank you kindly, sir." I reached in my reticule to withdraw my coins, but Mr. Prout's booming voice stopped me.

"No, 'tis a gift."

My gaze flew up to his. "You don't owe me any such thing." I smiled and reached for my reticule again, but this time, Timothy stopped me.

"Thank you for your generosity, Mr. Prout. We will be sure to repay you at a later date."

I scowled. Was that the correct way of accepting an unexpected gift? I had never been gifted anything by a stranger. I gave Mr. Prout a grateful smile before following Timothy back up the hill. When I turned around, Mr. Prout was still watching us—watching me in particular.

I walked a little faster.

"Well, then, you shall have a delicious fish dinner this evening, Anne."

"Wonderful," she said with a smile.

Timothy helped Anne up a steep rock, then me. "I think it might be prudent to invite Mr. Prout to dinner at some point before I leave Foxwell House," he said. His gaze searched my face, as if he were looking for something in my expression. "If only to repay him for the fish."

"Oh—of course." I wasn't certain I wanted Mr. Prout's watchful eyes on me for an entire evening, but Timothy seemed to be quite fond of him. I held his gaze, tipping my head to one side. "I have never heard of a fisherman dining with a duke. Do you think society would…judge you harshly for it?"

"Society cannot judge you for something they don't know." He kicked at a rock on the path. "That is the benefit of being so far north. The rules of propriety are at liberty to be ignored. Besides that, I'm a duke. I can do what I want." He tossed me a smile that was somehow still humble despite his words.

I narrowed my eyes as I studied him. Was that why Timothy had bought a manor here? Was it so he would have a place to come and ignore propriety? He was growing more mysterious by the minute. I had known him nearly my entire life, yet there were still times I felt like I was looking at a stranger. He had secrets, I was sure of it. A new determination rose in my chest.

I was going to find out what they were.

CHAPTER 11

Timothy was waiting for me in the drawing room. We had agreed to meet at twelve for my first dancing lesson. I might have imagined it, but the corridors were still permeated with the scent of fish. I tried not to breathe through my nose as made my way to the drawing room. Anne had enjoyed her entire fish, all the way down to the bones. I was grateful Mr. Prout had given me the smaller one so I wouldn't have to bear the smell all week.

I had spent the morning practicing my dancing in front of the mirror in my bedchamber, keeping my neck and spine straight and rehearsing the steps in my mind. There were many dances to be memorized, but today we would be focusing on the same cotillion that I had been practicing with Chesley.

My stomach fluttered, my palms damp. Dancing with a footman had been much less intimidating than this. The desire to prove myself to Timothy had kept me awake for hours in the night, as well as the determination to discover what he was hiding from me.

Dressed in a blue waistcoat and shirtsleeves, Timothy walked toward me with a smile. "I have spoken with Chesley, and his only task today is to critique my form." He glanced in the footman's direction. It was part of a footman's duty to be stoic and disappear into the walls, but I caught a smile twitching on his mouth.

"I suspect *your* form is not what will need critiquing." I drew a shaky breath, balling my hands into fists at my sides.

"You cannot be as graceless as you claim."

"You're right. I'm worse."

His smile was contagious. He had been smiling more of late. It was another cloudy day, so very little light came through the window. In the dimness, Timothy's hair was not blond, nor was it brown. It reminded me of the color of the wet sand we had stood on at the bay the day before. His eyes were the same shade, a perfect match.

I had spent far too long staring at his face, so I looked at the pianoforte instead. "Is Anne coming to play the music?"

"Not today. I think you will benefit from practicing the steps without music first. We shall take it as slowly as necessary."

"Very well." I scolded myself for being so nervous. This was Timothy, not a handsome stranger in a ballroom. I eyed his face again. Well, he *was* handsome, but not a stranger at all. He was familiar and safe, yet there was something new about him. I didn't know if it was his doing or mine, but there was an unfamiliarity in our recent interactions that heightened my senses. Had he changed, or had my perception of him changed? I shushed my heart before it could tell me something I didn't want to hear.

"I presume Lady Daventry has already introduced you to most of the steps?" Timothy asked.

I gave a reluctant nod. "Yes. But please do not ask me to demonstrate them." I paused. "Or name them."

He took a step toward me, a gleam of amusement in his eyes. "The balance, rigadoon, contretemps, chassé, pirouette, and gavotte step will be most necessary to memorize for a cotillion."

I nodded, swallowing hard. I had been practicing several of those steps, but still struggled to differentiate them or perform them in the correct order.

He must have sensed that I was overwhelmed, because he cast me a reassuring smile. "We will focus on just two today. Show me your best rigadoon."

I took a deep breath, rehearsing the movement in my mind as I performed it. *Right kick, step, left kick, step, together, plié, rise.* I looked up at Timothy for approval.

"That was nearly perfect." He gave me an encouraging smile and nodded toward the floor. "Do it again, but don't look at your feet."

I sighed. "My feet don't usually cooperate if I can't see them."

"When dancing, it's imperative that you keep your gaze up. With practice, the steps of the dance will become natural. You will then be able to give your full attention to your partner. Eye contact must be maintained." He stepped forward and took both my hands. His hands were warmer than mine, the change of temperature sending a shiver up both my arms. I had always worn gloves when his hands touched mine—into the carriage and out, or walking across treacherous ground. But today my gloves were absent, and so were his.

"Try again, but look at me," he said.

I filled my lungs and held my breath, fixing my gaze on his. When my feet began to move, he replicated the motion, moving in time with my steps. I finished without stepping on his feet or missing a step. I let out a gasp of delight. "Was that right?"

"Yes." His smile grew as he observed my excitement.

"May I try again?"

He nodded, keeping my hands tightly in his. I repeated the steps two more times, focusing on his face. I gave a breathless laugh. "That was not so difficult. It was much easier when you performed the steps alongside me."

"There is a reason dancing is for partners."

"Indeed." I cleared my throat and looked down at the floor. "As I understand it, there are certain steps that require a partner, and certain ones that do not. I practice my chassé and gavotte step alone in my room, but I have been puzzled by the many variations of a pirouette."

"Ah, yes, there are many variations." Timothy exhaled through this lips. "But I have full confidence that you can learn them all."

"I can't believe my father never hired a dance instructor for me." How could a marquess overlook the necessity of raising his daughter to enter society? Even if he had always planned to marry me off to the highest bidder, there would still come a time when my husband wanted to bring me into his social circles. I would be clueless.

"I can't believe it either." Timothy's eyes darkened. "But thankfully, you have one now."

I laughed. "You are an excellent instructor."

He gave a soft smile. "Why, thank you." He lowered my hands, interlocking his own behind his back. I chuckled as he paced in a line, fully embracing his role. "Now, for the pirouette. There are lively variations such as those used in the cotillion, and there are other more intimate variations performed in tune with a slow waltz, french waltz, or other andante selections." He stopped, meeting my gaze. "Which would you like to learn first?"

The word *intimate* thrummed in my ears, and they tingled with heat. Anne thought waltzes were improper, as did much of society, yet I knew they were still often selected at balls in London. The people of London, as it seemed, craved anything remotely scandalous. At the moment, so did I. A few months before, the idea of dancing a waltz with Timothy would have seemed so ridiculous that I would have laughed. So why was I not laughing now?

I swallowed against my dry throat. "Well, I have never practiced a waltz before. Not any variation."

He gave a slow nod. "It's perhaps the most important dance to practice with a partner." He leaned forward and whispered, "But I would advise you not to practice this one with Chesley."

I nodded. My heart thudded with restlessness.

He stepped closer, eyes soft and cautious as they settled on my face. I remembered his advice to maintain eye contact, but I was suddenly shy. His voice was deep and quiet. He was close enough to speak without projection. "The first and most common posture of the pirouette is as follows."

His right hand wrapped around the back of my waist, pressing against the fabric of my dress. I felt the pressure of each finger, and my mind blurred. "My right hand is at your waist, and yours is at mine." When I didn't move, he took my right hand with his left, sliding it into place around his ribcage. "Our left hands will form an arc as we turn." He took my left hand and raised it in the air above my head. The motion brought us closer. My right arm was fully draped across his torso, and my waist was tucked all the way to the crook of his elbow.

I drew a breath of surprise.

I held his gaze as I had been instructed and followed his steps as we turned, rotating in a graceful circle. It was strange to dance without music. All I could hear was my pulse, and it was certainly not providing the slow, andante rhythm that the dance required. I couldn't recall ever looking into Timothy's eyes for so long a period, especially not in silence. My stomach fluttered with butterflies so rigorous that I was more keen to call them a flock of seagulls.

When we completed our turn, I held perfectly still. He lowered our arms and released me a second too late. His jaw tightened as he took a step back. My skin tingled and burned on the places he had touched.

"Well done," he said, brushing his hands against the sides of his trousers.

"It is no wonder Anne calls the waltz scandalous." I laughed, but it sounded forced. "What are the other variations?"

He hesitated, as if questioning the wisdom of continuing. Did he realize how scandalous the dance truly was? He stood back, folding his arms across his chest. Was I truly so horrible a partner? The lesson had barely begun, yet he seemed prepared to end it. "Perhaps we save the others for a different day. Let us return to practicing the other steps of the cotillion. How is your contretemps?"

His unsettled expression was enough to earn my coopera-tion. He must have truly disliked holding me so close. I could see why it would be so uncomfortable for him. I imagined myself dancing a waltz with Charlie, and a wave of disgust passed through me. In comparison, I was like a sister to

Timothy. I willed my pulse to return to normal, fighting the embarrassment rising up in my heart.

We practiced for another hour, rehearsing all the steps of the cotillion, then the minuet. It was difficult to envision the other pairs of dancers that would be involved in the set, but Timothy explained it well, even fetching a sheet of foolscap and a pencil to draw a map. His disposition had shifted back to a professional one, and he kept his distance rather than holding my hands through each step.

Near the end of my lesson, I took a drink of water from the tea table, casting him a curious look. "Besides dancing, what else should I be practicing?"

Timothy's eyebrows lifted. "You gave me an extensive list of how you have been passing your time. I think you have a good understanding of the best accomplishments to improve upon."

"A man will not know that I am accomplished simply by looking at me or sharing a single conversation. I suspect I will need to flirt, but I don't recall ever trying." I eyed him and the surprise on his features. "Although I'm not certain you would be the best instructor for such a practice. I cannot imagine you flirting with anyone."

Timothy sighed. "First I am boorish, and now I don't know how to flirt?"

I laughed. "Well, I have never witnessed it."

"Perhaps I don't flirt in the way most men do. There is the method of superficial flirting—glances, touches, meaningless compliments—but there are other ways to show your feelings that are far more genuine."

"Are you claiming that you are superior to all other men?" I teased.

He scoffed, shaking his head with a smile. "Not superior. Perhaps more…reserved."

I tilted my head to one side as I studied his face. "Is that the way you flirt with Anne?"

He jerked with surprise. "I beg your pardon?"

The moment I recognized his annoyance, my voice went on with my thoughts anyway. "I was thinking that perhaps you and Anne would make a good match. She is the widow of a baron and very elegant, kind, and gracious. If you must marry, then she would be the perfect choice."

His eyes dropped from mine, landing on his feet. He scuffed the floor with one boot. I seemed to have taken my words too far, striking an unpleasant chord in him.

"Do you not agree?" My heart pounded fast. Why was I so eager to convince him? The odd sensations he had awoken inside me were frightening, and I needed to be reminded of my place. I needed to hear him say that he wanted Anne, Miss Grant—anyone.

"No, I do not." He looked up. The intensity of his gaze surprised me, and I took a step back. "Let us agree not to make *suggestions* about who the other should marry. I will make that decision for myself, and so will you."

Well, drat. My matchmaking career had only lasted one day, and I had upset Timothy in the process. I was grateful I had never presented the idea to Anne, because she likely would have been just as frustrated. "Very well. Forgive me." I looked down at my hands, wringing them together before my gaze snapped upward. "But you *have* expressed your disapproval of Mr. Ball. May I at least be permitted to express my disapproval for a lady if the need arises?" I raised an eyebrow.

Timothy exhaled sharply through his nose. "I suppose."

"Good." I pursed my lips into a smile, one that managed

to coax his grumpy expression into something more pleasant. I should have known his reaction would be so bristly. He had never liked being told what to do.

A knock sounded at the front door, echoing through the corridor to the drawing room. I strained my ears to hear the door creak open. I recognized the booming voice immediately.

Blast it. Mr. Ball had come calling.

For a few seconds, I remained rigid, frozen where I stood. I glanced at Timothy's face, but he was already staring at the drawing room door, jaw tight. He must have already gathered who the visitor was.

But where was Anne? She spent several hours each day in her room or in the library, so she must have heard the knock at the door as well. I slumped with relief when I heard her voice join Mr. Ball's in the entryway.

"Is Jane at home?" he asked, his voice carrying much louder than it should have given the distance between us.

"*Say no,*" I muttered.

"Y-yes. I believe so. One moment." Anne's light footfalls came closer to the drawing room. She pulled open the door, slipping inside. I rushed forward, leaving the provoked Timothy a few paces behind.

"Is he alone? Or is Mr. Elmore with him?" I asked. I could never be sure from eavesdropping since Mr. Elmore rarely said a word.

"He is alone." Anne hesitated, eyes flicking in Timothy's direction. "And he has another bouquet of flowers."

I didn't dare look over my shoulder. I could already sense Timothy's vexation. "Why did you say I was here?"

Anne sighed, scratching her head. "I thought his grace might like to make his acquaintance."

Timothy would certainly not *like* to make his acquaintance, but ensuring Mr. Ball would 'never come calling again' was part of his objective in staying at Foxwell House.

"Shall I send him in?" Anne whispered.

"Very well."

She nodded, disappearing into the corridor again. I clasped my hands together in front of me, squaring my shoulders. I had to show Timothy that I was not flirtatious with Mr. Ball so he would believe that I hadn't encouraged him. I also had to show that I could contend with a harmless gentleman on my own. Relying on Timothy for help with everything was my weakness, and I wanted to grow more independent. I held my chin high as Anne returned to the doorway with Mr. Ball in tow.

His dark curls were sculpted asymmetrically across his forehead, sodden with some sort of pomade. His large hazel eyes darted to me first, then behind my shoulder. His smile faltered, the roses in his hand rustling as he shifted his grip.

"Good afternoon, Mr. Ball." I gave a polite smile. I couldn't be unkind toward him. He seemed to like that. I also couldn't be too polite or he would consider his efforts successful. "I didn't expect your visit."

"I didn't think a calling card was necessary." He grinned, glancing at Timothy again with confusion.

"Mr. Ball, I am honored to introduce you to…" I paused. Was it wise to use Timothy's name and title? Or would he prefer a false identity like mine?

"The Duke of Heywood." Mr. Ball's gaze widened with recognition until his irises were like floating islands in the whites of his eyes.

So a false identity would not work in this case.

I swallowed. "Y-yes. He is." My experience with introductions was limited, but I still tried to make it proper. "Your grace, might I make known to you Mr. Christopher Ball."

Mr. Ball gave a flourishing bow. "It is an honor to make your acquaintance, your grace."

I cringed. He seemed far too pleased. Would my connection to a duke only make him more interested in me? I finally stole a glance in Timothy's direction. His expression was unreadable as he gave Mr. Ball a nod in greeting. I wasn't certain how to proceed, but Timothy hadn't spoken a word. How could I explain the Duke of Heywood's presence in our house? Anne and I had already presented ourselves as social recluses, so the fact that we had a duke casually standing in our drawing room would be sure to raise questions. I didn't know whether to claim Timothy as my guardian or my friend. Which would be most effective? I couldn't imagine that either one would successfully drive Mr. Ball away. He would be happy at the prospect of pursuing a match with a woman who was so closely connected to a duke.

"I wouldn't have guessed that you had such respectable connections," Mr. Ball said with a laugh.

I narrowed my eyes. "Why would you not have guessed?"

He gave a nervous chuckle. "Instinct. Though my instinct is not always correct. In this case, I am quite glad." He turned to Timothy with an admiring grin. "That is a very attractive waistcoat, your grace. From whence did you import the buttons?"

Mr. Elmore might be relieved to know that Mr. Ball had found a new gentleman to idolize. Timothy's voice came from just behind me. "France."

"I thought so." Mr. Ball's gaze dropped to the flowers in his hand, but he made no move to present them to me. It wouldn't have surprised me if he had presented them to

Timothy instead. "How are the three of you acquainted?" He glanced at each of us in turn, inviting anyone to answer.

My mind debated once again between using the term *friend* or *guardian*. If I said guardian, it would give Timothy the right to set limitations for how often Mr. Ball could visit. That made the most sense. I exchanged a glance with Timothy before opening my mouth to speak. "The duke is my—"

"Betrothed." Timothy took a step forward. "Miss Flowers and I are recently engaged."

CHAPTER 12

A wave of shock nearly made me topple. My breath caught in my throat. I managed to keep my expression composed, even if my insides were flopping like a fish out of water. I shot Timothy a glance, but he refused to look at me, keeping his gaze fixed on our guest.

"Is that so?" Mr. Ball's throat bobbed, his attention turning to me. "Did you not care to inform me of your previous attachment?" His eyes darkened, an expression I had never seen on him.

I gave him a pointed look. "I did try to discourage your visits."

Mr. Ball's voice rose in pitch as he addressed Timothy. "She has been accepting my flowers and notes. For your sake, your grace, I must discourage you from marrying a woman who will be so disloyal to you while you are away." A vein protruded in his forehead. "Additionally, in my humble opinion, a man of your standing could secure a wife far superior in situation, wealth, *and* beauty." He gave a mirthless laugh.

"What could have possibly drawn you to this woman in particular?"

My face burned with a mixture of shame and anger. I wanted to sink into the floorboards. Stunned silence overtook the room, until Timothy's voice broke it.

"I fell in love with her."

My heart pounded fast, my face burning all over again. It was part of the ruse, but I felt the words burrow into my skin nonetheless. Why could Timothy not have claimed to be my guardian? I would have been far more comfortable with that. At the moment, I doubted I would have the courage to look Timothy in the eye ever again.

Mr. Ball cleared his throat, nostrils flaring. "Well, then. I suppose congratulations are in order." His knuckles turned white on the hand that held the flowers, the paper crinkling under his grip. "It was a pleasure to make your acquaintance, your grace. Good day Mrs. Benson, Miss Flowers." He shot daggers at me with his gaze before turning on his heel and leaving the room.

I continued to face the door for several seconds, my insides twisting into knots. I willed my heart to slow. I could find humor in this. That was my specialty. However, I seemed to have lost the talent as I stared at the place Mr. Ball had been standing. Perhaps after my insults, I had deserved his, but Timothy's rescuing words echoed in my mind.

I fell in love with her.

It was clever of him to use a false engagement to put an end to Mr. Ball's pursuit forever. Very clever to pretend he loved me. Mr. Ball could not argue with that.

I met Anne's gaze first, reading her expression instantly. She was just as surprised as I was. With a steadying breath, I turned to face Timothy. His eyes met mine, heavy with caution. If he would laugh about what he had just said and heartily deny it, I would feel much better. The words he had just spoken hung between us like loose threads. My heart was already taking those threads and weaving together a daydream —one that I wasn't capable of ignoring.

"I thought he was going to break the flowers to pieces," I said with a skittish laugh, fidgeting with my skirts.

Anne took a shaky breath. "The flowers, or *Miss* Flowers? Did you see how angry he was?"

It was true. I had never seen that side of Mr. Ball. It had been almost as alarming as Timothy's unexpected strategy of sending him away. I glanced at Timothy again, willing myself to be bold. A slow smile crept over my lips, a bit of my teasing nature returning. Timothy looked far too serious, and someone needed to make light of this before it became even more awkward. "So, when is our wedding?"

His eyes narrowed slightly before shifting upward in exasperation. I laughed, poking him in the arm. That might have been too much. I stepped back, my laughter fading into silence. "I was about to call you my guardian."

He released a sigh. "I didn't plan to create such a sham, but in the moment, it seemed the best way to ensure he wouldn't continue his efforts to court you. If I were introduced as your guardian or friend, he would only view it as a beneficial connection and find you even more desirable." Timothy interlocked his hands behind his back. "I'm confident that was enough to ensure he never comes calling again."

It seemed too soon for celebration. I gave him a confused look. "But if you were to marry, your engagement would be announced in the papers. Everyone would know of it. Do you think Mr. Ball will be suspicious if he never sees the news? He might even attempt to spread the gossip and make it public himself."

"There is no harm in that," Timothy said with a sideways smile. "Miss Jane Flowers doesn't exist. Better yet, the papers might reach my mother. She would be overjoyed to hear that I was engaged."

"Until you tell her that Miss Jane Flowers doesn't exist, and that the engagement is a sham." It made me feel much calmer to speak in terms of Miss Flowers and not myself. She was a character, a fictional one—a perfect match for Timothy's fictional declarations of love.

Anne's forehead wrinkled in confusion as she observed our conversation. I had forgotten that she didn't know about Timothy's mother and her influence in his decision to marry. Only days before, I hadn't known either.

"I am not concerned about the consequences," Timothy said in a dismissive tone. "I don't imagine Mr. Ball will be in a hurry to publicize *your* engagement. Rest assured that he should not call again."

"How can you be certain?"

Timothy crossed his arms. "If a man learns that a woman's heart beats for someone else, then he has no choice but to move on."

I snorted, raising my brows. I had never heard Timothy use phrases that were so...romantic. "Do you imply that my heart beats for you?" I teased. My face burned. How true was it?

His features remained serious. "Where Mr. Ball is concerned, you must pretend it does. If a man knows a woman's heart is yet to be claimed, he might find a reason to hope. He'll be trapped in his affection forever."

I couldn't hide my amusement. Timothy spoke like a

poet, and I didn't know whether to laugh or applaud. Had he stolen those lines from Byron or Shakespeare or someone? I eyed him with a curious look, but he seemed to be avoiding my gaze, a deep furrow in his brow. I wanted to tease him, but a set of reins somewhere inside my chest tugged me back, holding me captive.

"That does make sense," I said with a nod. "Thank you for helping us escape his further visits."

I was glad that I still had more dancing lessons to undertake, otherwise Timothy's work here would be finished. I wasn't prepared for him to leave just yet.

"The pleasure was mine."

There was a tension in the room that coiled around me like a rope, and I was suddenly eager to escape it. First I had danced a pirouette with Timothy, then I had upset him by trying to encourage him to court Anne, and then he had claimed to be my betrothed. It was too much. I glanced at the clock. "Oh! It's time for me to practice my languages. Please excuse me."

My legs couldn't move quickly enough as I took my leave of the room.

My head was still spinning, my nerves on edge. The afternoon had been far too eventful. It was absurd, but I could almost feel Timothy's hand on my waist, even now, as if an imprint had been left behind.

At least I could sleep soundly knowing that the skull of the poor dog Jeremy was not in my bedchamber.

I brushed dust from my knees and elbows as I stood from

the floor. I had been searching under my bed for any loose floorboards under which the skull might have been hidden. I had also looked behind every painting and tapestry, and in all the drawers and cabinets. Over the past several days, I had searched Anne's room, the two guest rooms, the kitchen, and the drawing room. I was beginning to doubt the tale of the dog's skull even more than I had when Timothy had first shared it. The only rooms I hadn't yet searched were the library, Anne's room, and the servants' quarters. I didn't plan to search Timothy's room, of course, not until after he left Foxwell House, which, to my dismay, was the next day.

He had stayed for a full week. Ever since the day of our first dancing lesson, he had been withdrawn. He went to his bedchamber between meals, working on ledgers, writing to his steward, or simply avoiding Anne and me. I wasn't certain what to believe. I practiced my dancing with him for an hour each day, but he hadn't suggested the waltz again. I had been too nervous to do so myself. Our lessons consisted of all the most common dances I would encounter in a London ballroom, and I was required to demonstrate each step. I drew figures, memorized groupings and positions, and danced more with Anne than with Timothy. He had invited her to join all our lessons, watching and critiquing as I performed each step.

My skill had improved, though Timothy's mood hadn't. He wasn't unpleasant, but he had become stoic again. His smiles were rare. I couldn't help but wonder if I had done something to offend him, or if he was simply growing eager to return home. I would have felt imprisoned too if I had an unwell mother to care for and a sprawling estate to return to without a commandeering father around every turn.

I personally didn't feel imprisoned at Foxwell House.

Despite the fact that I might have shared that home with the bones of a hunting dog, it was still a sanctuary. The North, with all its rugged beauties, had claimed a piece of my heart. Would it still feel the same once Timothy left? He promised to return in three months, but that seemed so distant, especially because I hadn't managed to unearth any of his secrets.

On his last night at Foxwell House, Timothy invited Mr. Prout for dinner. He would be joining us in less than an hour. I was determined to take the opportunity to discover more about Timothy's time in the North. My days of late had been scheduled tightly, so between searching for the skull and dressing for dinner, I managed to write a few lines in my diary.

Nora's Coming of Age Diary
September 22, 1816

Friends do not keep secrets from one another. That is what I have always believed. Yet there seems to be something Timothy is hiding. I have searched for a way to infiltrate his walls, but he is never vulnerable, and he never shows weakness.

He finally confided in me about his new endeavor to marry. Could that be why he is acting so strangely? Is he overwhelmed by the idea of marriage? His mother being in poor health must also weigh heavily on his mind. Perhaps I should not judge him so harshly for being withdrawn. He has explained his reasoning for purchasing Foxwell House, yet I have not been able to fully believe him. I still have questions about his frequent visits to the 'hunting lodge' when he clearly does not hunt. His familiarity with that small fishing village is also strange. If there is some burden he is bearing, I wish he would tell me so I could help ease it.

My heart stung to think of Timothy's pain. He did so much to help me—*too* much—but he never allowed me to reciprocate. It wasn't fair.

I prepared for dinner as quickly as I could, making up for the time I had spent lost in thought. I wore my red dress, hair arranged with the curls pinned back once again. Timothy had planned to serve mutton for Mr. Prout. Since he lived primarily on the spoils of his work, it would be heartwarming to offer him something to eat besides fish pie and fish soup. I only hoped the man had learned not to stare at people.

When I walked into the drawing room, Mr. Prout was already standing beside Timothy. Anne sat on the sofa nearby.

Their conversation fell silent, and all eyes drifted to where I stood in the doorway. Timothy looked handsome in his navy blue jacket, his eyes settling on me as I strode into the room. My heart leaped as it always did. It was becoming more difficult to face Timothy when I felt as though he was avoiding my company. I kept my shoulders square, my neck stretched high. I couldn't allow him to affect me. I couldn't allow my feelings to show. After all, with a guest joining us for dinner that night, I didn't need to act like myself at all. I was Miss Jane Flowers.

I curtsied, rising with a smile. "Good evening, friends." I paused, a sudden jolt of panic rising in my chest. How had Timothy explained our relationship to Mr. Prout? Had he claimed to be my friend, guardian...or betrothed? My mind traveled back to the bay, when we had first been introduced to

Mr. Prout. I couldn't recall being called any of those things. I had simply been Miss Flowers.

Surely Timothy had explained the origin of our acquaintance—at least the story he wanted Mr. Prout to believe. Once again, I would have to follow Timothy's lead.

Mr. Prout stood, a broad smile on his face. His skin had been washed clean, and his clothing was no longer covered in strands of seaweed and grains of sand. "Good evening, Miss Flowers. Did you enjoy the fish?"

"Very much. I thank you again for your generosity." I smiled, my gaze shifting to Timothy. The corner of his mouth twitched.

Mr. Prout leaned forward with a knowing smile. "You needn't lie to me. His grace has already informed me that you're not fond of fish."

A flush rose to my cheeks, and I jerked toward Timothy. "I—well, I was not intending to eat it myself. Mrs. Benson is the one who likes them, as does the duke." I narrowed my eyes at Timothy. What other secrets of mine had he confided in his friend?

Mr. Prout gave a hearty laugh, throwing his head back. "There's no shame in it. I'm not particularly fond of fish either." His nose wrinkled.

"You're not?" My brows shot up.

"No indeed. I catch them, but I prefer not to eat them. Of course, beggars can't be choosers. There are times when I've no other choice." He gave a warm smile. "But tonight I look forward to the kindness of his grace to provide a meal that doesn't have scales."

Timothy chuckled. "That you shall have."

Hmm. I quite liked Mr. Prout after all.

His laugh was contagious, and his stare was not nearly as

intense as it had been that day in the village. He had a very
agreeable countenance, and I could find no reason not to
like him.

We proceeded to the dining room, and my stomach
growled at the scent of the warm white soup that was served
first. The cook Timothy employed had the best recipe I had
ever tasted, and Mr. Prout agreed. The rest of the meal was
just as delicious. The conversation was focused on Mr. Prout's
occupation and the specifics of his schedule as a fisherman. I
wondered how he hadn't toppled over with fatigue given the
rigorous routine he undertook each day.

Despite my own worries and fears, I had nothing to
complain of. Though tedious and lonely at times, my life was
comfortable at Foxwell House. I may have been raised
without loving parents, but at least I had wonderful friends.

My heart sank as I watched Timothy's reserved smile, his
polite nods and kind eyes as he addressed Mr. Prout. Why did
he have to leave so soon? It had already been a full week, yet
the time had disappeared so quickly. He had responsibilities
to attend to, and I knew that, but my heart still stung with
longing. All I wanted was a few more days.

Anne and I returned to the drawing room after dessert,
leaving the men to their port. With a bit of luck, Timothy
would drink himself into an overly cheerful mood.

"What an odd friendship," Anne said as we sat on the
sofa.

"That's what I thought." I pressed my lips together,
rubbing my hands on my skirts. "It's peculiar, a duke and a
fisherman being so dear to one another. But I suppose
Timothy has never cared for the rules of propriety, and he did
say that society cannot judge you for what they don't know." I

sighed. "A duke can do whatever he wants and remain unscathed. It's entirely unfair."

Anne's laugh stopped short in her throat as she examined my face. "Do you feel that your dancing lessons have been successful?"

I crossed my ankles nonchalantly. "Yes. But Timothy has been a very strict instructor. I don't think he has enjoyed being here." My throat tightened with an unbidden surge of emotion. I swallowed, fighting it back. "He seems eager to leave. Ever since he fulfilled his objective of sending Mr. Ball away, he seems to have been...avoiding me. It might not be evident since you don't know him as well as I do, but I can feel it." I pressed a hand to my chest without thinking. My heart had been aching for days.

I stared at the floor, unwilling to look up at Anne. I could feel her watching me, her calculations burning on the side of my face. I forced a smile to my face, waving my hand with a laugh. "It's silly that I care so much. I should simply be grateful that he came at all."

Anne was silent for several seconds longer. "I don't think he is avoiding you for the reasons you think."

I glanced up with a frown. "What do you mean?"

She sat up straighter, her shoulders raising with a heavy breath. She seemed to be debating speaking again, as if she had already said too much. "There are some behaviors that I have...observed...that may have escaped your notice." Her dark eyes flickered in my direction.

"Oh, no, I assure you I have noticed. I thought I might have imagined how strangely he has been acting. I'm glad you have noticed as well."

She shifted uncomfortably. "I would not call it strange, but rather...troubled."

"Yes! That is precisely what I think. I wish to help him, I truly do, but he will never ask for help. I think he has secrets that he is not sharing with me. I thought that I might ask him directly, but even as his friend that feels a bit...untoward." I tugged on the fingertips of my gloves. "Do you have any insight? What do you think could be troubling him?"

"Good heavens," she muttered, putting a hand to her cheek. "Do you truly not have any theories of your own? Have you not noticed the signs that he..." Her words stopped short again, and she seemed to be biting her tongue to hold them back. She took a deep breath.

My heart thudded as I leaned forward. Had Anne been the answer to solving this mystery all along? "Signs?"

She slumped against the back of the sofa, her features wincing.

Voices in the corridor made her pause, and within seconds, the door opened. Timothy and Mr. Prout strode into the room. Blast it. A wave of frustration made my fists clench in my lap.

Could they not have entered the room ten seconds later?

CHAPTER 13

"How shall we entertain our guest this evening?" Timothy asked as he settled into a chair by the hearth. "We could play a game of whist? Or if the ladies would be so kind, we could hear a performance or two on the pianoforte."

Mr. Prout leaned his elbows on his knees as he sat down, casting his bright blue eyes in my direction before speaking. "Both sound delightful."

"Very well. Let us begin with cards."

We moved to sit at the card table, and Timothy sat opposite from Anne, immediately claiming her as his partner. I hadn't expected that he would choose me, but the action still left a weakness in my limbs as I settled into my chair beside Anne and across from Mr. Prout, who would be my partner.

"You must forgive me, Miss Flowers," he said. "I haven't practiced in quite some time."

"Nor have I." I gave a kind smile. Most of my efforts with learning strategy games had been focused on my chess matches with Anne. With Mr. Prout as my partner, we managed to win the first several tricks. I surprised the entire table by taking the fifth in a row. The sense of satisfaction brought a victorious grin to my face. If I wanted to spite Timothy for being so aloof, winning the game with Mr. Prout as my partner would help.

Mr. Prout cheered, picking up his cards. "That is it! Well done, Leonora."

"Thank—" I froze. I glanced at Anne, then at Timothy. Had they noticed too? I quickly covered my silence with a laugh. "Thank you, sir."

Leonora.

How had Mr. Prout learned my Christian name? A hint of suspicion crept into my mind. Had Timothy told him? Had he deemed Mr. Prout trustworthy enough to confide in? My brow scrunched as I tried to recall the events of the evening. No—that didn't make sense. Mr. Prout had called me 'Miss Flowers' just a few minutes before.

Another question made my heart race. Did he know my father? Had he been sent here to spy on me? A million fears drummed through my head, distracting me when it was my turn to play a card.

"Sorry," I muttered, laying down a ten of hearts, ultimately losing to Anne's queen.

The game went on for half an hour, but my competitive spirt had faded. Mr. Prout and I won, but I couldn't manage to celebrate, not when I was suddenly suspicious of my partner.

I gave a series of false smiles, acting polite and gracious as the night wore on. Anne and I both played two songs on the pianoforte, but my fingers slipped on the keys, throwing out clashing notes throughout both songs. My head spun when I took my bow, a sense of misgiving flooding my stomach at the sight of Mr. Prout's proud smile as he applauded. *Well done, Leonora.* How had I been the only one to notice?

When it was time for Mr. Prout to leave, we bid our farewells and sent him out the front door. I took a steadying breath. I was drawing conclusions from my own fears, but I couldn't help but feel on-edge. There was no reason to assume the worst of him, or to assume that he had any connection to my father. He was a seemingly amiable man, and if Timothy trusted him, I could too.

After the door had closed behind Mr. Prout, I walked to the third stair and stood against the bannister, holding on with one hand. Timothy stood with his back turned to me. Standing as I was on the staircase, he wouldn't be able to escape without answering some of my questions.

He turned around, and I felt the impact of his gaze as he noticed my stance. Anne's eyes darted between Timothy and me, and she seemed to make a swift decision to retire for the evening.

"Goodnight," she said, flashing a smile. The expression disappeared when she faced me. She threw me a look of concern. As she approached the staircase, I stepped aside, allowing her to pass before assuming my defensive position again.

Anne's footfalls faded into the distance, leaving the vestibule in complete silence.

Timothy tugged at his cravat, leaving a few inches between the fabric and his neck. The candlelight shadowed the valleys of his face and jawline, highlighting the confusion in his eyes. I considered drumming my fingers on the bannister, but I stopped myself. He didn't even know what I was waiting for him to explain. One of his dark brows lifted.

"May I help you?" The amusement in his voice was comforting, if not a little vexing.

There was no use skirting around the subject. "Did you reveal my true identity to Mr. Prout?" I asked. "He called me Leonora."

"When?" Timothy frowned.

"During the card game."

After a moment of hesitation, he gave a brief nod. "Yes, I did tell him. I didn't want to lie to so dear a friend. But he can be trusted with that information; you have my word."

My shoulders relaxed. At least that was reassuring. "But even if he does know my true identity, did it not trouble you that he called me by my Christian name? If he knows I am the daughter of a marquess, I should have been properly addressed as Lady Leonora, especially by a man of his station." I had been studying my etiquette and proper social behaviors for long enough to know that Mr. Prout's behavior had been entirely inappropriate.

Timothy nodded. "I hope you will excuse his folly."

I could excuse it, but that didn't stop me from finding it strange. "I suppose I can." Silence fell between us again as I searched for my next item of business. "I know you must leave tomorrow, but there are dances that you still haven't taught me."

"Such as?"

"The other pirouettes. You said there were two more that are commonly used in waltzes." My words spilled out quicker than I intended. "You said we would save them for another day, and tomorrow is your last day here."

He stared at me, a heavy look of reservation in his gaze. "I depart at noon tomorrow, but if you will meet me in the library at ten, I will give you your final lesson."

"Good. Thank you." I exhaled sharply, already regretting my request. Where was this sudden longing coming from—this longing to be close to him? The pirouette dancing lesson was what had *caused* the new distance between us, so why was I practically begging him for another? From the reservation in his eyes, it was obvious that he didn't want to. But I wanted to. I would have taken the lesson that very moment in the empty vestibule, surrounded by romantic candlelight. I shushed my thoughts, infuriated by the direction they had gone. Timothy was my friend. Friends did not fantasize about such things.

Before I could speak again, Timothy rubbed the back of his neck with a yawn. "I must retire. I have a long day of travel tomorrow." He walked toward the staircase, a determination in his stride that nearly made me step aside and allow him to pass.

My own determination awoke just in time. I planted my feet on the center of the staircase, both hands draped on either side of the bannister. Timothy stopped short at the base of the staircase, one foot on the first stair. He looked up at me with lifted brows. "Is this a toll gate?"

"Yes." I gripped the bannisters harder.

He withdrew his foot, standing back with a faint smile. The night he had scooped me up and carried me to my bed flashed through my mind. He could very well do it again if he wished. I couldn't waste a second.

"What is the toll?" he asked.

This was not how I envisioned our conversation starting, but he had made it easier. "A secret."

He stared at me as if I had lost my mind, and perhaps I had. His eyes glinted with amusement. It was rather empowering to be three stairs above him; the height added to my conviction. I held his gaze, keeping my expression serious.

"Unfortunately I don't have any." He stepped up to the first stair, and my arms twitch on the bannister. I tightened my grip again, refusing to let go. His dark lashes and brows framed his brown eyes, and when I searched them, I found him completely unreadable. Was he telling the truth?

"I know you do. It's clear that something has been troubling you, and friends don't keep secrets from one another."

He glanced up at me, his jaw tightening. And then he stepped up one more time, landing on the stair just below me. I could no longer look down at him. Our gazes were now level. His shoulders, his chest, his nose and mouth, all perfectly in line with mine, were just inches away. My balance faltered, and I nearly gave up my efforts to block him. A jolt of nervousness spiraled through my stomach, followed by an all-encompassing thrill that made my legs weak.

"I disagree." His voice was quiet and deep. His gaze flickered to my mouth, and I held onto the bannister to steady myself. "Some secrets must be kept in order to preserve a friendship, or to protect someone from harm. There are some instances in which remaining ignorant is best for everyone involved."

I swallowed, my heart racing. He was so close. We seemed to be in some unspoken competition of who would move away first.

Or who would move closer.

My surroundings melted into a blur, a wave of heat tingling over my skin and bringing a flush to my cheeks. My objective had faded, suddenly far less important than the fact that Timothy's face was closer than it had ever been to my own.

Well, besides the night I had kissed him.

I held his gaze for a long moment. And then it slipped. My eyes fell to his lips.

Our first dance lesson played through my mind, and suddenly I wanted his hands on my waist, his chest pressed against mine. I wanted to let go of the bannister and bury my hands in his hair. A fierce longing trapped my breath in my lungs as I stared at his lips. I had never noticed how perfect they were before.

I blinked hard, forcing my gaze away. "So you are confessing that you do indeed have secrets." To my own ears, my voice sounded as weak and distant as an echo.

"No."

Frustration surged inside me. "Now you really are being boorish."

"I am simply trying to go to bed. You are in my way." His eyes flashed with a passion I hadn't seen before—and I couldn't distinguish the emotion. It was muddled with frustration, yet his eyes roamed my face with an intensity that turned me inside out, laying bare all the emotions I had been suppressing. "If I must pay a toll," he said, "it will have to be something else."

It was late. My mind wasn't working clearly. Nothing made sense. I knew exactly what I wanted that toll to be, yet I couldn't ask for it. *A kiss.* His lips against mine, his arms around my waist, something that might finally make sense of the strange emotions I had been feeling since that night in the rain when he had fallen from his horse and I had been so afraid of losing him.

No. I couldn't ask him to kiss me. It would be far too embarrassing if he denied my request.

But would he deny it?

My logic told me that yes, of course he would, but when I dared a look at his eyes…I wasn't so certain. My courage was frozen, locked in a stalemate with my fears. No. He couldn't know I had even considered such a request. The fact that I wanted to kiss him now would have to remain as deep a secret as when I had kissed him the night he fell from his horse.

His words made sense now, raking across my skin, trying to wake me from this dream: *Some secrets must be kept in order to preserve a friendship.*

If Timothy knew I had a sudden desire to kiss him into oblivion, our friendship would never be the same. If he rejected me now, I would never recover. The fear paralyzed me, and I backed up a step, dropping my hands from the bannister. "There is no toll. Forgive me." I stared at the floor. "Goodnight."

Rather than stepping aside to allow him to pass, I turned around and hurried up the stairs, not stopping until I was inside my bedchamber.

CHAPTER 14

I awoke before the sun the next morning, my mind still ablaze as I stared at the ceiling. My final dance lesson with Timothy wasn't until ten o'clock. I needed to find a way to fill the time. It was clear that further sleep was impossible.

Despite my doubts of its existence, I needed to search one more time for the skull before Timothy left Foxwell House for months. Searching for answers and secrets was exhausting, but searching for a skull that was most likely imaginary was something I could manage.

After changing into a white morning dress and taming my hair, I made my way to the library. The house was quiet. Golden sunlight had begun seeping through the windows. When I made it to the library, I stopped in the doorway, taking in the peaceful silence and the way the sunlight brought out the golden tones in the dark walnut shelves and furniture.

I planted my hands on my hips as I surveyed the space. Where would an old man choose to hid his dog's skull? The library seemed to be the heart of the house. The only reason I hadn't searched it yet was because it seemed too obvious a choice. I had suspected the skull would be in my bedchamber, as it was obviously intended for the master of the house, but my search had been unsuccessful.

Starting at the shelves on the left side of the room, I pulled out all of the books. I checked the wall behind each one. It didn't seem likely that the old man would have gone so far as to cut an alcove into the wall, so I gave up on that effort after a few minutes. I moved the rug, crawling on my hands and knees as I felt the floorboards. Breathing in the unsettled dust, I sat up with a sneeze.

There was nothing out of the ordinary about the floor. My gaze caught on the writing desk by the window. It was old and worn, as if it were original to the house and had never been moved. I pushed aside the chair that was tucked beneath it, then pulled open the two small drawers and peered inside. A crusty inkwell and a few quills sat inside one, and the other was empty. I sighed, crouching down and peering underneath the desk.

A small hinge caught my eye.

Directly across from it was a locking mechanism of some sort. I crawled under the desk until I could see it more clearly. It was a hidden hatch, perhaps intended to hold confidential documents or objects. A giddy sensation bubbled up in my chest. I pried at the latch with my fingers, but it didn't move. There seemed to be a missing piece. I frowned, wrenching at it one more time. There was no longer any way to access the latch that would open the door. Whomever had last closed it had either broken the latch intentionally, or had given up on ever opening it again.

My heart pounded as I crawled out, brushing the dust off my hands. How could I open it? My mind raced. It would require tools that I didn't have. For some reason, I was *certain* the skull was inside that desk. How could it not be? It was the perfect hiding place. I couldn't ask Timothy to help me. I needed to find it on my own. How satisfying would it be if Timothy arrived for my dance lesson and I presented him with the legendary skull of that old hunting dog? I laughed at the idea, clasping my hands together with delight.

Anne would be no more capable of opening it than I was. An idea struck me, and I grinned, starting for the door. I knew the perfect accomplice.

"Chesley," I hissed as I walked into the corridor near the breakfast room. The staff had begun setting up the food, but Anne and Timothy were not yet downstairs. The footman's eyes rounded, his throat bobbing with a terrified swallow.

"Y-yes, my lady?"

"I require your assistance. Please make haste." I waved a hand for him to follow me, and he took a hesitant step forward.

"It doesn't involve dancing," I clarified.

He seemed to relax, following me as I led him toward the library.

I pointed at the desk, waving him closer. "There is a hidden compartment beneath that desk. It's very important that I find a way to open it. We'll need tools of some sort, but I'm not certain what the task will require."

He bent over, peering at the latch and prying at it the same way I had.

"That won't work." I cast my gaze around the room, pausing at the hearth. A long metal poker rested against the mantle. I gasped, crossing the room and picking it up. I presented it to Chesley. "Perhaps this could be used?"

He sat back on his heels, taking the poker and examining

the latch again. He wedged the tip into the crevice between the compartment and the desk, using the length of the poker as a lever. A satisfying crack split the air, followed by the creaking of hinges.

"Did it open?" I lunged forward, bending over to take a peek.

"Indeed." Chesley stood, replacing the poker and turning to face me. "Will that be all, my lady?"

"Yes, thank you!" I refrained from crawling under the desk until Chesley had taken his leave. The moment the door was closed, I dipped my head under.

The hatch had opened halfway on its own. I pulled it down farther until it locked into place. Touching a skull with my bare hands didn't sound appealing, so I didn't dare reach inside. I took a deep breath and angled my head until I could see the interior of the small compartment.

My heart sank. The skull was not there. All I could see was a dusty old book.

I groaned in disappointment, but withdrew the book anyway. A mysterious object was still a mysterious object, even if it wasn't exactly what I had been looking for. I brushed the dust from the blue canvas cover, checking the spine for a title. It was blank besides a design of intricate gold leaves and vines. I opened to a page near the beginning, shocked to find it filled with handwritten words.

My heart picked up speed.

The penmanship was familiar—the shapes of the loops and the slant of each word.

It was Timothy's writing.

I snapped the book closed, instinctively glancing at the door behind me. I rotated under the desk until my back was against the wall and I had a clear view of the door.

I stared down at the book, my heart in my throat. Was this…Timothy's *diary*? The thought of him documenting his life and thoughts in a book had never once crossed my mind. Many people kept diaries, including myself, but I had never considered him the sort to do so. He had always seemed far too busy with other tasks to have time for writing. The contents of that diary, however, must have been written during his visits to Foxwell House when he was away from his estate and had more time to think and reflect.

The contents of that diary could be the answer to all of my questions.

My hands traced over the cover. The temptation to open it again gripped my entire body, but my conscience fought against it. How would I feel if Timothy found *my* diary and took it upon himself to read its pages? I would be mortified. He had hidden this diary in the desk compartment for a reason. Had he broken the lock intentionally, or had it broken by accident? Did he even remember the diary was there? My mind spun. Before I could stop myself, I wrenched open the cover.

One page.

It was fair, I assured myself. I had never received his toll at the staircase the night before. I would read one page and put it back in the compartment and never open it again.

My hands shook as I held the diary on my lap. I ran my finger along the inside, at the raw edges where two pages had been torn out. What had been written there that he had later decided to remove? My eyes raced over the first remaining page. If I didn't act quickly, my conscience would win and I would snap the book closed again. I looked at the date first.

. . .

October 11, 1812

Four years ago. It was the year Timothy's father died—the year he became the duke and bought Foxwell House. I closed my eyes, debating once again the morality of reading further. If Timothy wouldn't tell me, how else would I know the truth about his strange decision to purchase the manor, his frequent escapes to Northumberland, and his odd friendships with the people of that village? I had to know.

One page.

I opened my eyes and began reading before I could stop myself.

Is it horrible to confess that I do not mourn my father? Mother doesn't mourn him either. Since the day of his death, Mother's mood has lightened, and though she wears black, she smiles with the new freedom she has won. I am pleased to see the relief his death has brought her, even if his death has left me with unanswered questions and more responsibilities than I know how to bear.

His conversation with Lord Swindon lives in my mind day and night. My father denied the accusations, but he was not known for his honesty. He could have lied.

A flush of surprise washed over me, and I pressed one hand to my chest. Lord Swindon? That was my father's title. My eyes carried me to the next paragraph.

. . .

Not even Charlie knows the truth, and I dare not confide in him what I overheard. I didn't even dare leave the pages in this diary after I recounted the conversation. The pages are burned, but I still remember every word. Even without knowing what I overheard, Charlie has unwittingly given me a place to look for answers. I hired a steward to manage the estate while I spend a few months in the North. I purchased an old hunting lodge, and I believe I will be comfortable here while I investigate the matter as extensively as I can. I will return to Foxwell House as often as it takes to discover the truth. I refuse to believe what I have heard. I cannot accept a future that prevents me from any measure of happiness. If proof can never be found, and I am left hopeless, only then shall I accept what cannot be changed.

I stared at the page, shaking my head in confusion. "What did he overhear?" I muttered. Whatever it was had been written on those pages that he had torn out. How was Charlie involved? And my father? My head buzzed, overflowing with new information. At least one of my suspicions was confirmed—

Timothy hadn't purchased Foxwell House for hunting.

I had almost made it through the first page. I swallowed, my throat dry, as I continued reading. The next paragraph was a new entry. My brows shot up. One year later? So he was not a consistent writer after all.

December 15, 1813

. . .

I have met countless people in the nearby villages this year, but none were able to give me the answers I seek. I enjoy the solitude of the manor, even if my purpose in coming here has yet to be fulfilled. I must travel back to my estate soon, but I will return as soon as possible. There are several villages I have yet to explore, but I promised Nora I would return for Christmastide. I cannot disappoint her.

I stopped and held my breath. I hadn't expected to see my name in his diary, and my gaze was frozen on the elegant curve of the N. I had made it to the bottom of the page, but now my curiosity tugged even harder. If the paragraph continued on the next page, it was fair to at least finish the passage.

Wasn't it?

I hesitated before turning the page.

If I had never fallen in love with her, I wouldn't even be here in the North. My heart continues to beat for her, yet I know it should not. Next year I will continue to look for a reason it still can. I will resume my search for hope and answers.

My vision blurred, and my heart pounded so hard it hurt. I read it again.

And again.

I flipped back to the previous page, reminding myself that it had indeed been my name he had written. My hands shook, my face on fire. I held the diary with a grip like a vice as I read it yet again. I expected the words to change, but they remained the same, written in the black ink that had soaked into the page nearly three years before.

If I had never fallen in love with her, I wouldn't even be here in the North.

My heart continues to beat for her, yet I know it should not.

"Why should it not?" I whispered, my voice breaking. I could hardly sit still, my pulse racing so quickly I felt as if I might faint or vomit, or both. My arms weakened, and I lowered the diary to my lap, slumping my back against the wall in shock. A torrent of emotions wracked my body, and I couldn't think clearly. It must have been a dream, a forgery, anything but the truth. But how could I deny what was clearly written in front of me? Of all the mysterious things he had written in those passages, the lines about his love for me were by far the most shocking and prominent. How had he kept such a secret from me for so long?

I uncovered the diary again. I couldn't stop reading now. My eyes flew over the page.

December 2, 1814

My search has once again made little progress, though I have come to enjoy my time in the North. Foxwell House has become a refuge for me, and my steward manages my estate well while I am away. My duties here are beginning to feel like a fool's errand,

and I have nearly given up. If it is true that I can never marry Nora, then I will not marry at all.

I have been trying to put an end to my feelings, but it is exhausting trying not to love her. It is painful and futile. I will not try any longer. Instead, I will go on loving her despite the foolishness that it is to love someone who does not love me in return. Despite the possibility that we cannot be together, I will go on loving her. I will go on loving Nora, because that is all I know how to do. If not for the promise that I will see her again, I would live out my days in this manor, visiting my friends in the village, and I would never return to Somerset. As it is, however, I must return. I prefer her company above any other, her laughter, and her conversation. She is beautiful in every way. She is always smiling when I cannot, and she has no idea how long I have lived for those smiles.

I could hardly breathe. These words—these achingly romantic words—how could they be from *Timothy*? And how on earth could they be about me? I flipped to the next page, my hand creeping up to my throat to subdue my emotions.

"No," I blurted. The page was blank.

I flipped through more, but found them empty. There was nothing from the next year. Had he not come back to the North in eighteen-fifteen? Or had he accidentally locked the diary in the desk before he could create another entry? I should have been focusing on the mysterious quest Timothy had written of in such vague terms, or his reason for his recurring visits to Foxwell House, but my heart shushed me each time I tried. In the quiet of the library, hiding beneath the desk, I reread the other words—the romantic ones—over and over again.

My skin burned, my cheeks warm to the touch. It wasn't real. It couldn't be real.

The sound of footfalls came from the corridor. A jolt of panic made me drop the diary, but I grabbed it and snapped it shut, sliding it back into the compartment and forcing the door closed.

Had Timothy come for our dance lesson early?

The thought of facing him now made my stomach lurch with terror. I had never been afraid of him in my entire life.

I misjudged the height of the desk as I crawled out on shaky limbs, striking my head on the underside. "Blast it," I gripped my forehead in pain, sliding out from under the desk and staggering to my feet. A volatile energy raced through my veins, making my legs quake beneath me.

I barely had time to sit on a chair and pretend to be reading a poetry book before Timothy opened the door.

CHAPTER 15

I didn't have to look up to know it was him.

I could sense him in the doorway—feel his gaze against my face just as surely as I felt the warmth of the sunlight from the window. I didn't trust myself to stand or to look at him. My heart pounded wildly, beating against my ribs. A cold sweat sent a chill over my skin, and I kept my gaze fixed on the book for a few more seconds. My fortitude had scattered like leaves in a storm, and I struggled to gather it up.

"You're early," I said, my voice far too loud and cheerful. I flashed a smile, finally daring a look at him.

He had always been handsome, but now some barrier had been lifted from my eyes. It was ridiculous that the diary had given me permission to admit he was attractive, but now that was all I could notice. His height, broad shoulders, solid jaw, perfect lips and kind brown eyes. The golden brown of his hair, and drat—the wayward strand was out today, curling softly over his forehead. Was this the reward for all the misfortune I had endured—to have somehow, unwittingly, captured the heart of a man like Timothy? How was it possible? How could I ever behave normally around him again?

I stared at his face—for far too long—and his words from the night before came crashing back to mind. *Some secrets must be kept in order to preserve a friendship.*

I exhaled a shaky breath. My mind was not spacious enough to contain all of these sudden realizations. I felt like I might burst.

"As are you," he said, his voice sending a jolt up and down my spine.

"I am what?" My throat was dry, and I was suddenly lightheaded. I had already forgotten what he had said.

His brow furrowed. "Early?"

"Ah, yes." I laughed, pushing myself up from my chair and finding my balance. The right side of my forehead throbbed where it had struck the desk. I tucked my shaking hands behind my back. "I wanted to read a little before the dance lesson." I gulped. I would never tell him *what* exactly I had been reading.

He walked closer, the crease deepening between his brows. "Are you all right?"

"Me?" I pressed a hand to my chest in shock. "Yes. I am well. Very well." I grinned before softening the expression and letting out a slow, calming breath. What I needed was a glass of cold water and a fan. My face was still on fire—and everything else from my head to my toes. I didn't know whether to hold still or move, for fear of setting the entire room ablaze.

Timothy didn't hide his skepticism, and his worried expression persisted as he studied my face. His brow furrowed. "Your head."

"My...?" I froze. Ah, yes. "Oh, that is nothing." I waved a dismissive hand.

He stepped forward, and to my dismay, he brushed his thumb across my forehead, softer than a feather. A shiver followed his touch, and a series of alarms blared inside me. He leaned close, examining the injury. It provided me with an opportunity to look at his face again.

It felt like I was seeing him for the first time.

There had been Timothy the duke, the friend, the protector. But this new Timothy was a romantic, a keeper of secrets —a mystery. He was a man who was loyal without fault, easily wounded but skilled at hiding it. And he was in love with me? I prayed he couldn't see how quickly I was breathing, or how uncontrollably my hands and legs were shaking.

"What happened?" He still didn't lower his fingers from my face.

"I—I arose early this morning and tried to navigate the corridors without a candle."

Timothy's brows lifted. "Did you walk into a wall?"

"Y-yes. Yes, I did indeed." My attempt at sounding confident in my answer had the wrong effect, making me sound proud of the mishap.

Timothy's lips twitched, a smile breaking through his facade. He laughed, and it calmed some of my nerves. "I would advise you to bring a candle next time." His eyes settled on mine, and I watched the smile fade from them. "Something else is wrong."

I really needed to stop staring at him. "No." I walked a few paces away. With my back turned to him, I squeezed my eyes closed in frustration. I was acting far too suspicious and strange. But had he forgotten our interaction from the night before? That alone could have been causing me to feel uneasy around him. There had been a palpable desire between us when we had stood on the staircase, and knowing what I knew now, it most likely hadn't only been one-sided.

The idea was thrilling and terrifying at once.

I turned to face him, interlocking my hands behind my back. The stranger—the romantic poet—that was looking at me through Timothy's eyes walked forward again, but I backed up a step. What was I doing? I squared my shoulders, fighting the nervous flutter in my stomach.

"You seem upset." Timothy frowned.

I laughed, but it sounded harsh. If my nervousness was so obvious, then I needed to think of a way to explain it, or he would remain suspicious. "I confess it is rather upsetting to think of you leaving Foxwell House." I swallowed. In truth, I needed him to leave at once. I might have pushed him out the door myself if I had to. My feelings were unfamiliar and jarring, and I needed to be alone to understand what they meant.

"I will stay longer if you need me," he said. The look in his eyes—the one I had always called compassion—was deeper than that. The sincerity of it made my breath catch. I had to look away.

"Your mother needs you more. You must look after her. Anne and I will look after one another." The thought struck me then: who would look after Timothy? He seemed to go about life all alone, and I had always assumed he liked it that way. Had he really been visiting the North all those years, searching for a reason he didn't have to be alone—a reason he could be with me?

What reason was he looking for?

My heart hammered. I couldn't ask him any of my questions, not without revealing that I had been wicked enough to read his private diary after enlisting Chesley to pry it out of a locked compartment with a fire poker.

That would not be an easy conversation.

"At least you'll be without my boorish company for a few months," Timothy said with a soft smile. He had been distant for days, but when he saw me in distress, his resolve to be aloof seemed to weaken. The line from his diary repeated in my mind. *I prefer her company above any other, her laughter, and her conversation. She is beautiful in every way. She is always smiling when I cannot, and she has no idea how long I have lived for those smiles.*

Was Timothy a skilled actor, or was I naive and daft? Perhaps a little of both. Even now I couldn't detect any adoration in his gaze that would indicate he had been in love with me for years.

I laughed, but it was delayed. "I shouldn't have called you boorish yesterday. I'm sorry."

"Perhaps I deserved it." His chest rose and fell with a heavy breath. "I'm sorry too."

I tucked a curl behind my ear, looking down at the floor. I felt ill. Timothy had come to the library to practice a waltz, yet I could hardly look at his face without blushing. I should have told him I was unwell, but instead I had claimed to be *very* well. In truth, I would never be the same. An hour ago, I had been the Nora who wasn't aware that her dearest friend, as well as her brother's dearest friend, was in love with her. I could never be that person again.

Timothy cleared his throat. "You wished to learn the other positions of the waltz?"

I could still change my mind. I opened my mouth to say no, but something else came out. "Yes."

He stepped closer. "Besides the pirouette that I taught you

last week, you will also need to know the marche position and change of hands."

I nodded, swallowing hard as he took another step toward me. I forced my mind to focus—to pretend I had never discovered Timothy's secret. If this had been a few days before, I would not have been so anxious.

"The partners face one another and hold right hands, after which it is up to the gentleman to choose which posture he will transition to." Timothy took my right hand. In my shocked state, my hands had gone cold and damp like a dead fish. His was warm and soft, and the look in his eyes matched it. "If you are aware of all three of the most common positions, you should be prepared for any situation."

My voice shook, but I managed to find a question. "What dictates the posture a gentleman chooses? Is it his own preference?"

"Yes, but it also indicates his intentions. He might choose the most common posture to either show his respect for propriety, or his lack of any special interest in the lady." He nodded toward our hands. "Let us practice that posture again. We will switch hands first." Our right hands dropped and we joined left hands. His arm wrapped around my waist, and mine around his. Our left hands formed an arc as we turned.

"Don't forget eye contact," Timothy said, his breath brushing my hairline. My skin erupted in gooseflesh as I tipped my chin upward and met his gaze. As we completed the turn, he took my right hand again. "The second posture might be selected if a gentleman is a little more daring. He might wish to indicate an attachment, or simply be closer to his partner."

Closer? I laughed, but the sound was cut short when Timothy turned to the side and slid his right arm around my waist, tucking me against him. "Now your right hand will come to rest naturally on my shoulder."

I nodded, reaching up and anchoring my hand on his shoulder. We stood, hip to hip, heads turned inward. His eyes traced over my face slowly before he spoke again. "Your left arm forms an arc upward, and my left is downward," his voice was deep and quiet. "Now you will dance slowly backward while I advance."

I obeyed his instructions, following the pace of his advancing steps.

"Well done," he said, releasing me and taking my right hand a third time. His arm around my waist had been steadying my balance, so now I felt weak.

"Is that all of them?" I asked in a quick voice. I didn't know if I could bear further instruction at the moment. I was too confused and shocked to remember any of what he was teaching me. By the time I went to London it would be long forgotten.

"There is one more," he said in his instructive tone, like I was nothing more to him than a pupil. "This is perhaps the least common posture, but one that still requires attention. A gentleman will only choose this posture if he has true feelings for a lady." He paused. "Or if he is a rake." He gave a half-smile at my shocked expression. "The gentleman takes the lady's right hand in his left. Opposite hands are at one another's waist." He assumed the posture, bringing us hip to hip once again, with our hands entwined in front of us. Slowly, he raised my hand to the air, bringing the arc over our heads. I took in a breath and held it, afraid to move a muscle.

"Lean your shoulder toward me," he said, "when you tilt your hips away, your head should nearly be resting on my shoulder." He leaned his shoulder down, and when I did the same, the stretch in my arm became much more comfortable. My pulse raced as I assumed my position, tilting my head up to maintain eye contact as he looked down at me. Our noses nearly touched, our lips the same, and the higher our hands lifted above our heads, the closer we were forced to stand. As we turned, my slow steps followed his, and our legs practically intertwined like the vines on the cover of the diary.

By the time he released me, my skin was on fire. How did he act so…unaffected? He turned to face me, his arm slipping away from my waist. "Do you have any questions?"

I started shaking my head, but stopped myself. "Yes. Are you a rake?"

He laughed. "No."

"You said a gentleman only chooses that posture if he has true feelings for a lady *or* if he is a rake. If you are so well practiced at it, you must have once had true feelings for someone." My words spilled out in a random burst of courage. "Have you ever been in love? Be honest."

What was I doing? Was I fishing for a confession of sorts, right here in the library? I searched his face for clues—for any sign that he was going to finally tell me the truth.

His features were vulnerable, his jaw firm and his mouth closed tight. "Yes." His throat shifted with a swallow, and he brushed his hands on the sides of his trousers. "I have."

My heart threatened to escape my chest. I managed to catch my breath, feigning a look of surprise. "Who did you love?"

Timothy looked down at the floor. "I will not tell you that."

"Timothy! Please tell me." I took a step closer, gaining confidence with each passing second.

He looked up. "No." His stoic expression had returned,

and I knew his mind could not be changed. Not right now. If he had gone so long without doing so, I couldn't expect him to lay his heart bare now. It would take time and coaxing, and further investigation. Was it because he still believed there was a reason he couldn't marry me? That was the only explanation I could think of.

Or was it because he thought me indifferent? I wasn't. I wasn't indifferent at all.

"If you will not tell me who, will you help me understand something? Will you explain it to me what it feels like to fall in love?" My voice was quiet. The words in the diary were so romantic and beautiful. I wanted proof that he had written them. I wanted to hear his interpretation of love. I wanted to hear, indirectly, how he felt about me.

He looked uncharacteristically shy as he laughed under his breath. "You should speak with Lady Daventry on the subject. Perhaps Charlie and Henrietta."

"I don't want to ask them." My voice was too quick. "I want to hear it from you."

He drew his lower lip into his mouth, biting it for several seconds. He released a heavy breath in surrender. "There's a reason it's called falling in love. Not walking into love, or jumping into love, or running into love. Most people don't fall intentionally. As I said with flirting, there is superficial flirting, and there is a way of flirting with deeper meaning. The same applies to love. A rake, for instance, can love many women, but he is not loyal to a single one of them. His love is superficial and it won't last. When you truly love someone, they are the sun, moon, and stars to you. No one else will ever compare. That love doesn't fade with time, nor does it erase even if you try. It is an ever fixed mark."

My heart pounded. "An ever fixed mark... 'that looks on tempests and is never shaken?'"

He nodded, shifting with apparent discomfort. "Turn to Shakespeare from now on for advice about love. He is much wiser than me."

"Yes, but he is not much for conversation." I cast him a smile. My body had finally begun to relax, though my mind was still spinning. I had far too much to think about.

Timothy smiled back, and I felt the same tug toward him I had felt the night before on the staircase. I felt like I was running, and I could hardly catch my breath.

"I ought to prepare for my journey to Somerset," he said, taking a step back. "Please write and keep me informed about your happenings here."

He had gone straight to business; even his expression had returned to his serious one. How could he leave so soon after I had just discovered that he was in love with me? I didn't even know what to do with that information. It was good that he was leaving. I needed time to think and plan before seeing him again—to sort through all the wild emotions spiraling around my heart.

In a moment of courage, I extended my hand toward him, palm facing down, a playful smile on my face. "Good-bye, Timothy." I waited, counting to five in my head. If he thought I was flirting, I didn't care. Perhaps I wanted him to think that. My neck and ears tingled with heat when his cautious eyes met mine. It was rather empowering to think that I made him nervous. I had never realized it before. My victorious feeling ended swiftly when he cradled my hand softly between his fingers, proving that he could make me just as nervous with one touch.

He lowered his lips to the back of my hand, pressing a

soft kiss to my skin. He looked up at me through his lashes, a slight furrow in his brow, and I thought of the line in his diary. *She is always smiling when I cannot, and she has no idea how long I have lived for those smiles.*

I never would have known.

"Goodbye, Nora." He lowered my hand, brushing his own on the side of his trousers as he took his leave of the room.

CHAPTER 16

I had been neglecting my language studies of late, and now that Timothy was no longer at Foxwell House to distract me, I had ample time to do it. I needed to think. Whether it was about Timothy or about Italian, the library was the best place to do it.

Anne often joined me for my lessons, and today was no exception. After Timothy had left the day before, I had taken my dinner in my room, too overwhelmed to attempt any normal conversation with Anne. My mind still refused to focus on anything but the fact that Timothy was in love with me. Or—at least—he had been two years ago. For some reason though, he believed we could never be together. I had always mistook his protective nature for a brotherly kindness —his attention as a courtesy. All his efforts to keep me safe, giving me the most comfortable room at the inn, remembering that I didn't like fish, remembering my birthday, the jealousy in regard to Mr. Ball, the change in his attitude since I had teased him for claiming that we were engaged—It all made sense.

Realization had crashed over me overnight, wave by wave, ending with the most forceful one of all.

I was in love with him, too.

I had always dreamed of the sort of love that sprung upon me like a whirlwind, taking all of my time and energy and thought. I had imagined it would be obvious and sudden, not a compilation of days and months and *years* worth of interactions. I had always viewed Timothy as my superior, a figure who could never possibly care for me as more than a friend. He had claimed he would never marry anyone at all, so of course I had believed that I was not excluded from that. From the very beginning of our acquaintance, I had known that. But the diary had done something I could have never done for myself. It had given me permission to admit that I thought he was the most handsome, kind, and noble man I had ever met.

After a few minutes of staring blankly at the pages of my book in the library, Anne entered the room. She joined me at the table, sweeping her peach skirts beneath her.

"Good afternoon," she said in a friendly tone. Her dark hair was threaded with a peach ribbon, her cheeks flushed from her daily walk. She was already proficient at both Italian and French, but she still enjoyed practicing with me. I was always glad to have her there to help with my inept pronunciation.

"Good afternoon." I flashed a smile before returning my gaze to my book. My face was already hot and I hadn't even confessed anything. I had been avoiding her for a reason. She was sure to be curious about why I wasn't at—

"I missed you at dinner yesterday," she said, interrupting my thoughts. "Did…the duke's departure upset you?"

I crossed my ankles under my chair, tucking a loose curl

behind my ear. My skin tingled with awareness. I looked up, finding Anne's nervous brown eyes fixed on me as I had expected. "I will miss him, but I am very grateful to have you here. In truth, I like it better when we are free to do as we please. Timothy can be overbearing." I chewed my lower lip. I was near to bursting with my secret, but I had promised myself the night before that I wouldn't tell Anne about the diary.

She spoke again, her voice inquisitive. "There *is* something troubling you. I can see it." She let out a long sigh. "There is something I want to tell you, but I don't wish to distress you." She interlocked her fingers on the table, looking at her hands instead of my face. "I nearly told you at dinner two nights ago."

Oh, yes. The night Mr. Prout had come to Foxwell House, Anne had been moments away from telling me her opinion on Timothy's change of mood. We had been interrupted. What had she wanted to say then? My heart thudded fast. A sense of dread sprouted up in my stomach. "What is it?" I leaned forward, drawing her gaze back to mine. Nothing could make me more distressed than I already was.

She scooted back in her chair, turning to face me. "I wouldn't mention it if I were not absolutely certain." She took a deep breath. "But I think the duke…has feelings for you."

I blinked, staring with shock at the apprehension in her features. I tried to speak, but all that came out was a gurgling sound. I choked, clearing my throat.

"There has been plenty of evidence to support the idea," she continued in a quick voice. "I have been noticing his attachment since last spring when you came to visit Charlie in Bath. The duke behaved differently around you. He was far more cheerful. Then, on our journey here, he waited on you as if you were the Queen, and continued to do so when he came to visit. All of that, of course, is secondary to the way he looks at you. That alone was all the evidence I needed."

My heart fluttered, unfolding a bloom of romantic whimsy. I pushed it aside for the moment. A laugh bubbled out of my chest.

Anne's eyes rounded. "You don't appear...surprised." She frowned. "Do you think I'm jesting?"

"No." I covered my face with both hands, a blush creeping over my cheeks. I shook my head, peeking through my fingers. "I already knew."

Anne shot up from the table, slapping her hands down upon it. "How did you know? Did he confess his feelings?"

Not even close. I laughed into my hands, my stomach aching. All the emotions I had been holding inside, combined with my lack of sleep, had brought me to a state of delirium. I laughed until tears welled up in my eyes. I couldn't say what was so humorous about the situation, but the sense of release from my laughter was addicting.

"Tell me at once!" Anne peeled one hand away from my face. "What happened yesterday?"

My laughter subsided, and I slumped back in my chair. "Something horrible."

Her expression twisted with worry. "Did he kiss you?"

"No!" I paused. "But I don't think that would be horrible at all."

Her jaw lowered, a laugh bursting out of her mouth. "Leonora!" She sat in her chair again, grabbing my forearm with delight. "So you care for him too?"

My chest tightened with fear. I had never admitted it to anyone. After a few seconds, I found the courage to nod.

I had never seen Anne so giddy before. She squeezed my

arm so tightly it hurt, a smile stretching wide on her cheeks. "How long have you been in love with him?"

The question rang in my ears. "I think I loved him long before I even knew what that meant. But I started to recognize it when he fell from his horse. I hadn't realized how much I cared for him. I needed him." I paused, debating spilling yet another secret. "I kissed him that day when I thought he was dying, and I didn't know what had come over me. Now I know." I gave a breathless laugh.

Anne's rejoicing only lasted a moment before her brows drew together. "But what is the horrible thing that happened yesterday?"

I could already predict the disapproval on her face when I told her what I had done. Disrespecting Timothy's privacy after all he had done for me had been wicked, and a fresh pang of guilt stabbed at my heart. He could never, ever know. Even telling Anne put my secret at risk. It was like those two pages Timothy had torn out of the diary and burned. If the secret only existed in one's mind, it could never be discovered.

I was silent for too long. Anne nudged me again. "Tell me, please. You can trust me."

It would be relieving to tell the truth. At the moment, the pressure inside me was making me ill. If the secret didn't burst out today, it would likely burst out tomorrow. I released an upward breath through my lips. "I was looking for the dog's skull in the library yesterday, and I found…something else."

Anne urged me to continue, squeezing my arm again. "What did you find?"

I scrunched up my face, closing my eyes to avoid Anne's initial reaction. "His diary."

"The *duke's* diary?" she squeaked.

"Yes. Timothy's old diary from the days he spent at Foxwell House."

She must have covered her mouth with her hand, because her next words were muffled. "And you read it?"

"To my shame, yes I did. He did not write much, but what he wrote was…" I nearly swooned, a fresh wave of heat rushing to my face… "romantic." I opened my eyes.

Anne appeared to be seconds away from leaping out of her chair. "What do you mean?"

I held up one finger. "I quote: 'My heart continues to beat for her, yet I know it should not.'" I held up another. "'I will go on loving Nora, because that is all I know how to do.'" I had read the lines so many times that they were etched in my memory. "'I prefer her company above any other, her laughter, and her her conversation. She is beautiful in every way. She is always smiling when I cannot, and she has no idea how long I have lived for those smiles.'" I put a hand to my forehead. "That is what I mean by romantic."

Anne's mouth hung open. "I knew it."

"*I* did not know it!" I groaned. "I didn't have the slightest idea. I have been pretending for years that I didn't think of him as anything but a brother, but I have been lying to myself. And all along, he has been in love with me?" I compressed each side of my face, shaking my head. "It feels like a dream."

Anne's smile faded, a frown taking its place. "But why has he never declared his feelings to you? Why has he never proposed?"

"That is another matter entirely." I took a calming breath. Perhaps if we worked together, we could solve the mystery. "From what I gathered from his diary, he overheard a conversation between our fathers before his father died. Whatever was said was what led Timothy to run away to the North. He purchased Foxwell House with the intent to 'investigate the matter.'" I sighed. "There is a reason Timothy believed he could not marry me, and he thought that answer was here in Northumberland. His last entry was two years ago. I'm not certain if he found his answer, or if he has simply given up. The diary is in a broken compartment under that desk," I pointed across the room. "I had to ask Chesley to pry it out with a poker. Now that I put it back, I cannot remove it again for further study." I shook my head. "I already memorized what I need to know, and I feel too guilty to read it again."

Anne listened with wide eyes. "Did your father consider the late duke a friend...or an enemy?"

I shrugged. "He has never spoken ill of him that I can recall, but there are not many people my father considers as friends." He didn't even consider his own daughter as anything but a gambling piece.

"Could there have been some dispute between the late duke and your father?" Anne asked. "If there was enmity between them, perhaps Timothy has been led to believe that your father would not give his consent for the marriage, even before he made his agreement to marry you off to Mr. Verwood. Timothy could be waiting until you come of age to finally declare his feelings."

The idea set my heart pounding. "But that doesn't explain why he was seeking answers here in the North. Year after year he returned. He wrote, 'my heart continues to beat for her, yet I know it should not. Next year I will continue to look for a reason it still can. I will resume my search for hope and answers.'"

Anne bit her lower lip. "That is strange."

"I have been perplexed," I said in a tone of defeat. "He

said, 'If it is true that I can never marry Nora, then I will not marry at all.' All I can remember since Timothy became the duke was hearing about how he never wanted to marry. Recently though, he told me that his mother is ill and her final request is that he select a wife so the dukedom can continue with an heir. He no longer says he won't marry. He said he plans to wait until London to find a wife."

Anne held up a hand, stopping me. "So he has suddenly changed his mind about marrying?"

"Yes."

"And he blames the change on his mother's request?" She scoffed and stood up again, gripping my shoulders with both hands and shaking slightly. "That must only be an excuse." I jumped, alarmed by her enthusiasm. "Surely he has found a reason you can be together! He must have found the answer he was looking for."

"Or he has given up." A pang of despair struck my heart.

"Is he as stubborn as you say he is?"

I nodded.

She quoted the diary in a deep voice, "'If it is true that I can never marry Nora, then I will not marry at all.'" She raised an eyebrow. "He has not changed his mind about that."

"Then why won't he tell me how he feels? Why did he avoid me so much of this week?"

"I believe that the only reason he hasn't yet declared himself to you is because you are not yet of age, and he would still require your father's consent. Not only that, but you are under his protection here, and your brother has entrusted him to that task. He must have been avoiding you because he was afraid of revealing too much about his feelings." She gripped my shoulders tighter, a grin pulling on her lips. "He is waiting until London to find a wife, indeed. He's waiting for you."

Telling Anne had been a mistake. She stared down at me with a giddy smile, my shoulders trapped in her grip. I shrugged them away, shaking my head fast. I wanted to believe that her suspicions were correct, but having hope for something I wanted so much was far too vulnerable. Cold fear shot down my spine. Timothy had already been my rescuer in helping me escape my father and Mr. Verwood. How could I expect that he would save me a second time?

"You mustn't say things like that." I rubbed a circle on my forehead in distress, wincing when I touched the spot I had hit on the underside of the desk. Thankfully, it had only left a small bruise.

"And why not?" Anne asked. We seemed to have reversed roles. She was now the cheerful, optimistic one, and I was begging her to see sense.

"Because it might not be true. He might have been avoiding me because he still knows we cannot be together. I *must* find out what that reason is." I gave a frustrated sigh. "I am still going to be here at Foxwell House for months longer, am I not? This is the very place Timothy came to investigate this secret. Perhaps I can find answers of my own."

Anne returned to her seat, and I was tempted to steal the ribbon from her hair and tie her down to the chair so she couldn't jump up and startle me again.

"If you must look for answers, do so, but don't stop preparing for London," she said. "You still have a husband to catch. Although I don't imagine you will have to try very hard." Her eyes gleamed, and I knew precisely what she meant.

All this time, I had been preparing to catch a husband when I came of age. In my mind, it could have been anyone. My objective had been simple: Find a man who would protect me and not repulse me. All I had hoped for was to find someone who was better than Mr. Verwood, but not nearly as wonderful as I had always dreamed of.

But now when I imagined who my husband might be, the only person I could imagine was Timothy. I didn't want just any new acquaintance in London to propose to me. I wanted only one in particular. No one else could ever compare to Timothy.

No one ever had.

I took a shaky breath, glancing down at the Italian book on the table. I pushed it aside with no small measure of satisfaction. Did Timothy even care if I knew Italian? There were other matters that now required my full attention, such as what Timothy had been looking for in Northumberland. I had no idea where to start, but at least I had time on my side.

CHAPTER 17

The seaside air grew colder by the day, the winds and rain less forgiving. The more time that passed, the more I missed Timothy. I missed Charlie too. I spent my days as I had all along, practicing my accomplishments and learning new skills, but my motivation had changed. I was not doing it to become more desirable for a man. I was doing it because I wanted to. I was learning to draw and paint with far more skill, and my work no longer looked like it had been created with my eyes closed. I played the pianoforte each morning before breakfast, and I even opened my Italian book again and set to practicing in the afternoons with Anne.

Even if the unknown obstacle that made Timothy think he couldn't marry me still existed, at least I knew that he wanted me. He had wanted me long before I had learned how to draw, paint, dance, or speak Italian.

I had been trying to put him out of my mind, but it was difficult with so little to occupy me. Thinking of Timothy and all his secrets had become part of my daily schedule. Between breakfast and dancing, I went on a walk, and that was when I was allowed to daydream of dancing with him, laughing, feeling safe and happy. The months ahead of me were far more daunting than they had been before. I had been dreading London, but now I looked forward to it. Anne's words refused to leave my mind. *He is waiting until London to find a wife, indeed. He's waiting for you.*

I had been waiting for an opportune moment to investigate Timothy's secret for myself. On a morning when Anne caught a cold, I left her in her room with a pot of tea and sneaked out the front door.

That one particular fishing village that Timothy had taken me to had been standing out in my mind, raising flags of curiosity. All the villagers had recognized him, and he had greeted several by name. Speaking to any number of them could provide me with a sense of direction. Julia accompanied me as the coachman conveyed us to the village.

The land was not as beautiful as it had been weeks before. Much of the heather had died, losing its color. When I stepped out of the carriage, I wrapped my shawl more tightly around my shoulders. The cold wind was strong enough to cut through even my wool pelisse. I shivered, leading the way down the cobblestones as Julia followed beside me. I had worn grey, but that still wasn't enough to conceal me from the many watchful eyes of the villagers. I could have singled out any one of them and asked if they knew Timothy, but it would be fastest to go straight to the man I knew to be his friend.

I stopped at the top of the cliff, looking down at the treacherous path Timothy had helped me navigate. There were several steep drops and declines, but I had worn my most sturdy boots that day. I could do it on my own. I steeled myself with a deep breath, wobbling a little as a gust of wind took hold of my skirts. Down on the beach it didn't look quite so windy, and if my eyes were not deceiving me, Mr. Prout was standing on the shore hunched over a boat filled with fish.

"Are you comfortable making the walk?" I asked Julia, whose face was ghostly white as she stared at the path ahead of us.

"Yes, of course, my lady." She took a few tentative steps, and I noticed her legs shaking.

I grabbed the back of her arm, stopping her. For one afraid of heights, the walk would not be pleasant. Fortunately I was not afraid of heights—only of spiders and vicious cats. I cast her a smile. "Will you stay here instead? Keep watch from above to ensure I am safe. If anything looks amiss, scream for help." I gulped. I didn't expect anything terrible to happen, but without Timothy by my side, I felt far more vulnerable.

I started down the path, crouching down and using my hands to descend the first steep section. After that, the walk was fairly easy. I tugged my bonnet ribbons tighter to keep it from flying away in the wind. The air was grainy with sand, wet from mist, and it smelled of fish. I made it to the beach and cast my gaze at all the fishermen. My presence had already attracted the attention of several. I tried not to panic as I searched for Mr. Prout. I had seen him, hadn't I?

"Goodday, pretty lady," a voice slurred from my left. A chorus of laugher followed the words.

I whirled toward the sound, my heart leaping to my throat. A man with two missing teeth stood a few paces away, a limp fish in one hand and a hatchet in the other. My stomach turned.

I squared my shoulders, holding my ground even though

I wanted to run back up the hill. "I am here to speak with Mr. Prout."

"Are ye now?" He chuckled, and so did the men behind him. "Or are ye here to see me?" He took a step closer, and I noticed a rim of red on the blade of his hatchet.

"No. Not you." I gave a nervous laugh, backing up a step. Surely he was just taunting me, but I was still unnerved. If Timothy were there, he would have thrown the man upside down into the sea by now.

"Would ye like ta know where Mr. Prout is?" the man asked.

I nodded, swallowing my terror. "Yes, please."

"Give me a kiss, or give one to me fish," he held up the slippery creature, "and then I'll tell ye where 'e is."

The three men behind him doubled over in laughter. I glared at them. I didn't have time to converse with these scoundrels. My heart pounded as I took a quick step forward. "I will find him myself."

The man took a large sideways step, blocking my path. "Ye must choose. Me or him." He moved the fish closer.

I nearly gagged, yet I still would have much preferred to kiss the fish. I shot the man a glare. "Move aside." It might not have been wise to tell a crazed man with a hatchet what to do, but my chest was constricting with panic. He didn't move, a wide smile revealing yet another missing tooth.

A commotion caught in the corner of my eye, and I turned to the right. Mr. Prout was running across the sand, eyes ablaze. When he reached the men who had crowded in front of me, he shoved them aside with both hands. The toothless man fell to the sand, scrambling back to his feet a few yards away.

"Back to work, all of you!" Mr. Prout's tanned skin

flushed red with anger, a sharp contrast to his pale hair. He didn't pay them any further attention, turning to face me instead. "Are you all right? What are you doing down here alone?"

I was too stunned to speak, my arms rigid at my sides. Mr. Prout's sharp blue eyes were ripe with worry as he led me farther from the other fishermen.

"I came to speak with you," I said in a dazed voice.

"You should not have come alone."

"My maid is just there." I gestured to where Julia stood at the top of the hill.

"I don't think she could protect you from harm," he grumbled, taking a deep breath.

Now he was sounding like Timothy. It was no wonder that they were friends. "I am fortunate that you were here."

Mr. Prout nodded, his mouth a firm line. "How may I be of service?"

My thoughts had been scattered by those unruly men, so I took a moment to gather them again. I had been nervous to come speak with Mr. Prout, but I couldn't banish the feeling that his friendship with Timothy was related to the secret he was keeping. If nothing else, I had hope that Mr. Prout would be able to shed some light on Timothy's frequent visits to that particular village.

"As you know," I began, "Tim—er—the duke, is a dear friend of mine. I have been curious about something, and I wondered if you might be able to help me."

A deep set of lines formed in Mr. Prout's forehead as he listened.

"How long ago did you first meet the duke?" That seemed a fair question to start with.

Mr. Prout's confusion persisted. "One year ago."

Only one year? That would have been after the final entry in the diary. "And under what circumstances did you first meet him?"

Mr. Prout laughed under his breath. "What's the purpose of these inquiries?"

"I'm curious, that's all." I blinked innocently, tossing a him a smile.

He chuckled. "Do you mean to say you came all this way simply because you were curious about how I met the Duke of Heywood?"

He was right. It did not sound convincing. "No. That isn't the *only* reason. I-I came to purchase another fish for Lady Daventry."

He narrowed his eyes with skepticism. "Ah."

"But you didn't answer my question," I said in a quick voice. "How did you meet the duke?"

He rubbed his jaw, pausing for several seconds. "He was purchasing fish."

I pressed my lips together as I shook my head. Mr. Prout's shifting eyes were enough to reveal his lie. Timothy liked fish, but not enough to go all the way to that particular bay. "There are many villages closer to Foxwell House that sell fish. What I am trying to understand is why he came to this particular village and how he came to be such a dear friend to you. He has been quite vague about the subject."

"Has he?" Mr. Prout raised his brows. "I can't imagine why. Which fish would you like today?" He started walking toward the nearest boat, but I followed him.

"I *know* he has a secret, and I know that *you* know what it is." In truth, I wasn't certain, but if I acted confident, Mr. Prout might crack.

His response was a hearty laugh. "Everyone has a secret.

I'd wager you have one too." He stooped down to pick up a large silver fish.

"I may." I put one hand on my hip. "I assume you have one too."

"I do." He smiled.

"What is it?" My boldness shocked even myself, but I was growing desperate.

"If I told you, it would ruin the point of it being a secret, would it not?" His bright blue eyes gleamed with amusement.

I fisted my hands, taking a steadying breath. "I will confess mine if you promise to keep it."

His brows lifted in surprise. "I didn't ask for your secret."

"I wish to share it regardless." My heart pounded. At the moment, it seemed the only way to appeal to his sympathies. If he knew my worries, he might be able to appease them. Considering Mr. Prout's reluctance to tell the truth, I was now certain he had been involved somehow in Timothy's investigation, or at least he might have known what Timothy had been looking for. I gripped the sides of my skirts as I spoke. "Do you promise to keep my secret safe?"

Mr. Prout gave a slow nod.

I took a deep breath. "I love him. The duke." I swallowed, looking at the sand as my face tingled with heat. What on earth had come over me? Why was I confessing this to Mr. Prout of all people? It was too late to change my mind, so I continued. "I love him, but I'm afraid that we can't be together. I have reason to believe that there is an obstacle between us, but I don't know what that obstacle is, or how it can be overcome. I know it is all rather confusing, but I suspect that he was here in the North in search of something. An answer, a reason to hope…I'm not certain." I looked up, a sudden tightness in my throat. "I came today to ask if you can give *me* a reason to hope."

Mr. Prout studied my face for a long moment, and then a warm smile curved his mouth. He took a step forward, and the tenderness in his gaze lifted a burden inside me, before he even said a word. He didn't seem surprised or oblivious, only calm. "You have every reason to hope."

My shoulders relaxed, a blanket of relief spreading over me. "Did he find what he was looking for?"

Mr. Prout nodded. "Yes."

I pressed a hand to my stomach, catching my breath as an overwhelming sense of joy seized my body. "That is very good to know. Thank you, Mr. Prout."

He winked. "And don't worry, I'll keep your secret."

I gave a shy nod, my cheeks burning with embarrassment all over again. I may not have had all the answers, but I had the most important one. Anne might have been right—Timothy might have just been waiting until I was of age and free from my father to declare his feelings. The idea sent a thrill of excitement through my limbs, and I nearly twirled and jumped on the sand.

Mr. Prout gestured at the fish in his hand. "For you 'twill always be free of charge."

I shook my head. "No, please—"

He gave a kind smile. "I won't yield."

I sighed. "That is too kind."

"Do you have a basket?"

My heart dropped. "No."

"That's no matter." Mr. Prout held up the fish, extending it toward me. "'tisn't heavy. Wedge your fingers in the gills and carry it like so." He demonstrated, and the fish's unblinking eye stared straight at me.

My gaze leaped to Mr. Prout's face with disbelief.

He threw his head back with a laugh. "It's that, or use your bonnet."

Or better yet, Anne could go without fish for dinner tonight. I touched my bonnet ribbons, nearly whimpering in distress. It was my favorite bonnet, and it would never, ever go on my head again after touching those slimy grey scales. I didn't want to wedge my fingers in the fish's gills either, not while wearing the gloves Timothy had given me.

I took a deep breath, deciding in an instant that the gloves could be more easily washed. I reached out and took the fish, holding it out in front of me. "I thank you, sir."

Mr. Prout chuckled as I started up the hill again. The fish dangled from my fingers, swaying with my awkward steps over the rocks. "You are a vile creature," I mumbled, examining the glassy eye a little closer. I shuddered. I did have sympathy for it. Just that day it had been swimming peacefully, and now it would be Anne's dinner. It had been plucked from the water without any warning. Helpless and hopeless.

On the contrary, my life had turned from hopeless to a dream that I didn't feel worthy of. I hardly knew what to do now but wait. My smile was so wide it made my cheeks ache. If Timothy could wait for me to come of age, then I could wait for him to confess his feelings. My heart hammered at the thought, a delighted shiver crossing over my shoulders. Suddenly I didn't need to know the mystery Timothy had been trying to solve. Mr. Prout had reassured me, and I felt calm. The answers would come in time. It would only be yet another exercise in patience. It was not one of my virtues.

As I approached the top of the cliff, I stumbled on a rock. I cried out as I lunged forward, catching myself with both hands on the dirt. The fish tumbled out of reach, landing a few feet below with a sickening thud. I glanced down at the beach, relieved that Mr. Prout hadn't witnessed my fall. With one eye on the fish, I stood, brushing the dirt from my skirts.

"Are you all right, my lady?" Julia called. She was close enough now that I could see the distress in her features.

"Yes!" I pursed my lips in frustration, staring at the fish. Abandoning it would be a disrespect to Mr. Prout's generosity. Not only that, but Anne was not feeling well, and she would be happy to have fish soup for dinner. I pivoted and started back down the path to retrieve it. I was only a few paces away when a seabird swooped down, clamping the fish's tail in its beak. I gasped as it flew away, wings beating awkwardly as it carried Anne's dinner into the sky.

"That was mine!" I shouted. The bird didn't listen, landing on a rock on the side of the cliff where I could never reach it. It pecked at the fish, thoroughly enjoying its spoils.

I sighed, marching back up the hill. My vexation shifted to determination. I tugged my skirts up to climb the steep outcropping, surprised by my own agility. I gave a breathless laugh as I reached the top, glancing back at that hateful, thieving bird. That was the last time I would let something take what was mine. Soon it would be *my* choice where I lived and who I would marry. The future I truly wanted—one filled with love and happiness—was finally in reach. My heart swelled with so much hope that it nearly burst.

I took in the view at the top of the cliff. There was a quiet, untouched feeling to the North, a desolation that was breathtaking. It was the perfect hiding place, an escape from the rest of the world. Here, the sea was louder than my fears and pains, the wind was stronger, and the expansive views reminded me how small I truly was. If such beauty existed, if such nature could be designed, then it was possible for me to find true happiness one day. It had to be. I was not lost or resigned to any specific fate. I could still design a different one.

I was going to marry my best friend, and nothing could stop me.

CHAPTER 18

Nora's Coming of Age Diary

December 22, 1816

I have been waiting weeks for the first snow, and it has finally come. December is more than halfway through, and so soon shall be my time at Foxwell House.

Anne and I do all we can to keep our spirits high. We have begun a chess tournament, and just last week, I won. With hours and hours of practice, my skills have improved immensely. I practice my dances each night before I sleep. When Timothy comes to Foxwell House again, I will have to insist that he practice with me again.

I hovered an inch from the window in the drawing room, my breath leaving fog on the glass. Large snowflakes spiraled down from the sky, landing softly on the ground, collecting there in a thin white blanket.

"Leonora," Anne's voice came from behind me.

I turned away from the window. She stood in the door-way, palms outstretched and cupping something small and round. Her face was half horror and half fascination.

I squinted at the object in her hands. "What is th—" My words cut off as I realized what she was holding.

"The dog." She gave a dazed laugh. I stared at it, too shocked to speak. It was yellowing and old, with dirt in the creases. The eye sockets, set of canine teeth, and a long snout came together to form old Jeremy's skull.

My first thought was to ask where she had found it, but the second question was a little more pressing. "*Why* are you touching it?"

She laughed, bringing it closer to her face to examine. "I'm not afraid."

I covered my mouth with a laugh, shaking my head. "I cannot believe it actually exists! Where did you find it?"

"It was behind my wardrobe. My gloves fell beneath it, and when I went to retrieve them, I saw it."

"How remarkable." I dared to look closer. "Do you think his ghost haunts this house?"

Anne laughed. "I hope so. I am quite fond of dogs."

"As am I. He shall be our pet." We both stared adoringly at the skull before bursting into laughter.

"Obviously you must take the credit," she said. "Tell the duke that you found the skull and claim your reward." She wiggled her eyebrows.

My face grew hot. When had I become so shy when it

pertained to Timothy? There had once been a time I wasn't shy about anything. "And what do you suggest?" I teased.

"A proposal of marriage would be an appropriate reward."

I bit my lip, fighting a ridiculous smile. Forcing Timothy to propose to me was not part of my plan, but I *had* been thinking about how I might encourage him without declaring my feelings first. There was no way to prove that he planned to court and marry me once we arrived in London, so until then, I needed to give him some indication that I would welcome such a drastic turn of events.

Distracted as I was by my thoughts, I didn't notice Anne grab my hand until it was too late. "Here, take it." She placed the cold, dirty skull in my palm.

I swiped my hand away with a gasp, causing the skull to fall to the floor with a thud.

Two of the teeth fell out, scattering across the rug. I screamed.

Anne screamed.

Chesley jumped.

From out in the corridor, a firm knock sounded on the front door.

I pressed a hand to my chest. "Blast and bother!" I caught my breath, exchanging a worried glance with Anne. "Who could that be?"

"I haven't the slightest idea." She stooped over to pick up the skull, and I grimaced as I gathered up the two teeth. Anne hurried across the room to an empty vase, setting the skull inside. I dropped the teeth in beside it.

It had been months since we had any visitors, and the only people I could picture standing on our porch were Mr. Ball, Mr. Elmore, or possibly Mr. Prout. Who would have ventured out in the snow? I hadn't given a great deal of time to my appearance that day. My long-sleeved morning dress was plain and white, and my wild curls hung loose about my shoulders. At least Anne always presented herself well. She looked regal as always, hair at the crown of her head and a pendant at her neck.

We listened as the front door creaked open. A familiar male voice made tears spring to my eyes. I raced out into the corridor, gasping with delight. "Charlie!"

My brother had only set one foot inside the entryway when I ran toward him, throwing my arms around his shoulders. I hadn't seen his face or heard his voice for half a year. His dark curls and eyebrows were dotted with snowflakes, a broad smile on his face as he pulled away to look at me. "We thought to surprise you for Christmastide."

I craned my neck around his shoulder. "We?"

His wife, Henrietta, peeked her head out from behind him, beaming as she stole me from Charlie's embrace. She was beautiful, just like Anne, their brown eyes nearly identical in shape and size. I squeezed her tight, laughing as my emotions threatened to overwhelm me. I blinked hard, a stray tear escaping down my cheek. I sniffed, rubbing my nose hard.

I heard Anne's quick footsteps from behind me. "Henrietta!" She gasped, rushing toward her sister. They hugged, and I stepped aside, my cheeks aching from my smile. I started to turn toward Charlie again, but I stopped. My heart leaped. Another person was walking up the steps. Though I couldn't see his face through the half-opened door, his broad shoulders and height betrayed him. I moved to throw the door open wider, but Timothy beat me to it. He stopped in his tracks, filling the doorway in front of me.

"Nora." His deep voice sent tendrils of warmth through my body. His soft brown eyes met mine. My heart pounded fast, a nervous energy making little explosions under every inch of my skin. He was here.

He was here and he was covered in snowflakes.

I laughed, covering my mouth with one hand. "Please come inside," I said in a breathless voice, waving him forward. I collided with Charlie as I made room for Timothy's entrance, stumbling like a clumsy fool. Timothy's cheeks were flushed from the weather, and I hoped the redness on my own face could be excused for the ten seconds I had been exposed to the cold. Timothy's smile completely unarmed me, and for a moment I forgot how to breathe or stand up straight. I touched my hair. Of all the days to leave it so unruly, this had not been the best choice.

I faced all of them with my hands on my hips. "You should not have traveled in the snow! It is far too dangerous." My voice was scolding, but it broke with emotion. I blinked fast as Charlie and Henrietta laughed.

"We missed you," Henrietta said. "Why would we not choose to spend Christmastide with our sisters?" She squeezed Anne's hand, then reached for mine. Though Anne was not my sister-in-law as Henrietta was, the sisterhood we had built over our time at Foxwell House was irreversible. She was just as much a part of my family as Henrietta and Charlie were. My gaze slid to Timothy, those nervous explosions starting up again under my skin.

"You even managed to convince Timothy to come." I cast him a teasing smile. "What did you bribe him with?"

Charlie chuckled. "It was his idea, actually."

Timothy looked down at the floor, a modest smile on his lips. "I knew it would please you to see your family."

"And to see you," I added.

Timothy looked up. I turned my attention to the floor,

feeling a sudden urgency to hide my fondness for him with Charlie watching the interaction. Was this the pressure Timothy had been feeling all these years? I didn't want to cause a stir of gossip in the house. It would be an awkward Christmastide if Charlie picked up on my feelings for Timothy too early. He would surely assume they were one-sided, and the only way I could explain that they weren't would be if I confessed to reading the diary. I gulped. That could not happen.

I looked up at my brother. "How did you explain your absence to Father?"

"I told him I was searching for you. Of course I will return unsuccessful." He smiled, but it seemed forced. This entire ordeal was taking a toll on him. He looked weary and burdened, but that could have been from the long journey they had just undertaken.

"Does he even think I'm still…alive?" I paused, gripping the ends of my sleeves in my palms. "Does he care?"

Charlie didn't speak for several seconds, his brows drawing together. "We made the fake ransom far more than he could afford. Fortunately for you, he has kept your disappearance as hushed as possible for fear of revealing his financial state to society. You are safe. That is all that matters."

I pieced together the information in my mind, my heart stinging with old wounds. "So he declined to pay the ransom rather than humbling himself enough to ask for help from his peers. He would rather I be disposed of by my kidnapper." My grief at being so disregarded by my father had turned into anger since coming to Foxwell House. My eyes had been opened. I had been mistreated, and it wasn't a reason to cry or to pity myself. It was a reason to disregard my father in return. He was not worth my tears.

"Perhaps not. He hopes that the kidnapper will eventually bring you home when he realizes the ransom will not be paid. He is hoping for a surrender."

I scoffed. "Is Mr. Verwood still waiting for such a miracle as well?"

Charlie sighed. "He doesn't know you are missing. All the neighbors have been told that you are visiting a relative in Kent. Father still believes I can find you and bring you home quietly, without any money having to be paid."

"Surely he has given up by now! It's been half a year."

"And we hope he will give up completely by the time the year is through. By then we will find you a husband and Father will have no say in the matter." Charlie released a slow breath, rubbing the side of his jaw. "That will be another challenge entirely." It was clear that the prospect overwhelmed him. What would he say if I told him that I had already made my choice? Would it put his mind at ease if Timothy claimed my hand now, just a few months in advance? It would certainly put *my* mind at ease.

I glanced up at Timothy. The snowflakes in his hair had melted, leaving it damp with a slight wave. He observed our conversation, arms crossed over his chest. His eyes settled on mine before he addressed Charlie. "Let us think of happier things for now. It's nearly Christmastide. It's Nora's favorite time of year."

He was right, as always. It was my favorite, and I had been picturing this year as a bleak and lonely Christmas. But not anymore.

The footmen had finished bringing in the trunks, so Timothy led Charlie and Henrietta through the house, directing them to the rooms upstairs. I trailed behind with Anne, listening to their conversation.

"Why the devil did you buy such a secluded manor for yourself?" Charlie asked Timothy with a laugh. "I still don't understand it."

I smirked. I had certainly had the same question.

"I told you. Hunting." Timothy's voice was dismissive.

"Why the North?"

"I like it here."

I narrowed my eyes. Was that really enough to convince Charlie? I stared at Timothy's back as he walked, confidence in every stride. He left no room for argument.

"My mother liked it here too," Charlie said. "I don't have many memories of her, but I do recall the stories she told me of the moors and the endless sea of blooming heather."

I caught up to them, nearly tripping up the staircase. "Mother visited the North? When?"

"She had a cousin who lived here who has since died." Charlie glanced over his shoulder at me. "But I believe she visited often. She loved Northumberland."

I held tightly to the bannister, letting his words sink through me.

I had never known her. I had never had the opportunity to see her face or hear her voice, but I had been told I looked like her. Father didn't speak of her. The only thing I missed about my home in Somerset was her portrait that hung in the upstairs corridor. Each time I looked at it, I knew she forgave me, even if Father could not. Because I had been born, she had died. I had been given so many of her qualities, including a love for the North and the moors. My heart flooded with pride. It was no wonder I felt such a connection to the place.

Henrietta paused in the doorway of my bedchamber, gaping at the furnishings. "Is this your room, your grace?"

Timothy turned, assuming a casual posture. "That's Nora's

room. I will be at the end of the corridor, and the two of you will be in the room opposite Lady Daventry's."

Henrietta whirled to face me. Her eyes rounded with awe, her limp dark curls framing them. "You must never want to leave this house," she said with a laugh. "I was expecting far worse."

"Pardon me?" Timothy said, one eyebrow raised.

Henrietta raised a hand in defense. "Well—you did call it an 'old abandoned hunting lodge.' This is grand. I didn't realize Leonora was living like a princess."

It was my turn to be defensive. "I didn't expect it either. Timothy insisted that I have this room." The memory of him scooping me up and dropping me on the bed flashed in my mind. That was one way of *insisting*. His eyes met mine, and butterflies surged once again in my stomach. Was he thinking of that moment too?

"As he should." Henrietta said with a wink. "Men do not need beautiful rooms." She flitted down the corridor to Charlie's side, linking her arm through his. He gave her a soft smile, pressing a kiss to the top of her head. It was still strange to see my brother so...adoring. Anne followed behind them, showing them which bedchamber they would occupy.

Timothy's lips twitched with a smile as he took a step toward me. "How do you feel?"

A jolt of panic shot through my body. "How do I...feel?"

"To see Charlie and Henrietta."

I exhaled sharply with relief. "Oh. Yes. I...I am overjoyed. Truly. I didn't expect to see them at all."

"We will stay until Twelfth Night."

"Not longer?" I asked.

"That *is* more than a fortnight," he said with a laugh.

I sighed. "I suppose you're right."

He eyed me with exasperation. "Are you not satisfied?"

I took a deep breath, willing myself to be brave. *Encourage him.* That was my duty during this unexpected visit. I had been playing the role of little sister for far too long. I shrugged. "If I had my way, you would never leave."

His soft smile undid me, thread by thread. "Well, then. I'm glad to hear that you've finally learned to appreciate me."

Appreciate was an understatement. He had no idea how many hours I had spent thinking about him and the romantic words in his diary, dreaming and planning and hoping. I was terrified that he could see all of it in my eyes. I must have been looking at him differently than I always had. I couldn't help it.

His head tipped to one side, a grin tugging on his mouth as he studied me.

"What?" I asked.

"Your hair."

My face flamed. I took two handfuls of it, hiding the knotted curls. "I didn't expect any visitors."

He continued staring at me, ripe amusement in his eyes.

"It's not my fault my hair looks like a bird's nest."

He laughed. "It doesn't look like a bird's nest."

"That's what Miss Grant told me."

His brow furrowed with sudden vexation. "Why would she say that?"

I shrugged. "She must value honesty." My heart pounded. His eyes would not leave my face and hair. "If I had known we would have guests, I would have had it properly arranged. *You* are the one who chose to come unannounced."

"I'm glad I did."

I stopped my rambling, my fingers going limp around the ends of my hair.

He inhaled slowly, then looked away fast. "It suits you."

I didn't have the opportunity to reply before he turned his attention to Charlie and Henrietta, who had apparently finished examining their room. I was rooted where I stood, stunned by his passive compliment. Timothy's business-like expression returned, and he walked away without a backward glance.

There he was again, ever unromantic and stoic.

A slow smile pulled on my lips.

But I knew better.

CHAPTER 19

Even after singing countless Christmas carols about good tidings of great joy, Charlie continued to bring up bad tidings without joy—such as all the men he planned to introduce me to in London.

At nearly every meal, it was the subject of discussion. There were so many lords and sirs and misters that I lost track of all their names. He had even made a list, numbering them in order of desirability.

Timothy was not on the list.

If he had been, he would have been in first place, but Charlie was under the same impression that I had always been —that Timothy would never consider marrying me, not even under such desperate circumstances.

As the days went on, I was beginning to be fooled again.

Timothy performed his charade far too well. He greeted me with polite smiles, always choosing a seat across the room, not too close and not too far. He participated in Charlie's conversations about London. Over the course of Christmas

Eve, Christmas day, and the week beyond, Timothy ensured we were never left alone together. He was always the last to arrive at meals, and we never spoke privately.

Doubt crept into my mind as I lay in bed each night. What if his feelings had changed since he wrote the diary? What if Mr. Prout had been wrong to give me hope? I shook the doubts from my mind. Timothy had said that love doesn't fade with time, nor does it erase even if you try. It is an ever fixed mark. He was simply good at hiding it. But I already knew that.

It made sense that he would hide his feelings during Charlie's visit, and while he was still trusted to protect me at Foxwell House. He was acting with propriety, but I was beginning to fear that he always would. Would everything really change when I turned twenty-one?

On the morning of Twelfth Night, I pulled Anne aside in the corridor, motioning for her to follow me to the drawing room. I needed her advice, and Henrietta had been lovingly stealing her time over the past two weeks. Our guests would be leaving the next afternoon, and my fears were weighing on my chest like a stack of bricks. I took a deep breath, closing the drawing room door behind us.

"I have been meaning to speak with you." I wrung my fingers together.

She nodded her agreement. "A conversation is long overdue."

"Charlie is overbearing with his plans for London," I said with a sigh. "I don't know whether to voice my agreement with the choices on his list or to outwardly object. I don't know whether I should be planning on securing one of them, or if I should wait patiently for Timothy to finally make his intentions known. As of now, he is not even close to doing so." I released an anxious breath. "Do you think he even plans to marry me?" I asked, dropping heavily into the sofa like an anchor. "Am I imagining all of it? Has his old diary created some sort of fantasy in my mind?"

Anne sat down beside me, shaking her head. "You are not imagining it. He is acting as he always has. This visit has been no different, and why should it be? If anything, he would be acting more distant because your brother is here to observe any interactions he has with you."

"I suppose that's true."

"When you walked into the drawing room in your red gown for dinner yesterday, he could not stop staring at you."

My brows flew upward. "Truly?"

"Don't be so surprised!" Anne swatted at my arm.

"Well, he is a very skilled actor." It was vexing that he had accused me of being a horrible actor the day he had pretended to kidnap me. But with his skill, I supposed he had the right to criticize me.

"Wait until London," Anne reassured me.

I frowned. "But Charlie has other plans. When we arrive in London, will Timothy step aside and allow all these gentlemen to court me? Will he allow Charlie to choose my husband from his list? I don't understand why Timothy won't explain his intentions now. It would save us all a great deal of trouble."

"Because he's essentially acting as your guardian. It would be inappropriate for him to continue his visits here if there was anything romantic between you. He knows it would betray Charlie's trust."

I puzzled over her words, staring at the floor. Why did it

feel like there was still another reason? "He did mention yesterday that he won't be visiting in three months as planned. His next visit will be with Charlie when they come to fetch me for London in the summer."

"Oh?" Anne scowled.

"He's avoiding me again." I sighed.

She grinned. "Perhaps he doesn't trust himself to keep his feelings hidden through another prolonged visit. He also doesn't know how you feel," she added. "I'm certain he plans to display his affections with great care so as not to scare you. You mustn't forget that he is completely unaware that you even know how *he* feels." She raised an eyebrow. "He likely still believes you are indifferent."

I stood, folding my arms as I paced in a straight line. "But I want him to know that I'm not. I want him to know before he leaves again. Perhaps I ought to give him reason to believe that I have no interest in all those gentlemen Charlie is suggesting."

Anne's eyes rounded. "Are you going to tell him?"

"That would be far too bold." I bit one fingernail softly as I passed the vase in the corner of the room. I peered inside where we had left the dog's skull. I hadn't even told Timothy that we had found it—I had been waiting until the right moment, but now my time with him was almost spent. The next time Timothy came to Foxwell House, it would be time to go to London. There was no longer a need for him to keep his distance and act as my noble protector.

"Then what are you going to do?" Anne asked.

"I'm going to give him a birthday gift." I stared into the vase again, my heart pounding as an idea sprouted up in my mind. Timothy's birthday was in January, later that very month. If I showed him I remembered, he would know that I cared—even if I had nothing to give him besides the dusty old skull of a hunting dog.

The skull was also an opportunity to ask him for something that he couldn't refuse. 'Your wish shall be my command,' he had said.

I would have to see if he was truly a man of his word.

CHAPTER 20

I tied the red ribbon a third time, adjusting where it was positioned on the box. I had left a note outside Timothy's door before dinner the night before. As long as he had received it, he would be meeting me in the library at any moment.

He hadn't confirmed his receipt of the note at dinner, but I trusted that it hadn't gone unnoticed. I had written that I had a surprise for him, and to not tell anyone. The secretive nature of the missive would have either terrified him, or intrigued him.

Or both.

It was early, the sun barely coming through the library windows. It had been days since the last snowfall, so the roads would be safe for Charlie, Henrietta, and Timothy as they started the long journey home later that morning. This was my last chance to speak with Timothy before he was gone. I couldn't ruin it.

I took a deep breath, leaning on the courage that had

brought me to the library in the first place. Unfortunately, it seemed to have scattered. There was no telling whether or not I would follow through with my plan. I had learned over and over again that Timothy would not be told what to do.

My heart leaped when the library door opened. Timothy slipped inside, rubbing sleep from one eye with a cautious smile. "What the devil are you doing up so early?" He wore his shirtsleeves and a green waistcoat, a lazily tied cravat at his throat. My spine was rigid. I sat at the table like a queen, ankles crossed beneath me, hands perched atop the gift box. He looked as nervous as I felt, standing close to the door as if he might need to make a swift escape.

I grabbed the box and stood on shaky legs, accidentally stepping on the hem of my dress. I tripped, catching myself with one arm on the table. I cringed, stealing a peek at Timothy's reaction. He looked thoroughly entertained, a curious tilt to his head as he noticed the box in my hand.

If I couldn't even stand or walk properly, then how was I going to find the strength to follow through with my plan? I fortified myself with a deep breath. "I knew that you were leaving this morning, so I wanted to give you a birthday gift." My hand shook as I approached him with the box.

A smile twisted his lips, but he seemed to be fighting it. His eyes shifted from the box to my face. "My birthday isn't for weeks."

"Yes, but you won't be here."

His gaze was softened by the early morning light, and I was nearly drowning in it. The curious look he gave me was far too endearing, and he looked far too handsome with his casual manner of dress. "Shall I wait to open it until then?" he asked.

"No." My mouth stretched into a wide grin of anticipation. "Open it now." I pushed the box toward him until he finally took it.

I fought the laughter that bubbled in my chest, keeping myself composed. He eyed me with suspicion before tugging on one end of the ribbon. It fell away, and he lifted the lid. His face contorted in shock.

I burst into laughter.

He reached into the box and withdrew the skull, gaping at it with horrified fascination. "The dog. How—" He tipped his head back with a laugh of disbelief. "Where was it?"

"Behind the wardrobe in Anne's room."

He shook his head in awe. "I was certain the old man lied to me."

I planted a hand on my hip. "Yet you convinced me to spend hours searching for it?"

"Your search wasn't in vain. That's all that matters." He put the skull back in the box, closing the lid behind it. "Thank you for the birthday gift. I shall treasure it forever."

I laughed, temporarily forgetting my nerves. "I expect it to be displayed at your estate in Somerset."

"It shall be the first thing one sees when they enter the front doors."

My laugher came simultaneously with his, interrupting the quiet of the library. This was the Timothy I had been missing. He seemed to only show this side when we were alone, which hadn't happened at all during the last fortnight. My heart thudded against my ribs as I formulated my next words. "You did say that if I found it, you would give me anything I asked for."

His brow furrowed. "Did I say that?"

"Yes. Don't deny it."

He looked down at me, a playful grin on his face. "Very well, what will it be?"

He wouldn't be smiling so much if he knew what I intended to ask for.

I took the box from his hand, walking back to the table to set it down. I rubbed my palms on my skirts, gathering my composure before turning around. I had been rehearsing what to say all night, but now the words had fled my mind.

"I'm worried about London," I stammered. "Besides all the dancing and parties and manners, I will be expected to enter a courtship. I will be expected to flirt and encourage a gentleman and...well, I want to be prepared for what might come next."

Timothy's smile had already faded, a scowl replacing it. "And what is that?"

I bit my lower lip, a fresh wave of nervousness pooling in my stomach. Anne would hate me, but I needed to blame her in order to sound convincing. She had been married before. She had been through what I would soon face. "Anne told me that when I am courting a gentleman, he is likely to seek an opportunity to kiss me. When the time comes, I want to know what to expect." I had planned to walk closer to him at this point, but I was still frozen by the table.

Timothy crossed his arms tightly over his chest. I didn't dare look at his face for too long, so I continued rambling. "I have never kissed a man before." I laughed. "Well, I suppose I did kiss..." my voice trailed off. What the devil was I doing? This had not been part of my script. I had sworn I would never tell him. I snapped my mouth closed and searched for a way to cover my words. "Well, never mind." I laughed.

Timothy interrupted before I could speak again. "Who did you kiss?"

My cheeks burned. "I cannot tell you."

"Mr. Ball? Did he make such advances toward you?"

"*No.*" I let out a huffed breath.

"Who?"

I shook my head, my cheeks burning.

Timothy fell silent, and when I looked at his face, he looked prepared to duel the man responsible for my first kiss. The jealousy in his features gave me a burst of confidence. I folded my arms to match his, daring to walk a few paces closer. "Still, I cannot consider myself properly trained for what I might encounter in London."

My heart galloped when his gaze flickered to my mouth. He looked at my eyes again, and I dared another step closer. His arms were still crossed, his posture tense. He released an exasperated breath. "You shouldn't plan to kiss every man you meet in London."

"Suppose I do." I met his eyes. Preying on his jealousy was not the wisest way to navigate the situation, but it seemed to be the only thing that worked. "If I am to catch a husband in so short a time, I will have to use whatever means necessary for the sake of my future."

I sensed the frustration building in him. "Nora—you will not need to do that."

"I may."

"No." He shook his head. "The right man will love you for everything that you are. He will love you for your heart, and he will show you his love without asking for anything in return."

My heart fluttered, my nerves spinning out of control. "Suppose I do find that man. If he is as wonderful as he sounds, surely I will *want* to kiss him. I think it's still wise to practice beforehand."

Timothy's chest rose and fell as he released a hard laugh. "Are you asking me to *practice* with you?"

My face burned, but I nodded. That was exactly what I was doing. "You said if I found the skull I could ask for anything I wanted."

"Not this." His eyes found my lips again, lingering there a little longer than before. "You may ask for something else."

"Why not?" I eyed the the faint crease that marked the center of his full lower lip, and when I looked at his eyes again, the intensity within them caused a wave of longing to spiral through my stomach. This was more than just a trick to convince Timothy that I loved him. I needed that kiss, and I needed it now.

"It isn't proper, and you know it." He spoke with such finality, that I was certain I had failed. Even so, his eyes still burned into me, keeping me captive. He said one thing, but wanted another; I knew it. I felt his desire as surely as my own —in my heart, my bones, under every inch of my skin.

I had only one more idea, but I wasn't certain I was prepared for the consequences.

"Very well," I said in a passive voice, backing up a step. "After you leave today, I shall have to ask Chesley. Or Mr. Ball. I'm sure he would be just as willing."

Timothy's jaw tightened. With an exasperated groan, he took two steps toward me. His hands captured me by the waist, and then his lips captured mine.

I had wanted this to happen—I had expected it, but I was too stunned to move. My mind banished all thought and reason. Timothy was kissing *me*. Despite all my devising, nothing could have prepared me for this. My heart dipped and soared like a bird, but it might as well have been a limp fish for how easily he seized it. His fingers pressed into my lower back, gathering me against him until I couldn't possibly be closer. His mouth moved slowly against mine with a passion that sent chaotic, beautiful shivers down my neck and shoulders.

My hands slid up to his chest, climbing to the sides of his neck. I anchored myself there for a moment. Rising on my toes, I found the courage to kiss him back. I wasn't certain if I did it right or not, but Timothy didn't seem to have any objection. There was no way to undo what was done. I was in his arms, and he was in mine, and I was going to seize every moment of it. If either one of us came to our senses, the kiss would end, and Timothy would leave, and I would have to wait months to see him again. Before I could lose my nerve, I took two handfuls of the fabric of his waistcoat and tugged. With three backward steps, I stumbled against the edge of the table.

"Nora," he sighed, only managing to create an inch between us before kissing me again. His face came into view, but my vision was blurred. I blinked fast, my head spinning as his soft brown eyes gazed into mine, more vulnerable than I had ever seen them. He was shaking his head.

"Please don't stop." My lips tingled and burned, my voice breathless. This was far more dangerous than a dance lesson, but it was also far more enjoyable. I pulled on his waistcoat, my mouth colliding with his again. Kissing Timothy was beautiful and perfect, and a sense of belonging had overtaken all the rest of my sense. It wasn't the North, or Foxwell House, or the moors that felt like home. It had always been him.

He responded as I had hoped. His hands gripped my

waist, hoisting me up onto the table. He dipped his head down to kiss the skin behind my ear, and a shiver followed each touch of his mouth as it moved down my neck and the hollow of my throat. His lips pressed firmer, burning a map across my skin until they found mine again. He pressed his thumb to my chin to deepen the kiss, and I sighed in the back of my throat. It only seemed to encourage him.

He buried his fingers in my hair, undoing my haphazard pins from that morning. If my hair wasn't a bird's nest before, it surely would be one now. But I didn't care. Not one bit. The weight of his chest leaned against mine, and his arms were all that held me upright as he kissed me again and again.

I gave an involuntary gasp when his mouth grazed my ear, feathering one last time to my throat. Each kiss was slow and intentional, worshipful even. I didn't dare breathe for fear of interrupting him. His gaze roamed my face, and his thumb brushed my lower lip with a reverence that shattered me. His chest rose and fell quickly. "That's enough practice for one day," he whispered. There was venom in the word *practice*—a resentment and sadness that broke my heart. How could I tell him that it hadn't been practice at all? He was the only one I wanted to kiss for the rest of my life. I was in love with him.

Regret marked his expression as he backed away. The crease between his brows deepened.

"Timothy—" I lowered myself carefully to my feet, unsure of the steadiness in my legs. What could I say? I couldn't declare my feelings to him first, not when there was still so much time until I was even free to marry him. I searched my muddled mind for something I might say.

He stared at me, and I could only imagine how I appeared with my kiss swollen lips and bird's nest hair. "I'm sorry," he said, shaking his head. "That should not have happened." He swallowed, raking a hand over his hair in frustration.

My heart hammered with disappointment. "I asked for it." My insecurities interfered, and I was desperate to defend myself. "I'm not trying to ensnare you if that's what you are afraid of." A wave of heat flushed my cheeks. "I won't tell Charlie. I won't tell anyone."

I heard footsteps in the corridor beyond the library, and we both turned toward the door. Henrietta's voice sounded in the distance, then a laugh from Anne. With the others awake and out of their bedchambers, we could be discovered at any moment, and I didn't think I could hide the fact that I had just kissed Timothy. I felt the flush of my skin and the rawness around my lips. And my hair was a mess.

"I should go," Timothy said, taking a deep breath. His vulnerable eyes held mine for a few seconds before he retreated to the door. "I will see you soon. Be safe while I am away."

Soon? Did he think several months was soon? I gave a slight nod, confusion spiraling through my head.

He grabbed the door handle, and his eyes drank me in, as if to memorize how I looked just moments after being thoroughly kissed by him. I wanted to do it all over again. His brow furrowed as he turned around, leaving me alone with the books, skull, and his old, hidden diary.

I sat on the edge of the table, listening to the rapid beating of my heart as silence filled the library again. Timothy must have had a sense for my feelings now. How could he not?

I fell backward until I lay on the table like an open ency- clopedia, limbs and hair splayed out without a care. Kissing Timothy had been the most perfect moment of my life, but would it ever happen again? He obviously felt guilty for kissing me, even when I had practically begged him to. I could hardly contain the giddiness that bubbled inside me. I needed to tell Anne. The moment the idea crossed my mind, I thought better of it. That kiss ought to remain a secret for now.

It wasn't just my secret, nor was it Timothy's. It was ours.

CHAPTER 21

D*ear Leonora,*

I hope the weather has taken a turn for the better. Father seems to have given up his search for your kidnapper, but I have urged him not to publicize your disappearance yet. He still claims you are visiting a relative, but Mr. Verwood is losing patience. If I can manage to appease them for a little longer, you shall be free.

It is strange to think that you will come of age in just two short months. As soon as Father learns that I have found you, he is sure to make an attempt to bring you home and convince you to marry Mr. Verwood if his offer still stands. Refusing Mr. Verwood will anger him enough to make you unwelcome at his home. We cannot ask Lady Daventry to remain your companion forever. I hope you understand why your swift marriage is so essential. I feel that I haven't properly explained my role in that. As your brother, I must do what is best for you. I don't want you to be left unhappy, nor to be in a loveless marriage, and that is why I have compiled my list of respectable gentlemen to introduce you to. One of them is sure to make you happy if your heart is open. Rest assured that they are all far better than Mr. Verwood. You may even fall in love with one of them.

I shook my head, creasing the letter with a sigh. All Charlie spoke of in his letters was his list of gentlemen, and from what I had gathered, the rest of this letter would be no different. He did want the best for me. He had once nearly sacrificed his chance to be with Henrietta in order to obtain the money necessary to pay the sum Mr. Verwood was offering. I could not be upset with him—only with Timothy for not adding his own name to the list by now.

There must have been a reason he was waiting. It could have been honor, fear, hesitation, or that Mr. Prout had been wrong to give me hope that Timothy had found an answer. The words of the diary still haunted me, causing fresh worries to sprout up in my mind like the wildflowers on the cliffs outside.

My heart continues to beat for her, yet I know it should not.

Why should I trust the words of a fisherman I hardly knew, when such proof had been written by Timothy in his own diary? What if that kiss hadn't been the beginning, but a farewell? The more time that passed, the more uncertain I became. January felt like an eternity ago, yet I knew it was only April. It wasn't *so* long ago. My mind played tricks on me, preying on my fears. Until Timothy spoke his feelings aloud—until he asked me to marry him—I would still be worried. The diary, his behavior toward me, his kiss—it might have all been evidence of his *love*, but it still wasn't evidence of his intentions.

I set the opened letter from Charlie on the salver in the entryway, making my way upstairs to my bedchamber. I had just taken a walk with Anne in the sunshine and wind, and I needed to change my dress. I was proud of myself for keeping the kiss a secret from Anne, though she *had* seemed suspicious in the days following Timothy's departure.

I chose my favorite pink morning dress with short sleeves, even though the weather was still too chilly to venture outside without a shawl. Spring was in the air, but I was counting down the days until summer, my birthday, and my freedom.

I hummed a tune I had been practicing on the pianoforte as I made my way down the stairs. I stopped halfway, choking on a breath. My feet stopped abruptly, and a bitter taste filled my mouth.

Mr. Ball stood in the entryway. I could only see the top of his head, but he held a letter in one hand. Realization crashed over my shoulders, followed swiftly by anger. "Mr. Ball?" I marched down the stairs, making him jump. He dropped the letter onto the salver on the table. *My* letter from Charlie.

I reached the bottom of the stairs, planting my hands on my hips. My eyes darted to the letter, then to his face. What had he seen? Had I caught him in time? His round hazel eyes were far from innocent.

"What are you doing?" I asked in an accusatory voice. The last time I had seen him, he had been furious at me, and his insults were still fresh in my mind. I couldn't shrink with fear though. I would have to contend with him alone. Anne had taken a longer route home, so she was still outside.

Mr. Ball lifted his chin. "I recently returned to town and I thought I would inquire after the residents of Foxwell House." His nostrils flared, a smirk on his lips. "I didn't see the Duke of Heywood's engagement announced in the papers. At first, I thought he might have married you in secret. But you are here still, months later, and he is not." He coiled one of his fingers around a curl in his hair. "Peculiar, is it not?" His eyes slid to the letter on the salver.

I clenched my jaw as fear crept over my spine. I hid it. I couldn't allow Mr. Ball to see any signs of panic. "Why were you reading my letter?"

"*Your* letter?" His brows shot up, but that smirk remained. "I thought your name was Miss Jane Flowers?" To my dismay, he picked up the letter again, pointing at the introduction. "Dear Leonora."

I lunged forward, snatching it from his grasp.

He let go willingly, laughing in his throat. "Take it. I already read the entire thing."

My heart sank. I looked down at the page again, at the address on the back. The wax had been stamped with our family seal, and the letter was filled with all Charlie's incriminating words about Father and my need to marry.

"If your brother is the Earl of Guildford...then your father would be the Marquess of Swindon. It appears you are hiding from him?"

I didn't answer, keeping my mouth clamped shut. Why had the butler let Mr. Ball inside, and why had he left him unattended with my letter? Hot anger boiled in my veins, making my eyes sting.

"Don't cry, my lady." He took a step toward me, his eyes soft and sympathetic. I wanted to stomp on his toes. "I can help you."

I narrowed my eyes at him. He lifted his hand to my chin, pinching it between two fingers. I could no longer hide my panic, dipping my head out of the way as he leaned down to kiss me.

I jumped back to dodge it, my heart in my throat.

A flash of anger crossed his expression as he straightened his jacket. He recovered his wits, brushing a curl from his forehead. "It would seem you require a husband." He gave a deep laugh. "And since your charade with the duke is over, I would like to offer you my hand. I found you enchanting even before I knew you were the daughter of a marquess, but now I must confess my attraction has grown. I can save you from your father's plans to have you marry this *Mr. Verwood.*" He chuckled. "I should have known the Duke of Heywood wouldn't marry you. It didn't make sense."

Mr. Ball had only gathered pieces from Charlie's letter, but he didn't have the completed puzzle. His eyes gleamed with triumph, as if he had just made me an offer that I couldn't possibly refuse. How had he just so casually picked up my private letter and read it while I was upstairs? He was mad.

Was I just as wicked for reading the contents of Timothy's diary? Was this how Timothy would feel if he discovered that I had? My stomach writhed with dread, and I wiped an angry tear from my cheek. "I do not accept your offer, Mr. Ball." I lifted my chin. "I *am* going to marry the duke."

He laughed, but the sound faded quickly. If he hadn't heard it from Timothy first, he might not have believed me. His eyes darkened. "I don't think that will be possible. Not if your father finds you first."

His threat hung in the air, scratching over my skin with icy fingers. I glared at him. "What do you mean?"

"If you reject my proposal now, I will ensure your father knows that you have run off to the North to evade him." He walked closer, wrapping one hand around my wrist. "I will ensure he finds you." He squeezed tight over my bracelet. I twisted my arm, struggling to free my wrist, but he only gripped me tighter. The letter fluttered to the floor. "Would you like to revise your answer?" He smiled, and it chilled me to my core.

"I would rather have all my meals served in a chamber pot." I wrenched my wrist free, ignoring the throbbing pain that was left behind.

He gritted his teeth, nostrils flaring. My heart raced with terror, but then the front door opened. Anne stepped inside, taking in the scene as she removed her bonnet.

"Mr. Ball." She gave an alarmed curtsy, hurrying to my side.

He brushed his hands over his jacket, each of his rapid exhales shaking with anger. "Very well, my lady." He bowed in my direction, ignoring Anne's entrance. "It would seem I have a letter to write." He started to walk away.

"Mr. Ball, please don't." I searched for any words that might convince him. "You mustn't take such offense to my rejection of your offer. I am in love with someone else. If my heart were free to give away, only then could I accept you. Surely you must understand."

He sneered from the doorway. "I sympathize more with your father. If he is looking for his daughter, I am bound by honor to help and serve him."

I scoffed, glaring at him. "You are doing it to spite me!"

He smiled. "Need I only have one reason?" He marched out the door, and I considered fetching Chesley to chase him down and tie him to a tree on the property. The dread in my stomach was overwhelming. Fresh tears ran down my face when I looked at my wrist and the angry red welt that followed the curve of my bracelet, encircling my entire wrist. I buried my face in my hands, my shoulders shaking.

I felt Anne's hands on my shoulders. "What on earth just happened?"

I uncovered my face and retrieved the letter from the floor. I explained everything, terrified sobs shaking my body. My father could *not* find me. Not after all this time. Not when we were so close to succeeding. When I finished speaking, Anne took the letter and read it herself.

"I sh-should have s-said yes to Mr. Ball." I wiped my nose. "I should have pretended I would marry him just to appease him. But he made me so angry."

"You must write a letter to Charlie at once." Anne's face was flushed with panic as she retrieved writing supplies from the drawing room.

"But he might not receive my letter before my father receives word from Mr. Ball!" I took a steadying breath. "If my father leaves before Charlie does, he will reach me and fetch me home." Terror seized my body, and I nearly lost my composure again.

Anne squared her shoulders. "Then we shall have to make a plan of our own."

"We have to leave," I said, reading her expression.

She nodded. "Tell Charlie what has happened and that we will meet him in London. The letter didn't mention London specifically. Mr. Ball won't be able to tell your father where you are."

"But now my father will know Charlie was involved in my disappearance."

"What is the worst your father can do to him? He can't disinherit him from his birthright. Your father is in debt and has no money to take away from Charlie either. If he chooses to involve the law, then you will testify that you were not kidnapped and that you went of your own free will. The only danger you face at the moment is being found by your father." She gave a distressed sigh. "We were so close. *Blast* Mr. Ball."

"Blast him to Cornwall and back," I muttered, hot anger burning on my neck.

Anne handed me the foolscap and quill, directing me to the nearby table. "Tell Charlie that we will be in London. We can attempt to hide you for another two months until Timothy is able to marry you without your father's consent. It will be difficult, but not impossible. You will have to avoid being named in any gossip papers." Her nose wrinkled with distaste. "Henrietta was not very skilled at evading those."

I gave a swift nod, blinking the moisture from my eyes as I dipped the quill. I hated being so helpless, so desperate for rescue. If Timothy didn't actually plan to marry me as I hoped, then what?

"After the letters are sent, go pack your trunk," Anne said. "If we can reach London near the same time your letter reaches Charlie, then he should be able to make the journey to London and arrive just a few days later than we do, perhaps less. We must leave tomorrow, and we must ensure Mr. Ball is none the wiser." She squeezed my arm. "Everything will be all right."

I gave a tight-lipped nod. "Thank you, Anne. I don't know what I would do without you."

I would cross the country on foot if it meant I could avoid my father. Mr. Verwood's leering eye flashed in my mind, his wet tongue flicking over his mouth. I shuddered, closeting my emotions for long enough to focus on my letters.

Everything will be all right. I had always strived to be optimistic. So why was that suddenly so difficult to believe?

CHAPTER 22

L ondon was much like Bath, but larger, more crowded, and far more intimidating.

I was eternally grateful for Anne's experience living and operating in Town, and the title her late husband had given her. I had spent nearly a year in Anne's company, but she had transformed into someone else entirely the moment we set foot in London. She was Lady Daventry. I was certain she could ask for anything she wanted and never be declined. Her elegance turned heads on every corner. She knew how to navigate the crowded streets just as well as she had navigated the many inns we had stopped at on our journey there.

I was exhausted, but tried not to show it. Anne was just as weary, her eyes drooping only when we were behind the doors of our townhouse. She had secured a lease within our first hours in Town, and it came fully furnished. Charlie had anticipated the expense of living in London for my season, so I hoped he would reimburse her as he planned to reimburse Timothy for all his contributions. Accepting charity in the form of time, money, and other resources was taking a toll on me. I didn't want to continue to burden anyone. Anne's money had only come as a result of her marriage to Lord Daventry. As a single, penniless woman with a father who hated her, I was not capable of providing for myself.

During the journey to London, fear had taken over most of my optimism yet again, so I had been planning what I would do if Father found me.

If he tried to force me to marry Mr. Verwood again, I would first ask Timothy to elope with me to Gretna Green. If that didn't work, I would run away a third time. After my birthday, I would find work as a governess or maid, because if Timothy would not marry me, then I didn't want to marry at all.

Doubts crept into my mind. If Timothy wanted to elope with me, he could have done it by now. He could have done it nearly a year ago. But a year ago, I reminded myself, he didn't know how I felt. He thought I would have laughed at the idea of being his wife. He knew I dreamed of falling in love, and he had hidden me away in that house so I could prepare for London and have the opportunity to find it. Perhaps he had hoped that I would recognize my feelings before then. Or perhaps he loved me enough to want my future happiness regardless of whether or not he could be part of it.

The mystery raged on.

I could hardly wait to see him. If he and Charlie had received my letters when expected, then they would be arriving in London any day now. We expected they would be staying at Timothy's London townhouse in Berkeley square. Each evening, Anne and I walked by, checking to see if it was occupied.

On the fourth day, we saw light in the window.

My nerves sprung to life. I had been anticipating seeing Timothy again for what felt like an eternity. Our parting had been living in my mind without rest for months on end. That kiss hadn't been practice. It had been real for both of us. I knew it. How would I feel to see him now? Had he been just as haunted by our farewell as I had?

Anne and I approached the front steps of the townhouse. My heart pounded fast as she knocked thrice on the door. After a few seconds, Charlie opened it.

I rushed toward him, and he hugged me. "You're safe," he whispered with relief, squeezing tighter. I hadn't noticed Henrietta step up beside him. She hugged Anne, then me, her eyes round with worry.

"We came as quickly as we could," she said. We followed her to the nearby drawing room. The corridors were lit with dim candlelight, and the dark red furniture added to the gloom that had been hovering over me for nearly a fortnight. Seeing Charlie and Henrietta lightened my spirits, but there were still many reasons to fret. I hadn't seen Timothy yet, so I assumed he was still on his way.

Anne sat beside me on the red sofas, and we relayed to Charlie how we had arrived and what we had done in the days since. I gave him more background on my interactions with Mr. Ball, however, I left out the part about Timothy pretending to be engaged to me.

"Mr. Ball threatened me," I said. "When I refused him, he wrote the news to Father as his revenge. I couldn't stop him."

"Are you certain he followed through with his threat?"

"I don't have proof of it, no, but it was too great a risk to stay at Foxwell House."

"Of course." Charlie leaned his elbows on his knees, rubbing his jaw with one hand. He buried his fingers in his dark curls, groaning with frustration. "We nearly made it the entire year. It would have worked. I know Father. The moment he learns that you are in the North, he is going to send servants to retrieve you. It was wise to leave when you did."

"Do you think it's safe here?" I wrung my fingers together.

"For now. London is a vast place." He sighed. "I would assume that Father has received word by now if Mr. Ball sent his letter when he said he would. After Father's servants journey to the North and back without success, another fortnight will have passed. I can't predict what he will do next, but I don't imagine London will be high on his list of places to search. It's too public. If anything, he might try Bath since he knows you have traveled there before." He rested one hand on Henrietta's knee, puffing out an anxious breath. "By my estimation, we have at least a month before he would think to send a search to London. At that point he may even abandon his efforts."

I deflated with relief, grateful to hear such comforting words. I had been on-edge, half-expecting my father to be knocking on the door at any moment.

"But in one month, you won't yet be of age," Charlie said. "You will be short only a few weeks."

"Drat it all," Henrietta muttered beside him, pursing her lips. "But if your Father *does* find Leonora before her birthday, she could still refuse to go with him. If she has nothing to lose, she cannot be coerced into marrying Mr. Verwood."

Charlie shook his head, pinching the bridge of his nose. "She does have something to lose. He will never allow her in his home again now that he knows she defied him in such a manner. As I haven't yet inherited the estate, and our father still lives there, I cannot give her a place to live. Only a husband could. She will be left to rely on Timothy's charity until we find her someone to marry. Timothy has offered to fund her season, but after that, we cannot ask for more of his help. The current issue has less to do with whether she is twenty-one or not. Father will know the truth, he will be angry, and if he knows he cannot control her decisions for very much longer, she will surely be cut off and disowned." He met my gaze, as if just remembering I was there. "The most urgent matter is still finding you a husband. A month is plenty of time to begin a courtship. I fell in love with Henrietta within such a short amount of time. You very well might find success with one of the men on my list. I can arrange introductions to all of them this week."

I dragged my fingers down the sides of my face, panic tightening every muscle in my body. Certain measures were taken only in the most desperate times, and this felt like one of them. I sat forward on the sofa. "Perhaps I should elope to Gretna Green. I have heard of young lovers escaping in the night and marrying underage."

Charlie's brows shot up, a laugh escaping him. "Well, that would certainly resolve the issue." He sat back, raking a hand through his curls with a sigh. He seemed prepared to be entertained. "Did you have a gentleman in mind who might be so willing? Besides Mr. Ball?"

I grimaced. Nothing sounded worse. I exchanged a glance with Anne. For a fleeting moment, I considered asking her if *she* had anyone in mind so I could evade answering for myself. Anne's eyes were round, and she gave a discreet nod, urging me to continue.

My throat was dry, and my next swallow was prolonged. "Timothy."

A smile broke through Charlie's anxious expression, and he laughed again. "Leonora."

"What?" I snapped.

He exhaled through his nose, his laughter subsiding. He seemed to notice my vexation. His voice softened. "You know I could never ask so much of Timothy. He is the sort of friend who would do anything to help us, and do anything I asked of him. He has already provided you with a home for a year, and offered to fund your season. That is a debt I could never repay him."

I held my tongue against what I truly wanted to say. How could I tell them about the diary when I hadn't even told Timothy? I couldn't spill all his secrets to Charlie and Henrietta. Until I heard Timothy say aloud that he loved me, I ought to pretend it wasn't true. "Did he tell you about his mother's wish for him to marry?"

Charlie hesitated. "Yes, but I will not attempt to be his matchmaker."

I raised one eyebrow. "Yet you will happily be mine."

"You are my sister."

"He is your friend."

Charlie sighed. "It isn't so simple."

"If he requires a wife soon, and I require a husband, why should he not choose me? When he arrives in London, could you not offer the idea as a casual…suggestion? Please?" My voice was weak. I was moments away from spilling everything about the diary.

Charlie frowned, shaking his head. "Timothy isn't coming to London."

CHAPTER 23

My heart dropped, the impact so intense I pressed a hand to my stomach. "What?"

Charlie's eyes flickered with concern. "I asked him to stay in Somerset to keep watch over Father. If he sees any action being taken to find you, he will try to discover the details. In the meantime, I will be the one to assist you in finding a husband here."

I felt the blood draining from my face. "But—Timothy has always planned to come with me."

Charlie leaned forward with a frown. "I'm sorry…I didn't know it would disappoint you so greatly."

"No—I," I gathered my wits about me, a heavy stone of dread settling in my stomach. "I'm surprised, that's all."

"Even if Timothy isn't here, you won't be alone," Charlie emphasized. "Henrietta and I will be here, as will Anne. They will both act as your chaperones at balls and parties. I will continue my efforts to introduce you to every respectable man I know in Town."

Henrietta's eyes flashed with sadness, and she squeezed Charlie's hand to stop him. "Leonora—do you *want* to marry Timothy? I mean…do you…have feelings for him?"

Charlie's sharp blue eyes returned to my face. Anne was looking at me. Henrietta was looking at me.

Everyone was looking at me.

The silence of the room threatened to swallow me whole. My face burned hot. If Timothy knew of Charlie's plans to find me a husband, yet had chosen not to come to London then…

He must not have wanted me after all.

If he did, he would have said something. He would have tried to claim me by now. Instead, he had agreed to stay back in Somerset while Charlie introduced me to his list of gentlemen. My heart cracked open slowly, emotions spilling out and forming a lump in my throat.

"No." I laughed, swallowing hard. "I don't. Eloping with him was a silly idea." The lie stung, flooding my mouth with bitterness. Tears hovered behind my eyes. I sensed Anne's distress beside me. Had all of my hope been for nothing? I had allowed myself to dream and plan for the day I would arrive in London and Timothy would finally confess his feelings for me—rescue me from the doom of choosing a man I didn't love. One month was too short a time to fall in love with someone else. It had taken years to recognize that I was in love with Timothy, and that love was steadfast. It was an ever-fixed mark now, one that would leave behind an ugly scar.

Charlie seemed relieved at my answer. A pang of grief spread through my chest, and I nearly excused myself from the room. But if I did, Charlie would know I had lied.

Insecurity stitched my mouth closed. If it was true that

Timothy didn't want me, then Charlie could never, ever know what I wanted. It was too vulnerable. It was too painful to see the amusement on my brother's face at the prospect of Timothy choosing a wife like me. I was not the obvious choice. I was not regal and intimidating like him. My manners were not in line with a duchess. I couldn't blame Charlie for laughing. Nor could I blame Mr. Ball for laughing as he had. It wasn't plausible for me to be Timothy's wife, and I had been a fool to think otherwise.

Charlie gave me a reassuring smile. "I will set to work with my introductions at Hyde Park tomorrow. I am confident that you are capable of capturing a man's heart within a month."

But none of of them were capable of capturing mine.

I gave a bleak nod, holding my emotions together by a string.

Henrietta still looked concerned, dark brows pinched. Women were generally more observant of emotions than men. Did she not believe me? Thankfully, she changed the subject. "We must take care not to observe any croquet matches while we're there," she said with a grimace. "There are many watchful eyes at Hyde Park, and you cannot risk being written into Lady Teignmouth's gossip column."

Charlie raised an eyebrow at her. "Leonora doesn't share your habit of observing men's haunches."

Henrietta narrowed her eyes, swatting at his arm. A smile twisted her lips. "Charlie is still jealous, even after a year."

"So you don't deny that you were ogling him?"

"His breeches were torn and I was trying to be polite by informing him!" She groaned, stopping her words. "I will not defend myself again."

Anne laughed, but I sensed her worried gaze on the side

of my face. I tried to join in the merriment, but my chest felt hollow. There was nothing inside—no hope, no laughter, and no heart.

I sat rigid, faking a smile. That was now the most important skill I would need to practice.

My gowns were not nearly as intricate as the gowns of many of the other young ladies in Town. Despite being the daughter of a peer, we avoided attending any of the Queen's drawing rooms. A formal presentation would draw far too much attention. Under normal circumstances, attention was desired by every young lady in London. But the more people who knew *I* was in London, the greater risk I faced. So instead, we relied on Charlie's connections and the gentlemen on his list.

Lord Ramsdell, Mr. Walker, Mr. Calcot, and Sir Daniel were first in line. I had no desire to know any of them, but I also understood that I couldn't afford to disregard them. I had been relying on words that had been written in a diary years ago. I had clung to them, and I had concocted a fantasy with those words. I had made assumptions, and my hope had soared to a height that made the fall all the more painful. My imagination had run away with me, but this time it hadn't been harmless.

I awoke from my cruel daydream to a walk through Hyde Park with a man whose jacket was covered in cat fur.

"Fine weather, is it not?" Mr. Walker asked. He sniffed, wiping his nose with the back of his sleeve. The action left a few cat hairs dangling from his nostrils. He sneezed. "My apologies. The flowers tend to give me an allergic reaction."

"How unfortunate." I studied the blossoms on a tree as we passed. "They are so beautiful."

"Indeed." The word was rather sultry, and when I looked up, he was staring at my face. Those cat hairs on his nose were staring at me too.

I gulped. Charlie, Henrietta, and Anne walked several paces ahead. If anyone was bound to be eavesdropping, it was Anne. She had been just as confused as I was about Timothy not coming to London, and she had felt guilty for contributing to my high hopes. She wanted to help me, but in truth, I was beyond help.

"What is your favorite flower, my lady?" Mr. Walker asked.

"A rose."

He frowned at the grass ahead of us. "That is very unoriginal. Why such a boring choice?"

I blinked, shocked at his forthrightness. "Well…a rose is the most romantic flower."

His thin lips pursed into a heart shape. "You seem the sort to favor daisies or lilies. Perhaps you should change your preference to better suit your…" he paused, fluttering his hands around me, "…air."

Vexation prickled over my skin. "I would rather not, thank you."

He seemed to be searching for another question, taking several seconds to find one. I was content to walk in silence. The sooner the outing was over, the better. "Are you fond of cats?" he asked finally.

"No, not particularly."

"Why not?"

"They are not fond of me, so why should I love something that will not love me in return?" My voice was bitter. I laughed to hide it. "I was attacked by one."

He scoffed. "Well, you must have done something to deserve it." His tightly curled hair, piled high atop his head, rustled with the breeze.

Why must all the most disagreeable men have curly hair? Mr. Ball was one of them.

Charlie was the other.

At the moment, I was not particularly fond of him either. I scowled at his back as he walked, blissfully in love with his wife, taking in the scenery. What had made him think I would be attracted to Mr. Walker? Perhaps attraction was out of the question just as love was. Mr. Walker was a reasonable choice because he had a moderate income, a quaint property in the country, and a respectable family. But being more advanced in years, with a propensity for carrying cat fur everywhere he went, he was rather desperate for a wife. It occurred to me that *all* the men on Charlie's list were likely in a similar state of desperation. Timothy was only a few years my senior, but Mr. Walker was at least a decade and a half.

Stop. I demanded my thoughts to change course. I was not allowed to think about Timothy. Despite his mother's wishes that he marry, he would never actually reach a desperate state. Being a wealthy, handsome, young, and kind duke, he had his pick of any woman in the country.

If it wasn't me, then who would it be?

The thought stabbed a dagger through my heart. Mr. Ball's words about my inferiority flitted through my mind. Where had my newfound confidence gone? Had it really been so tied to Timothy and whether or not he wanted me? Mr. Ball was not worth a single one of my thoughts. In fact, if I ever saw him again, I would throw a facer at him. Lady Teignmouth could write all about it in her gossip paper, and I wouldn't even care.

I glared down at the grass.

"Are you otherwise engaged the afternoon of Wednesday next?" Mr. Walker asked. "I should like to take you out for a ride on my phaeton." He beamed with pride. "I might even introduce you to Archibald."

"Archibald?"

"My cat. He enjoys rides as well."

I laughed, an anxious weight pressing down on my shoulders. "Oh, I see." I wanted to bite my fingernail, but I was wearing gloves. Timothy's gloves.

Charlie glanced back at me with an encouraging nod.

I took a shaky breath. It wouldn't be wise to throw away my prospects so soon. I hadn't yet properly investigated the specifics of becoming a governess. "I am not otherwise engaged."

"Capital!" Mr. Walker grinned.

If he began pursuing me, Charlie would encourage it. I couldn't deny that he *was* better than Mr. Verwood, although that wasn't difficult to accomplish. His small estate sounded lovely. However, I had written my requirements for a husband in my diary long before I had ever had hope for Timothy. It was required that my husband of choice protect me and not repulse me, but Mr. Walker was repulsing me more by the moment.

He sniffed, and the cat hairs disappeared somewhere inside his nostril. "Is something amiss?" He stared at me through cautious eyes. Lost in thought as I was, I hadn't noticed my strides growing faster.

"Not at all." I flashed a smile that felt as fake as Chesley's wig. A few more stitches ripped in my heart as a wave of despair struck my chest. *Everything* was amiss, and I had no idea how to fix it.

CHAPTER 24

Tucked against the wall at Almack's, my mind erased every dance lesson I had received from Anne and Timothy. I could hardly breathe in the crowded, humid air.

It smelled of perfume and sweating people.

The candlelight encompassed the vast assembly room, glittering on the gowns of all the beautiful young ladies who hoped to make an impression. Many of them were several years younger than me, yet they danced with far more grace.

Julia had arranged my hair with a string of pearls, pinning back my wild curls enough to add elegance to my presentation. I had insisted on not having new gowns made, especially not since it was Timothy who was lending the money to Charlie. Instead, Anne had given me one of her ballgowns to wear, and Julia had stitched a few alterations. It was white with blue embroidery that matched my eyes. I looked like I might have belonged in a London ballroom—like I wasn't an imposter. When I had looked in the mirror, I wanted to feel beautiful, but I felt the same emptiness that had been persisting for days. None of Julia's work could ever make me feel more beautiful than I had when Timothy had kissed me and undid my hair to resemble a bird's nest.

Just as the thought crossed my mind, my gaze caught on a familiar face across the room. Two faces, actually.

Miss Grant and her mother, Lady Shaftesbury.

It had been nearly a year since I had encountered them at the Lion's Crown Inn. In truth, it came as a surprise that Miss Grant hadn't married in the time since. She had a sizeable dowry, and she was decidedly pretty. Her dark hair was like silk, shining in the candlelight. The curls around her forehead were perfectly formed, unlike mine, which had a mind of their own.

Anne stood beside me, wearing a peach gown and surveying the crowd. "Do you remember your dances?"

"No."

The alarm on her face made me laugh, which was a balm to my heart. It had been too long since I had laughed.

"Mr. Walker is here," she said. "He is sure to claim at least one."

I shrugged, leaning toward her with a whisper. "Perhaps I should tell him I am not fond of dancing."

"I didn't spend hours teaching you for nothing, and neither did—" her voice cut off. She knew how sensitive the subject was. Her features shifted to a look of compassion. "Only say yes if you are confident, of course. It would be better to refuse him than to embarrass yourself publicly."

My forgetfulness wasn't entirely true. As I watched several couples begin a dance at the center of the room, I recognized most of the steps. But dancing in this room with so many watchful eyes would be far different than dancing in the drawing room or library at Foxwell House. And far less romantic.

"Drat it all," I muttered as I looked up and saw Charlie on his way toward me with Henrietta and three unfamiliar gentlemen in tow. I glanced to the right, then the left. There was a particularly tall gentleman nearby. The temptation to scurry behind him to hide flitted through my head.

It was too late. It was only a matter of seconds before Charlie reached me, introducing each of the gentlemen in turn. There was a Lord Ramswell, Mr. Calcot, and Sir Daniel. Of the three of them, Sir Daniel was the most handsome, with a kind smile that put me at ease.

"A pleasure to meet you, my lady," Sir Daniel said. His black hair was combed neatly, and to my relief, it didn't have the curls I had developed a negative association with. That was a very good sign.

I curtsied, offering a smile in return.

"Your brother has informed me that this is your first ball," he said. "It is my opinion that a lady should not be left alone for a single dance under such circumstances." He gave a charming smile. "May I have the honor of the next dance?"

My nerves sprung to life, but I nodded, finally finding my voice. "You may."

His smile was contagious, and the tightness in my shoulders relaxed a little.

Perhaps I had judged Charlie's list of gentlemen too soon. I would not object to being Sir Daniel's friend. Dread sank through my stomach. I had grown accustomed to the idea that Charlie's list would only contain unattractive, strange men, and that my decision not to marry would be entirely valid. But if one of them was kind and handsome, what excuse did I have? I should have found Sir Daniel's sincere attention comforting, but instead it awoke a new sense of panic. The door to my heart was shut tighter than a hatch under an old library desk. Except not even a poker could pry it open.

Lord Ramswell was polite enough, but he didn't ask for any of my dances. His critical eye swept over me, and he seemed to make an assessment of my worthiness of his attention within five seconds. I could have easily guessed what his unspoken conclusion was. Mr. Calcot asked for my second dance before dispersing with the other two gentlemen.

"Well done, Leonora," Charlie whispered. "I thought I saw Lord Fulshaw walk through the door a few minutes ago. I'm going to see if I can introduce you to him as well."

I felt no sense of victory, giving a bleak nod. As Charlie walked away, Henrietta squeezed my arm. "Sir Daniel was agreeable. Handsome too." Her encouraging voice raised my spirits a little.

"Yes." I gave a bright smile, knowing full well it was the only way to appease her. She had noticed my dreary mood, and it had obviously concerned her. The people in my life were accustomed to me smiling all of the time, pretending I wasn't hurting inside. I had done so my entire life. Even while wishing my days away that my father would forgive and love me, or that my mother would live again, or that I was not a burden, I had smiled.

I smiled now, even though I was wasting my first ball still wishing for something I couldn't have.

Henrietta followed Charlie in his pursuit of Lord Fulshaw, and I huddled against the wall yet again. My heart sank as I caught sight of Mr. Walker, fluffy curls moving through the crowd toward me at an alarming speed.

That tall gentleman was still there near the same wall, his back turned to me. It was not too late to hide behind him. I took a closer look at his broad shoulders and golden brown hair. Then he started to turn around.

The music from the loud stringed instruments faded in my ears.

It was Timothy.

I struggled to breathe, to speak, to think. How long had he been standing there? I blinked hard, convinced my mind was fooling me, but when my eyes opened again, he was still there. Knee breeches, blue waistcoat, black jacket, pure white cravat, eyes locked on mine. My heart beat a wild rhythm in my chest.

Anne noticed him too, clenching my arm so tightly it hurt. I was grateful. It made me aware that I wasn't dreaming. Timothy was there, and he was walking toward me.

I didn't know whether to be angry or happy, the conflict bringing a wave of heat to my skin. There was a weight on my chest, compressing my lungs as he drew closer. Reservation and fear battled for control inside me. Hope had begun its own escape strategy, rattling the bars of its cage.

"What are you doing here?" I choked under my breath.

Timothy had never looked more handsome. I searched every inch of his face, and it occurred to me that the last time we had seen one another, I had practically begged him for a kissing lesson. My ears tingled with heat.

"I couldn't very well miss your first ball." His soft gaze was making rapid work of unraveling my grudges against him.

"Charlie said you weren't coming to London at all." I heard the broken shards in my voice. "He said he asked you to stay in Somerset near my father."

"He did ask me to do that." His eyes roamed my face for a long moment, his lips slowly forming a smile. "But I'm a duke. I can do what I want."

My bewilderment persisted, and he persisted in his intense study of my face. It had been months since we had seen one another, and the memory of our last parting was forcing its way to the front of my mind. His arms around me, his lips on mine. My stomach swarmed with butterflies at the depth of his gaze. Was he thinking of it too? Was it with longing or regret? I had spent days undoing my assumptions about his feelings, and now I hardly knew what to believe.

I edged toward the ballroom doors, motioning for Timothy to follow me. I had far too many questions that couldn't be answered in such a crowded place. I weaved through the crowd until I was in the corridor, and I continued walking until I was outside the facade of Almack's. The cool outside air made me aware of how hot my skin had become. I tugged off my gloves, fanning my face with one hand as Timothy caught up to me. For a moment, all I could do was stare at him. He was here. He was real. I wanted to reach out and touch him, but my arms went rigid at my sides.

"Where is my father?" I asked. "Has he tried to make a journey to the North?"

Timothy's gaze was relentless, but I could hardly look at his face. The shock of his late arrival still vibrated through me, making my legs shake.

"I stayed long enough to see that he is still at his estate. Although, he did appear to send servants on the journey."

I tried to imagine Timothy spying on my father. Would it have been the first time? According to his diary, he had overheard a conversation between my father and his father several years before. "Does Charlie know you've come to London?" I glanced behind me, half-expecting Charlie to have found me already. He had been far too attentive of late.

"Not yet. I arrived an hour ago to find my townhouse

empty. I guessed that if Charlie had succeeded in securing your entry, you would be at Almack's." He gave a soft smile. "Has your first dance been claimed?"

I nodded. A burst of satisfaction followed the motion. "Yes."

"And the second?"

I brushed a curl from my forehead. "Yes."

He froze. His brow creased as he stepped forward, snatching up the hand I had just lifted. He turned over my wrist.

I followed his gaze to the angry red lines that had been left behind by my bracelet. The welt looked even worse in the moonlight, and a green bruise had started to form around it.

"Who did this to you?" Timothy's eyes flashed.

I swallowed hard. "It doesn't hurt anymore. I nearly forgot it was there."

"Who did this?" he repeated. His voice was dark, his eyes blazing.

I looked down at the cobblestones. "Mr. Ball."

He cursed under his breath, but kept my wrist in his hand, pulling it closer to his chest. "When you refused his proposal?"

I gave a grim nod. I dared a look at his face. He had nothing short of murder on his mind, that much was certain. His jaw tightened, every feature of his face rigid, wired tight with anger. The contrasting softness with which he cradled my hand didn't match. "I'm sorry." His voice was hoarse. "I shouldn't have assumed he would stop calling on you."

"I didn't expect him to call again either. I certainly didn't think he would have the audacity to read my letter from Charlie."

Timothy's anger returned. He shook his head, frustration

boiling over. "I can think of nothing more odious, yet it represents his character perfectly. The immaturity alone is bewildering. Not to mention the disrespect for your privacy. Did he really think that he could proceed to win your hand in marriage after that?" He cursed again.

A pang of guilt spiraled through my chest. Shame burned on my cheeks. What would Timothy think of me if he knew that I had read his diary? I didn't dare wonder.

I started to pull my hand away, but Timothy didn't let go. The rigid lines of his face softened, and he traced his thumb across the bruise. "I will never allow him to hurt you again."

My skin reacted to his soft touch, shivers cascading up and down my arm. I watched him, desperately wishing I could read his mind. All at once, he lowered my hand and his eyes found mine again. He still looked angry—not at me, but at himself. Frustrated, just like when he had kissed me. It didn't matter what the torrent in his gaze meant—it still set my heart pounding.

"I-I should return for my dance," I said in a nervous voice.

Timothy nodded. "I nearly forgot we were in London now. Being alone, even you and I, without your chaperone should be avoided at all times."

I frowned as he led the way back to the ballroom. *'Even you and I?'* Vexation rose up in my chest. Did he not remember that he had kissed me—quite fervently—the last time we had parted? Anger coiled inside me like a snake ready to strike.

Shortly after we walked inside, Sir Daniel approached with a smile, a look of surprise crossing his features when he noticed Timothy.

"Your grace, what an honor to see you in Town."

Timothy greeted him with a smile. "Sir Daniel."

"You must forgive me for interrupting your conversation with Lady Leonora." He turned his attention to me, motioning toward the dance floor. "Shall we?"

I nodded and followed him, taking a deep breath to steady my nerves. It was a cotillion. All the steps I had practiced raced through my mind, flooding back to me at the opportune moment. Thank the heavens. I drew a nervous breath, trying to forget about all the eyes that could potentially witness my mistakes.

Just before the music began, I glanced back at Timothy. His arms were crossed, intent gaze focused on me. Had he wanted to claim my first dance? I hoped so. It would be beneficial for him to see that I was not gathering dust on a shelf, available if he ever wanted my time or attention. The residual feelings of abandonment from his late arrival in London might have been making me a little more bitter.

I smiled, focusing my attention on my partner.

The dance began, and I put into practice all that I had been taught over the past year. At first, my focus was on my feet, but then I remembered Timothy's advice about eye contact. I met Sir Daniel's gaze, sharing a smile with him as the steps became more lively. He gave me a nod of encouragement. My curls bounced, the pins loosening a little in my hair. By the time the dance ended, my head was light with exhilaration.

I met Timothy and Anne, putting a hand to my hair with a grin. "I didn't step on his toes!"

Timothy watched me, a wide smile on his face. I caught my breath, searching his face for approval. "Did I miss any steps? I don't think I did."

"You were perfect." The compliment brought a flush to my cheeks.

"Why did you not dance?" I asked, placing one hand on my hip. "I should like to make an assessment of your dancing skills as well."

His eyes glinted with amusement. "Have you not already?"

Drat, now I was thinking of the waltz again, and the various postures of the pirouettes and how progressively intimate they had become. His dark eyes set me ablaze, and it was all I wanted to tug him away to the nearby gardens and be reminded how it felt to kiss him. I shook myself, willing my mind not to wander back to its favorite destination.

"I think I require further proof," I teased. "Please don't tell me you usually lurk in the dark corners of the ballroom without dancing." I raised an eyebrow. It felt good to tease him. I had been worried I would never be able to do so again, not after we had kissed. The dance had given me courage and energy, lightening my spirits.

"I usually do."

"Timothy." I groaned. "Why would you be so boorish?"

His smile grew. It seemed to be his favorite thing when I called him that. "The only lady I wanted to dance with has always been absent at balls I've attended."

My heart fluttered, but I shushed it. "Oh?" My voice cracked. I would die or faint if he continued looking at me in such a manner. His searching eyes seemed to reach deeper than my skin, and I had to look at his cravat instead.

I sensed a gentleman step up beside me, and I jumped when I realized it was Mr. Walker, and not Mr. Calcot as I had expected. I detected a few cat hairs, even on his finest black jacket. "Good evening, my lady."

"Good evening, Mr. Walker." I clasped my fingers together. Ever since agreeing to the ride in his phaeton, I had been regretting it. I still had a few days to think of some excuse. I could claim an allergy to cats just as easily as he had claimed an allergy to flowers.

"I came to ask the privilege of your next dance." He straightened his sleeves, eyes flickering in Timothy's direction. His throat bobbed with a swallow as he focused on me once again.

My next dance had been claimed by Mr. Calcot, and I had never been more relieved. "I'm afraid not. My next dance has been spoken for."

He didn't falter. "May I have the next after that?"

"Oh—er—yes."

"Capital!" He gave a deep bow, sucking in a breath through his teeth as his eyes grazed over my figure. "I believe it's a waltz."

An involuntary shudder assaulted my shoulder blades. "Wonderful," I choked.

He walked away with a mood that was far too cheerful, and I turned toward Timothy again. His eyes followed Mr. Walker as he retreated, a crease between his brows.

"Who was that?"

"Mr. Walker. He has an estate in Kent." If I could instill a sense of urgency in Timothy, my misery might be put to an end. Just minutes before, my hope had been shattered, but now it crept back in. "He is desperate to find a wife, and he has already made plans to take me on a ride in his phaeton. Charlie thinks he might be a good match for me."

I watched for Timothy's reaction. He scowled, but that was not uncommon. He let out a hard breath. "I disagree."

"You've been in his company for a total of ten seconds," I said with a questioning smile.

He didn't seem to find humor in the situation. His jaw tightened. "Charlie has lost sight of what he wanted for you." He shook his head. "He shouldn't be throwing you into situations that could result in a future just like the one you are avoiding with Mr. Verwood."

"Perhaps you should speak with him, then."

Timothy's gaze found mine, and I held it for several seconds. My words held various meanings, but I hoped he detected the one I wanted him to.

Before Timothy could say another word, Mr. Calcot arrived to take me away for the second dance.

When the first steps began, I noticed that Charlie had found Timothy. He looked surprised. I watched their interaction, missing a few steps throughout the dance as I tried to read their lips.

When the dance ended, Charlie met me halfway back to the wall. "Leave it to Timothy to make a dramatic entrance." He smiled, and I was relieved that he didn't seem upset with the change in his plan. "His being here will only help your chances of securing a match. If you are seen associating with him, it will improve how other gentlemen perceive your connections."

I hardly heard him. I wanted to steal a few more moments of conversation with Timothy before Mr. Walker claimed my next dance, but Charlie pulled me in the opposite direction. "I spoke with Lord Fulshaw and he would like to make your acquaintance." He gave a cajoling smile. "Come with me."

The atmosphere was overwhelming as we crossed the ballroom, my senses struggling to take in all the faces and scents and glittering jewelry. Loud laughter and whispers behind fans followed us as we weaved through the crowd. Lord Fulshaw was tall, with pale blond hair and a long nose. Our introduction passed in a blur, and then Mr. Walker took me away for the waltz.

Which posture would he choose? Timothy had taught me what each one could mean about a gentleman's intentions. I glanced around the room, my head spinning. Anne had found a partner with Mr. Calcot. And then I noticed Timothy with his own partner.

Miss Grant.

My stomach dropped. I snapped my gaze back to Mr. Walker. *Focus, Nora.* But my heart was suddenly in my throat. Timothy had asked for my dance, but it had been claimed, I reassured myself. It was perfectly reasonable for him to seek another partner, even if it was for the waltz. The most romantic of all dances. The insecurities and doubts in my head danced with more vigor and precision than I ever had.

Lady Shaftesbury stood nearby, a grin on her face that could easily be called wicked. For all I knew, ensnaring Timothy for her daughter could have been her new objective for the entire season. My heart sank further as I noticed how regal Miss Grant looked beside Timothy. She was tall, her satin blue gown shimmering in the candlelight. Her long neck and perfect curls gave her an elegance that could only be matched by Anne. She had been raised to ensnare a duke.

I turned my attention back to my own partner as we held hands. The first measure played out, and then Mr. Walker took me in the posture I had least hoped for. The closest one. The most romantic. I tried to keep my body from touching him as we turned, but in order to maintain eye contact, my head was forced closer to his shoulder. His arm wrapped me up tight. I saw the cat fur on his jacket close to my face, and I held my breath to avoid inhaling any bits and pieces of Archibald.

I broke eye contact only once.

I had to know which posture Timothy had chosen with Miss Grant.

My heart raced as I spotted him over Mr. Walker's shoulder. He held Miss Grant in the most traditional posture, keeping her at a distance. Relief rained down on me.

Not only that, but he had broken eye contact as well.

I looked away fast, forcing myself to gaze back into the vibrant blue irises of Mr. Walker. His pupils were dilated, nearly engulfing the blue with black. "You are an excellent dancer, my lady."

"And you are an excellent liar, sir."

He laughed, pulling me impossibly closer. My spine stiffened, and I stepped on his foot. He grunted in pain, a bead of perspiration escaping his fluffy curls and trickling down his brow.

"I'm sorry! Forgive me." My frantic whisper was nearly lost in the final notes of the waltz, and I practically leaped away from his embrace.

He smiled, swiping away his perspiration with one finger. "I shall forgive you if you grant me your next dance."

Two dances in one evening with the same gentleman? I wrung my fingers together. I had heard that two indicated an attachment, and to dance three was practically announcing your engagement. Mr. Walker was not wasting any time, and according to Charlie, I didn't have time to waste either.

I tightened my jaw, glancing in Timothy's direction. He had just parted ways with Miss Grant. She rushed back to her mother's side, beaming with pride. My heart spiraled down, nearly becoming buried once again. "Of course," I said, lowering into a curtsy before leaving Mr. Walker's side.

Henrietta and Charlie had also danced the waltz, and they met Anne, Timothy, and me at the edge of the ballroom. Charlie nudged Timothy with his elbow. "You rarely dance. What came over you?" His eyes gleamed with mischief.

"Miss Grant was without a partner, and her mother insisted."

Charlie laughed. "How noble of you."

Timothy didn't smile, nor did he defend himself with any further comment. Was he considering her? She was the sort of woman I would have always expected to be a match for Timothy. Even now that he was here, I couldn't repeat the mistake of convincing myself that he was here to propose to me. He could have been here to help find me a different husband, and to find a different wife of his own. I had learned that it was foolish to assume anything about Timothy's intentions.

If I had never read the diary, I never would have assumed anything. It would have been much easier that way. I cursed myself for ever opening those pages. What a mess they had made of my heart..

Jealousy seemed to work on Timothy. The men on Charlie's list were helping make that tactic possible. My heart surged with determination. Now that Timothy was here, I had no choice but to do all I could to get him to propose. Suggesting the idea to Charlie hadn't worked, and suggesting it to Timothy was out of the question, at least for now. Despite the urgency I felt, I still had time. My straits weren't so dire yet.

Charlie turned to me. "Did Mr. Walker just ask for a

second dance?" His eyes were wide with congratulations, as if that were something to be celebrated.

I cringed inwardly, but nodded with a smile.

Charlie rubbed his hands together with a thoughtful nod. "And he's not the only one with obvious interest in you. I would predict that Sir Daniel and Mr. Calcot will come calling this week as well. You are doing so well, Leonora. Continue with your charming smiles as you have been, and you will have at least one proposal within a fortnight."

"Excellent," I muttered.

"Mr. Walker is the most proactive though," Charlie added. "This is only your second time meeting, yet he is making no secret of his interest in you. His intentions are clear."

"They are indeed." I dared to look at Timothy before turning my attention to my brother again. "And I find it quite refreshing."

Like an angel from heaven, Sir Daniel swooped down, landing himself directly between Timothy and me. He too claimed a second dance, and I thought I caught a muscle twitch in Timothy's jaw.

CHAPTER 25

I rushed through the front door of the townhouse, slamming it behind me. I tugged my bonnet strings, unveiling my wind tousled curls. There had been a strong breeze that day, and I had just endured an hour on Mr. Walker's phaeton with Archibald. The cat had been much more tolerable than its owner, even if it had climbed onto my lap for most of the ride, depositing half its coat onto my dress. I brushed aggressively at my skirts. The fur stuck to my gloves instead.

Anne had been my chaperone, but we hadn't had the opportunity to discuss the outing. "How was it?" Anne's lip curled with distaste.

"As dreadful as I expected." I gave up my futile attempt at cleaning my skirts with a huffed breath. "He asked me if I would like to join him for a walk next Monday."

"I heard that." She shook her head with a frustrated sigh. "Why won't the duke propose? I don't understand."

"He doesn't want to." I stared at the floor, my mouth

clamped shut. "That can be the only reason." I tugged my gloves off and set them on the nearby table, placing my bonnet beside them. "Please put the subject to rest as I have." I swallowed hard. It was easier to pretend I didn't want Timothy than to show how disappointed and confused I was. My efforts to make him jealous might have worked that night at Almack's, but the jealousy hadn't forced him into action of any kind.

"I will not." Anne raised an eyebrow. "I still believe he is waiting for the right moment."

"And when will that be? After I am already engaged to Mr. Walker or Sir Daniel? Perhaps when I am walking down the aisle at a church?"

She pressed her lips together, apparently at a loss for words. "You will see him again at Sir Daniel's soiree tonight." Her eyes shone with mischief. "When all the gentlemen there fight for your attention, perhaps the duke will finally join them."

I scoffed. "No one will be fighting for my attention."

"Sir Daniel and Mr. Walker will at least."

I planned to attend, but my stomach had been sinking all day. Sir Daniel was someone I couldn't so easily excuse. How could I deflect him that night without Charlie noticing? It was foolish. Why should I hold out hope and wait for Timothy if he had given me no reason to?

My only reason was gathering dust in a hatch under a desk in Northumberland.

Charlie and Henrietta took their own carriage to the soiree, so Timothy came to fetch Anne and me. I opened the front door of the house, letting in the cool night air. I took a deep gulp of it. My nerves couldn't be subdued.

Timothy stood outside the carriage. I pulled my shoulders back, willing my confidence to remain beyond the threshold. I felt his gaze on my skin as I approached. Anne led the way, and Timothy helped her into the carriage.

When it was my turn, I looked up at his face. His jaw was freshly shaved, his hair combed neatly. His eyes took me in, and he seemed to forget to offer me his hand.

"She looks beautiful, does she not?" Anne said from inside. I heard the smile in her voice.

So she wasn't putting the subject to rest after all.

Timothy's gaze could have set a fire to my new blue gown. "She does."

My ears tingled with heat.

He helped me into the carriage and sat across from me. His knees brushed mine the entire way to Sir Daniel's townhouse.

When Anne and I walked inside the drawing room, I caught sight of Charlie and Henrietta. Sir Daniel was there, as well as Lord Fulshaw. There were several other men and women I had never seen before, and a few of them glanced our way when we walked through the doors. Lady Shaftesbury and Miss Grant stood in the center of the room.

Before we had made it ten paces in, Miss Grant and her mother were already on their way to Timothy.

"Devil take it," he muttered under his breath.

Lady Shaftesbury wasted no time with her greeting. "Your grace, how *unexpected* to see you here this evening."

Miss Grant fluttered her lashes, looking down at the floor before giving him a demure smile. I was certain I had never made that expression in my life. Was that what I had been doing wrong?

I released an upward breath into my curls. The room was far too hot. My chest itched beneath the embroidery of my gown, and my lungs could hardly expand. I didn't want to listen to their conversation, so thankfully Charlie came to retrieve me.

Henrietta gaped at me as she approached. "You look stunning, Leonora. Truly. That color matches your eyes perfectly."

"Thank you." I said with a smile, my voice a little breathless.

Lady Shaftesbury was still rambling on about something to Timothy, but I caught him looking in my direction.

Charlie brought me to Sir Daniel, then to Lord Fulshaw, allowing a brief conversation with each of the men. I was introduced to everyone in the room before we all proceeded to dinner. Timothy sat in the seat of honor, and I was on the long side of the table between two strangers. The first course was a vegetable soup served with bread.

When the doors opened to serve the second course, my nose wrinkled.

Plate upon plate of fish were brought in. My stomach turned. Could the evening be any more painful than it already was? Thankfully my stays were too tight to fully inhale the stench as my meal was placed in front of me. The silver skin of the fish was still intact, and when I poked it with my fork, the flesh flaked off onto my plate.

I looked up, catching Timothy's gaze. A smile twitched on his lips.

"After my days in the navy, I fell in love with this particular meal," Sir Daniel said to the entire table with a proud smile. "I hope you enjoy it."

The other guests began eating. I poked at my fish with my fork, moving the pieces around as I conversed with the gentleman beside me. My gaze wandered to Timothy. I expected to see him happily devouring his meal, perhaps throwing me an amused smile, but instead, I found his fish untouched.

I watched him pick up his fork and move a piece of fish to one side of his plate, then the other, before setting it down again.

He caught me watching, and only then did he take a minuscule bite from his plate. The man beside him asked him a question, and I saw the grimace on Timothy's brow as he swallowed. He immediately picked up his water and took a large gulp.

My eyes narrowed.

By the time dessert was brought in, that one minuscule bite was still all he had taken.

The women removed to the drawing room after dinner and the men stayed back for port. I tapped my foot on the rug, staring at the open doorway with a scowl. Miss Grant and her mother stared at the same doorway with perfect smiles, as if Timothy might materialize at any moment.

When he did finally step through the doorway, Miss Grant fluttered her lashes again, throwing a flirtatious glance in his direction. There was an open seat beside her, and I wouldn't have been surprised if she reached out a hand and patted it.

I watched him with narrowed eyes as he made his way across the room and sat in that very chair.

My head ached. I had laced my emotions up tight, but

they threatened to spill over. I tried to fill my lungs, but they wouldn't fully expand, my ribs aching. I needed a breath of fresh air.

I stood, rushing toward the open drawing room door. I escaped into the corridor, not stopping until I was all the way outside in the night air. My senses diluted when the voices of the guests were far behind me. I reached the side of the row of townhouses, tucking myself into the dark corner.

"Nora?" The deep voice came from down the street, nearly lost in the clamor of horse hooves from a passing carriage. How had I known he would follow me? I peered out from around the brick wall, my heart racing.

Timothy rounded the corner, his rushed movements halting once his gaze settled on me. "Is something wrong? Are you unwell?"

I ignored him, shoving both hands against his chest. He staggered back a step, and I glared at him. "You don't like fish!"

His eyes widened with shock. "Nora—"

"You didn't touch your fish at dinner." My eyes stung with sudden tears.

"I wasn't hungry."

I found his eyes in the dark. Backlit by the moon, I could hardly make out the features of his face. I, on the other hand, felt completely exposed by the moonbeams. "When you traded your meal for mine at the inn, you claimed that you loved fish. You said that *I* was doing you a favor." I bit back tears of frustration. "You must have been so hungry." I sniffed, recalling the pallor of his face the next morning when he had slept on that old, sunken bed with the spiders and gone without dinner so I could eat beef and sleep comfortably. Angry tears seeped out of my eyes. I advanced toward him. "Why would you do that? *Why* would you do that for me?" I knew the answer, but I was desperate to hear him say it.

I had never seen him more vulnerable. I had caught him with one secret of many, and he couldn't escape this time. He looked down at the cobblestones. "We should not be seen together. Come back inside."

His demanding tone snapped a cord inside me. Just months before, I had been determined to show Timothy how I felt. I had even been brave enough to ask him to kiss me. So where had my determination gone? I didn't want to marry Mr. Walker, or Sir Daniel, or Mr. Calcot, or Lord Fulshaw. Who was I trying to fool? If it was a choice between sacrificing my pride by declaring my feelings to Timothy first, I would do it. No one else could do it for me. After a year of relying on Timothy to protect and educate me, I couldn't rely on him any longer. Confessing my feelings was my risk to take, just as much as it was his.

All he ever did was give. Give, give, give.

It was my turn.

"What would happen if we *were* seen together?" I asked. "Would a scandal be assumed? Would you be honor bound to marry me in order to spare my reputation?" I took a step closer. "I must confess, I am not afraid of that outcome." I tilted my chin upward. My face burned, but the words could not be unsaid. "In fact, I welcome it." I held his gaze, daring him to cause a scandal if he wished to. Every inch of me wished to. Desire coursed through me in waves. I had spent days thinking he had abandoned me, and now he had come to London only to confuse me further. "Admit that you hate fish as much as I do." I shook as I drew my next breath. "Admit that you love me as much as I love you." My voice was quiet enough to pass for a whisper, and for a moment I wondered if he had even heard me.

His eyes flooded with shock. He stared at me for several seconds. And then he took one step forward, both hands surrounding my face. Within my next breath, he was kissing me, fingers buried in my hair. His lips were firm and determined, but they couldn't have been more so than mine. I clung to his jacket, gathering him closer and closer, kissing him until I couldn't breathe. He pulled away suddenly, keeping my face between his hands. "I didn't know you—" His voice broke, and his fingertips traced my eyebrows, then the curve of my cheek. The adoration in his gaze wasn't masked by anything, not even the lack of light. "I didn't know you felt this way."

My fists were still full of his lapels. I loosened my grip, resting my palms on his chest. My throat was raw, my heart beating so hard it hurt. "I have loved you for a long time. I just never thought...well, I thought you would prefer a woman like Miss Grant. Someone regal and well-mannered who would not embarrass you. I never thought you would want...me." My face burned as those words rang true in my ears. My heart was completely bare.

He shook his head, eyes locked on mine. "I have always wanted you."

Tears streamed down my face now. A lifetime of feeling unwanted had led me to this. With each word, Timothy was lifting boulders off my heart.

"I must add that Miss Grant's hair looks like a bird's nest this evening," he whispered.

I laughed, even though I knew it wasn't true.

"I love you." His words brushed an intoxicating breeze against my skin. "And I hate fish."

"I hate it more." I made a sound—a choked laugh, and his lips found mine again in the dark. This kiss was deep and fast, and then he pressed me against the wall. My hands wrapped under his jacket and around his back. He seemed to have something to prove—to create a testament to his words, to ensure there was no doubt in my mind that he loved and wanted me. His kisses trailed across my cheek and jaw, but he stopped short of my neck. The restraint in his eyes set my heart racing all over again.

He pressed a gentle kiss to my lips, and his thumb swiped away a stray tear. "We should go back inside," he said in a quiet voice. "If I marry you, I don't want it to be to spare your reputation."

My head spun. I wasn't thinking clearly. He had still said *if.* The question that had been bothering me for months spilled out of my mouth. "What were you searching for in the North?"

His brow furrowed, and I realized my mistake.

"How did you—"

With my face between his hands, I felt safe. Perhaps too safe, but the truth spilled out just as easily as my question. "I found your old diary when I was looking for the skull. It was stuck in the compartment under the desk in the library." The reality of what I was confessing made my face burn. "I didn't intend to read it, but then I saw my name. I saw how you felt about me, and I saw all the things you wrote about your time in the North. I know that you overheard a conversation between my father and yours before he died." I caught my breath. "I'm sorry, Timothy. I should not have read it." I stopped my words short.

His eyes flashed with realization, and his hands slipped away from my face. The cold air slapped me. He was silent for a long moment. "How long have you known?"

I swallowed, my throat suddenly dry. "Since the day you gave me my final dancing lesson and left Foxwell House. Once I knew how you felt, I couldn't give up hope of marrying you. But I also knew that there was a reason you doubted we could be together."

His scowl made my heart race with regret. "Did you start loving me before or after you read my diary?"

"Before! Long before. I was too afraid to hope that you could ever feel the same. I was shocked. I hardly knew what to do or how to behave around you."

His eyes flashed with pain. "So you asked me to practice kissing you? That wasn't the innocent request you pretended it was."

I gave a frustrated sigh. "I wanted you to finally tell me how you felt. I had read those words, but I still couldn't believe them when you carried on treating me like your ward."

He rubbed one side of his face. "I had to."

"Why?" I begged. "I know you have a secret that was too deep to even share in your own diary. What did you overhear between my father and yours? What answers were you searching for in the North?" My voice shook.

A passing carriage drew us apart, and Timothy nudged me back toward the street. "It is better that you remain ignorant. At least for now."

I shook my head in confusion.

"Go back to the house. Please." Timothy's brow furrowed.

He was angry with me, I could feel it. Could I blame him? He must have been embarrassed and hurt that I had read such personal words. He looked down at the cobblestones, jaw tight. He wouldn't even look at my face.

My cheeks burned as I rushed down the street alone.

CHAPTER 26

My head ached as I prepared to attend my second evening of assembly rooms.

It had been a busy day, yet Timothy's words from the night before still echoed in my mind. I still felt his kiss, but I also felt the betrayal I had seen in his eyes. It stabbed at me, driving a knife of guilt into my chest. Despite my confession of reading his diary, he still hadn't revealed his secrets. If anything, he seemed more determined to keep them.

Anne had purchased me a new gown, despite my reluctance to accept it. It was a deep navy blue, and the neckline scooped lower than anything I had ever worn. I had been assured it was all the rage in London.

Julia tugged the laces on my stays tighter.

"Must you lace me so tightly?" I felt ill, pressing a hand to my ribs. I glanced at my reflection. My eyes bulged even more than my bosoms. I hadn't known they existed so fully until that day. I winced. "If you don't stop tugging, you will slice them in half."

Julia cracked a faint smile before helping me into my dress. I hated to admit it, but her efforts had been worthwhile. The gown flattered my figure. Julia had managed to smooth and pin back my curls. I didn't look like sweet Leonora, who could be molded and controlled, who depended on others to achieve any possible thing. I looked like Anne. I looked regal and elegant, like someone who couldn't be argued with. I looked determined. Strong.

On the inside, I felt ill.

There would be dancing in the ballroom, and the other rooms would be opened to various activities, such as music, gambling, and other games. Henrietta had encouraged me to flirt with Sir Daniel, but I knew Anne had other meddlesome plans. Now that I was wearing the gown she had purchased for me, it became clear that she had chosen that particular dress for a reason. It was stunning, eye catching, and Julia's work with my stays would not hurt my chances of being noticed. Anne didn't know about my conversation with Timothy from the night before. I hadn't breathed a word of it to anyone.

This assembly was even more crowded and far less exclusive than Almack's, and the humid heat of the room stuck to my skin. All my life I had dreamed of attending a party like this, but that dream had become more of a nightmare. The main character of that nightmare was Mr. Walker, who had already spotted me.

He claimed my first dance before I even made it to the other side of the room. I searched the crowd for Timothy, but I didn't see him. Disappointment sank through my stomach. Had I driven him away?

Charlie and Henrietta found us, and Charlie set to work

introducing me to more gentlemen. My head was spinning, my lungs tight and constricted by my stays. I gave polite smiles, but I felt close to vomiting.

After my first dance with Mr. Walker, I was lightheaded. When I started back toward the wall, I stopped in my tracks. Timothy was there, and Lady Shaftesbury and Miss Grant surrounded him. Miss Grant laughed at something he said, and her mother looked like she wanted to devour Timothy like a fairy cake. I cringed. I knew how he felt about me, and that there was nothing between him and Miss Grant, but there was still nothing that could tempt me to join their conversation.

I missed the days when Timothy and I could be alone together, when we could talk whenever we pleased. Here in London, it was impossible. I wanted to apologize again, but I knew I would end up begging him to tell me what he was thinking and planning. Was he going to marry me or not? A pang of grief struck my heart. What if there was still a reason he couldn't?

Waves of heat washed over my skin, and I nearly lost my balance. I couldn't see where Anne had gone, so I wandered out of the ballroom alone. That was becoming a habit of mine.

I made my way down the corridor. The cool air sent chills over my arms, and I caught my breath in the open doorway of one of the other rooms. An empty sofa near the door looked welcoming, so I stepped inside. All my training had taught me not to wander away from my chaperone, but the risk of fainting in the middle of a ballroom called for an exception.

With deep, slow breathing, I managed to relax, but the feeling didn't last long.

Across the room, a group of men sat around a table, a chess board at the center. A jolt of panic shot through me when I saw that one of them was familiar.

Mr. Ball. His gaze locked on mine before I had a chance to hide. What the devil was he doing in London? He must have left the North shortly after we had. Of all the hoards of people in Town, how did I end up in the same room as my worst enemy? My face drained. My muscles twitched, unsure if it would be better to stand, leave, or remain where I sat.

He had seen me, that much was certain. A smile of disbelief curled his lips upward into a sneer. My heart pounded.

There was nothing that would stop him from informing my father of my whereabouts. Dread pulsed through my veins. It was over. I could run away from London again, or I could face the people who wanted to hurt me with all the confidence I had been searching for. If Father found me at this point, what threat could he use against me? Only weeks remained until my birthday. He couldn't threaten me with anything that I wasn't prepared and willing to lose. Even if he wouldn't marry me, Timothy would ensure I was safe. He wouldn't abandon me.

My thoughts swirled fast, and I stood on shaky legs. I was no longer lightheaded. I didn't want to run or hide anymore. And after thinking it through, I realized I no longer had anything to lose.

I squared my shoulders and walked toward Mr. Ball.

At my approach, the other gentlemen at the table glanced up, and I felt their gazes sweep over me. I didn't make eye contact with any of them. Only Mr. Ball. Anger boiled inside me, and I hoped it was reflected in my eyes.

"Lady Leonora, what a surprise to see you in Town." He

stood, walking around the table to approach me. His large hazel eyes were glazed, and I smelled the brandy on his breath. I examined my emotions, and the absence of fear was empowering. His eyes traced over my figure with a gleam of approval.

My stomach lurched.

"What brought you here, I wonder?" he asked in a sardonic tone.

My nostrils flared. "I wanted a change of scenery."

"Did you? Hmm. I think your father should like to know about that."

"He would." I held my chin high. "Perhaps you should tell him."

A twinge of confusion marked Mr. Ball's brow. "Where is your chaperone?"

"Dancing." I shrugged, as if it were completely acceptable to be all alone at the assembly rooms. I scanned the table, passing a glance at all the men who Mr. Ball had been sitting with. Mr. Elmore was among them, as well as many strangers I had never seen before. They all observed our conversation. I nodded toward the chess board. "I should like to challenge you to a match, Mr. Ball."

Two of the men laughed under their breath.

"You would like to challenge *me*?" Mr. Ball gave a deep cackle.

I nodded. "Yes. Unless you are afraid you'll lose."

The men had turned in their chairs now, watching with rapt attention.

There was no question that he was skilled at chess, but I had played countless matches with Anne at Foxwell House. And it was clear that Mr. Ball was drunk. Drunk enough to be a little less adept at the game, but unfortunately not quite drunk enough to forget that he had seen me in London.

"Not in the slightest." Mr. Ball motioned toward an open chair, and I took it. He sat across from me. My heart raced, but I sat tall, hiding any nerves from my expression.

I made the first move. Mr. Ball followed. The men at the table leaned forward to catch a closer glimpse of the board. My senses heightened as I focused, applying all the tricks Mr. Ball had taught Anne and me, but with a twist that I hoped he wouldn't recognize. The strategy I used was the same one I had used against Anne when I had beat her.

After fifteen minutes, a bead of perspiration had formed on Mr. Ball's forehead. It was clear that the crowd favored me, because each time I made a clever move, they laughed or cheered, and each time Mr. Ball moved any of his pieces, he received nothing but silence. I held back my smile as I made yet another move toward trapping his king. Several other men and women from the room had gathered to see what had drawn the crowd.

As focused as I was, I hadn't noticed Timothy among them until I glanced up. My heart leaped. He stood at the back of the crowd. When I met his gaze, he started making his way forward. I shook my head ever so slightly. I needed to finish the game.

Timothy's anger was obvious. From his perspective, he would think Mr. Ball had forced me into this match and that I needed rescuing. I needed to prove that I could contend with Mr. Ball on my own—that I wasn't afraid of him, or my father. Determination rose in my chest.

When Timothy reached the front of the crowd, he stopped, crossing his arms. He was itching to lunge forward and tug Mr. Ball up from the table by his collar, I knew it. I could see it in every inch of his face. I begged him with my eyes not to intervene.

And he didn't.

I moved another piece on the board. Mr. Ball wiped his forehead. The crowd applauded. And so did Timothy.

Mr. Ball made another move, but it was pointless. This was it. Mr. Ball was trapped. His teeth gritted as I captured his king.

The crowd applauded, and a few people exchanged money. Had they bet on me or Mr. Ball? There were several bouts of laughter, and no small measure of insulting words rang out about Mr. Ball's loss. I rose from my chair with a curtsy, fighting the smile that pulled on my lips.

Mr. Ball's hands curled into fists on the table. The dark look in his eyes was familiar. I tucked my wrist behind my back, taking a step away from my chair.

He stood, side-stepping away from the table. His glare could have impaled me. He took one step toward me, then another. Timothy pushed his way out of the crowd, moving to stand between us. I couldn't see his face, but I could very well imagine it. He had been eager to flatten Mr. Ball for months.

"Ah, your grace." Mr. Ball shrunk a little in front of Timothy, backing up a step. "I see you've come back for your *betrothed*. Or was she your ward? Did I confuse the two?" His anger seemed to be growing hotter by the second, splotches of red creeping onto his face. "I have never met a more contemptuous, ill-mannered woman in my life," he spat in my direction.

"Yet you wanted to marry her." Timothy said. I heard the quiet rage in his voice.

The crowd whispered at that.

I wrung my hands together, tugging on Timothy's sleeve. "Timothy—" I stopped myself. Addressing him so casually would not be deemed appropriate. As suspected, the room erupted in further whispers and gasps. I pressed my lips together.

Mr. Ball scoffed. "Not anymore. She is a disobedient, untamed little thing that has no business in London. It is good that her father will hear of this. He will take her home and free you of your inconvenience."

Timothy lunged forward, but I caught the back of his jacket. I flung forward, crashing into his back. It was enough to stop him from throwing his fist at Mr. Ball, but only just. "She is *not* an inconvenience to me," Timothy growled. "Why don't you tell everyone here what you did to her wrist? Tell them how she rejected your proposal and you couldn't bear it."

I flinched, half hidden behind Timothy's back.

Mr. Ball's eyes flashed. He threw his fist toward Timothy, but he dodged it, throwing his own directly into Mr. Ball's face. He fell backward, holding his nose.

I gasped. I hadn't even noticed Charlie walk into the room, but he rushed to stand between Timothy and Mr. Ball. Mr. Elmore pulled Mr. Ball away by the upper arm, and Charlie pushed Timothy back several feet. My face burned. I had caused this scene. Everyone whispered and watched as Mr. Elmore tried to calm his friend. A trail of blood seeped out of Mr. Ball's nose.

One woman with a large white feather on her turban whispered to the woman beside her. They were looking in my direction. I realized I still held onto Timothy's jacket.

Charlie raked a hand through his hair, muttering under his breath. "Is that—"

"Mr. Ball," I choked.

I expected Charlie's anger to be directed at me, but he had only arrived to witness Timothy's argument with Mr. Ball, not my chess match.

"Devil take it," Charlie muttered, pulling Timothy out to the corridor by the arm, holding onto my elbow with his other hand. When we were away from the crowd, Charlie whirled to face Timothy. "What were you thinking? He could challenge you to a duel."

"I hope he does." Timothy clenched his jaw.

Charlie gave an exasperated sigh. "Causing a scene like that is exactly what we are here to avoid. Regardless of the fact that Mr. Ball now knows where Leonora is, everyone in that room has something to gossip about."

"It was my fault," I said, stepping in front of Timothy. "I challenged Mr. Ball to a game of chess. When he lost, he was upset, and Timothy was only trying to protect me."

Charlie's eyes flickered to Timothy, then to me. His brow twinged. "You wandered off alone to play a game of chess with the man who poses the greatest threat to your safety?"

"I had to humble him." The excuse fell flat, and I covered my face with my hands.

"She succeeded," Timothy said.

I glanced up at him, catching a glimpse of a smile on his lips.

Charlie laughed under his breath, rubbing one side of his face. "He deserved it, and I'm glad you were able to have your satisfaction. But it does complicate matters." He closed his eyes for a long moment, taking a deep breath. He addressed Timothy. "I will take Leonora home now. Henrietta and Anne are in the ballroom. Will you see them safely out?"

Timothy nodded, his serious expression returning. I

thought of how I had grabbed his jacket and the whispers of the spectators.

Charlie didn't know about that part.

CHAPTER 27

Anne burst through the door of my bedchamber in her chemise the next morning, the front pieces of her hair still tied in rags. She thrust a paper toward me, and I rubbed the sleep from my eyes to read it.

BEHIND

THE FAN

By *Lady Teignmouth*

May 16, 1817

It is a terrible shame when a king loses his crown, but I find it rather more enjoyable when the thief is a woman. Mr.

Christopher ball was bested in a game of chess by Lady Leonora, the daughter of the Marquess of Swindon. As I understand it, Lady Leonora did not take a traditional route in entering the marriage mart, as she is nearly one and twenty, and hasn't yet been presented to the Queen. I consider it my duty to inform all the eligible gentlemen of London of this gem I have discovered. A word of caution, however. Without a dowry, proper chaperone, manners, or considerable beauty, Lady Leonora has only one thing to offer: an adept knowledge of the game of chess.

What more could a man truly want in a wife?

I gasped, glowering at the paper. "How unkind!"

"She was kinder to you than she was to Henrietta," Anne said with a wince. "But keep reading."

I returned my gaze to the page.

Do not be fooled, my dear reader. There is one man who seems to want just that. The Duke of Heywood threw himself between Mr. Ball and Lady Leonora after the match, and my sources have reported that the two men engaged in a fisticuffs match of their own. Lady Leonora clung to the duke's jacket and addressed him informally, which gives me no choice but to assume an attachment exists between them. My advice to the ladies who hope to catch the duke this season is this: Lady Leonora's crown is new. It could still be stolen again.

I dropped the page, and my jaw did the same.

There had been a very valid reason for Anne's wild

rampage into my room that morning. She sat on the edge of my bed. "Do you think this is enough to make him propose?"

I threw my hands in the air. "How could it be? He didn't even propose after he kissed me."

Anne gasped, lunging toward me. "He kissed you?"

I cursed myself under my breath. I had meant to keep that a secret. "Twice," I muttered, a bloom of warmth filling my cheeks.

She demanded more details, and I told her. When I finished, she laughed into her hands. "I cannot believe you were so bold. And I cannot believe that Lady Teignmouth thinks your crown can be stolen."

I flattened my palms against my cheeks to cool them. "I also told Timothy about the diary." I paused. "He might never want to speak to me again."

Anne untied the rags in her hair, shaping the curls with her fingers. "Don't be so dramatic. After seeing this publication, all of London will be expecting an engagement between the two of you. I predict that he will be at the door at any moment to propose."

I wagged a finger. "Your predictions have been wrong in the past."

My nerves were on edge as I changed and prepared for the day ahead. In my white morning dress, I hurried down the stairs, planning to perch by the front window to watch for any visitors. Before I reached the entryway, a knock sounded on the door.

My heart leaped.

Anne raced around the corner, meeting me just in time to see who stood behind the threshold.

A mixture of relief and disappointment assailed me. It was just Charlie.

He removed his top hat, slipping inside to stand on the checkered floors. He held a familiar paper in his hand.

"You saw it too?" I chewed my lower lip, wringing my fingers together.

"Everyone has seen it." Charlie marched inside, glowering at the floor. "And Timothy has subsequently disappeared."

I blinked, dread twisting my stomach. "Disappeared?"

"I awoke this morning and he was gone. He left a note telling me that he has traveled to Somerset to speak with Father."

"Someone needs to shackle that man to a chair," I muttered.

Charlie nodded his agreement. "I'm not certain if he plans to try to placate Father or bribe him. He thinks Father plans to do something drastic. This publication might reach him just as quickly as Mr. Ball's note, and he will be furious at both of us." Charlie grimaced.

"Why would Timothy leave without telling me?" I scowled at the floor.

Charlie released a tense breath. "The implications of the gossip column might have also made him want to escape. Now all of Town believes there is an attachment between you."

I closed my eyes, exhaling through my lips. "The implications are true." I stole a peek at Charlie's face.

He stepped forward, deep set eyes fixed on me. He seemed to be gathering a response, but I spared him the effort.

"I'm in love with Timothy," I blurted. "And he is in love with me, too."

Charlie was silent for several seconds. It seemed he was finally taking the idea seriously. "How do you know?"

"He told me. And…I read his diary."

Charlie's brows shot upward. "Timothy keeps a diary?"

I scoffed. "Is that really the most surprising part of what I just told you?"

Charlie shook his head. "Sorry. I—" He gathered his wits about him. "I am going to need more of an explanation."

I told him everything. Well, besides the two times Timothy had kissed me.

"There is a secret he's keeping," I said. "That is the only reason I can think of that he hasn't told you about his feelings for me, or expressed his intentions to marry me. It doesn't make sense."

Charlie scowled. He had hardly said a word, absorbing every detail of the story. "If he has always felt this way, he could have eloped with you from the moment he learned of Father's plan with Mr. Verwood."

"He never knew how I felt." I tugged on the fingertips of my gloves. "Perhaps, like you, he wanted me to have the chance to fall in love."

Charlie sighed. "I will speak with him."

"No!" I practically jumped out of my seat. "I think he is angry with me for reading his diary. He might not want to marry me at all anymore." My heart stung.

Charlie laughed under his breath. "Do you know him at all? He is nothing if not steadfast. If he loved you two days ago, I assure you, he loves you today. Knowing that you read his diary is not going to change that."

Anne piped in. "That's what I said."

I paced in a line with my hands on my hips. "But if there's a reason he can't marry me, then even his love for me can't change that."

A deep crease marked Charlie's brow. "What the devil could it be?"

"In his diary he mentioned that you unintentionally gave him direction to seek the answers he was looking for. That was shortly before he bought the hunting lodge in the North. Do you recall what you might have said to him?"

Charlie rubbed his jaw in thought. "The only connection I have ever had to the North was Mother. I do remember Timothy asking about her."

I practically jumped toward him. "What did he ask?" It was the first hint I had ever collected.

"He asked how often she visited Northumberland. I was too young to remember her absences, but after growing up to see the sort of man our father is, I imagine she traveled there as often as she could to escape him."

"Father must have loved her though," I said. "If he hadn't, then why would he resent me and blame me for her death?"

Charlie pinched the bridge of his nose. "He might have loved her, but that doesn't mean *she* loved *him*. He has always been cruel. I can't imagine that cruelty didn't extend to his treatment of her."

My heart ached for my mother. She had fled to the North to escape him just as I had. A chill ran over my spine. What connection could that have to Timothy's secret?

"Are you going to follow Timothy to Somerset?" I asked.

Charlie shook his head. "No. I am going to stay here with you to ensure you are safe. No harm shall come upon you. If Father comes, we will contend with him together. Let us hope Timothy can do something to prevent it. Only heaven knows what he's planning."

I gave a slow nod, even though I disagreed.

I was fairly certain heaven didn't even know.

CHAPTER 28

I stared at the droplets of rain on the window of my bedchamber, counting them one by one. It was how I entertained myself while I watched for Timothy's carriage on the street.

He had been gone for a week.

A week without invitations, callers, or parties. Not even Mr. Walker had come calling. At least I could thank Lady Teignmouth for one thing.

I didn't know who to expect on my doorstep first, Timothy, or my father, but I was prepared for either one. I checked Lady Teignmouth's columns each morning, and since I had started staying away from public gatherings, the passages had been focused on other poor victims who had misbehaved in one way or another. My reputation had been hurt, but it wasn't beyond repair. In time, society could forgive my follies.

I prayed that Timothy could forgive my follies as well.

As had become my daily routine, I gathered at the breakfast table with Anne and picked up the latest issue of Behind the Fan.

. . .

BEHIND

THE FAN

By *Lady Teignmouth*

May 23, 1817

Just when I thought I had served you the most delicious tea of the Season, I now realize I have neglected the sugar. At the bequest of the Marquess of Swindon, I bring to light yet another layer to the failings of Lady Leonora.

Although it would seem we shall no longer call her that.

Young Leonora is the child of no one. Her own father has declared her illegitimacy, no longer claiming her as his own. Was it her behavior in the assembly rooms that caused him to make this shocking revelation? It should come as no surprise that she does not behave as a marquess's daughter ought. She is, in fact, not one.

The Duke of Heywood has not been seen in London since the evening of the chess match. I must therefore conclude that he came to his senses, or perhaps learned of Lady Leonora's illegitimacy before the rest of us. Rejoice, young ladies of the ton, the duke remains a bachelor, and a sensible one. If he ever returns to London, catch him while you can. He never stays for long.

. . .

I stopped reading. My head was light, and I had to hold onto the edge of my chair. I pressed a hand to my chest as I tried to comprehend what I had just read. I knew what the words implied, but I could hardly believe it was true. Dozens of questions battled for attention in my head, and my stomach threatened to cast up my breakfast. "Anne—" I turned to her, my voice a weak whisper. "Do you think it's true?"

Her face was pale. "If it's true, it would explain how you were raised." Her brows contracted, and she wrapped an arm around my shoulders, pulling me close. "I'm sorry, Leonora. You should not have found out this way. But why would he publicize this?"

I was rigid, my senses completely overwhelmed. "To ruin me." My voice sounded far away, and Anne was shrinking into a blurred ring in my vision. If I wasn't the daughter of a marquess, then I wasn't Lady Leonora. I was just plain Leonora. I had been hidden away in my room my entire life because *Lord Swindon* hadn't cared to give me the opportunities that he would his real daughter. He didn't resent me only because my mother had died giving birth to me—he resented me because even after all of that pain, I wasn't even his.

My heart pounded.

I could hardly grasp onto any of my spinning thoughts for long enough to understand them.

Anne continued trying to understand though, speaking her guesses aloud. "He must have either heard from Mr. Ball that you were in London, or read Lady Teignmouth's column about your chess game. He might have been ashamed of your behavior and angry that you defied him by hiding in London, so he thought to ruin your chance of marrying anyone else."

My chest ached, deep inside. I kept my hand pressed to it,

fighting the tears that stung my eyes. "Because no one would risk their own reputation by marrying someone illegitimate."

Not even Timothy?

The question rang in my head, over and over.

For the first time in my life, the way my father had treated me made sense. It was still cruel, but it explained why he treated Charlie as his own and me like I wasn't.

I stared at the floral wallpaper across the room, unable to blink or even draw a breath. Part of me sagged with relief at the idea that I was not the daughter of Lord Swindon. The other part made me feel like an imposter in my own skin. I wrapped my arms around myself to keep the broken, confused things inside me from spilling out.

"If not the marquess, then who could your father be?" Anne asked. "Could this be the secret Timothy was keeping from you?"

The thought had already crossed my mind, but it hurt. Pain spread through my chest and burrowed in my heart. If Timothy had known for years that I was illegitimate, had that been the reason that he couldn't marry me? A duke marrying an illegitimate woman would attract no small measure of scorn, but it hurt to think that scorn was enough to keep him from choosing me.

I sat for several minutes, my mind racing, until Charlie came to the door with a copy of his own of Lady Teignmouth's article. His curls were askew, his features full of shock.

"Did you know?" I asked in a weak voice.

"No." He sat down heavily on the chair beside me. "I had no idea."

"It makes sense." I swallowed hard, reaching for a glass of water. My hands shook as I brought the cup to my lips. I set it down with a clatter. "He has never treated me like his daughter. Why would he not publicize this sooner?"

"My guess would be that he still thought he could benefit from you. Mr. Verwood was willing to pay a high price to have you as a wife. Father has been raising you to bargain with. I assume he kept your parentage a secret all this time because it would reflect badly on him if society knew that his wife…" Charlie looked down at the table.

"Had someone else." I twisted my hands together. My head hurt as I tried to put the pieces of the puzzle together.

"Yes." Charlie scowled. "Mother was mistreated by Father, but I never would have guessed that she had been involved with another man."

I blinked, wiping the tears that escaped my eyes. I had been holding my emotions together, but now it was too overwhelming. Charlie was my half-brother. We no longer shared a father. I was not a marquess's daughter. In the eyes of society, I was the child of no one. Charlie and I had both inherited our mother's curls, but the lightness of my hair had seemingly come from nowhere. Both our eyes were blue, but my short nose and wide smile didn't look like Mother's, nor Charlie's, nor the man I had always believed to be my father's. Those parts of me, and countless others, had come from somewhere else. From *someone* else.

It shook me.

"No one will marry me now," I said in a broken voice. "This news has ruined me."

Charlie didn't deny it. He rubbed one side of his face. "It doesn't bode well for your success, no. But look at the positive side of the situation. Father has made it so he can never threaten you again. If he no longer claims you as his daughter, then he has no right to sign on your marriage papers. You are free of him earlier than expected."

I wanted to smile, to celebrate the supposed victory, but I couldn't. Pain enveloped me from head to toe. My tears continued to fall, and Charlie wrapped his arms around me. "I'm sorry, Leonora. I wish I would have known."

"I don't have a father." The numb words spilled out. Was not having a father any worse than having a cruel father who didn't love me? The answer was simple, but the feelings in my chest were too complicated to sort through.

"But you still have a brother." Charlie pulled back, meeting my gaze. "I am not any less your brother than I was yesterday."

"Half less." I mumbled, wiping my cheek.

"No." He gave me a stern look. "Do not say that."

I laughed a little, and it made me feel lighter. I scrunched my forehead in thought. This secret must have been related to what Timothy had overheard between my father and his, and why he had gone to the North in search of answers. What could have made Timothy believe that he could never marry me?

Dread spiraled into my stomach, settling with a heavy thud. Calling Charlie my half-brother had sparked a horrible thought. I didn't dare say it aloud.

Charlie and I still shared a mother. But had Timothy believed...we shared a father?

I choked on a breath, shaking my head.

The late Duke of Heywood had been known for his constant search for new mistresses. Could my mother have been one of them? Is that what Timothy had overheard—my father accusing his of such an offense?

"Leonora?" Charlie turned my face toward him with one hand, staring into my eyes. "Are you unwell?"

My skin was cold, and I couldn't speak for fear of interrupting my thoughts. They were finally moving in the right direction, and they raced faster than the horses at the Epsom Derby.

If Timothy had overheard that I was illegitimate, and that the late duke was accused of being my father, he would assume he could not love me.

He would assume we could never marry, just as he had written in his diary.

But then Charlie had given him hope by stating that our mother often escaped to the North to visit a relative. After his father's death was when Timothy bought the hunting lodge. Had he been searching for *my* father in Northumberland?

That must have been how Timothy knew so many villagers. He had been searching for anyone who had known my mother.

My heart galloped when I recalled my conversation with Mr. Prout. He had confirmed that Timothy had found what he was looking for.

I pictured the fisherman's pale, wild hair, blue eyes, and wide smile—the way he had stared at me on our first meeting. He had called me by my Christian name that night at dinner. Timothy had seemed determined to introduce him to me, and had even invited him to Foxwell House. I pressed a hand to my chest, taking a deep breath.

"Anne," I choked out, whirling in my chair to face her. "I think I know who my father is."

CHAPTER 29

I took a rather vicious bite of a tea cake. I had never been so impatient in my life.

Charlie and Henrietta had joined Anne and me for afternoon tea. I hadn't left the house in three days. Ever since the publication of the gossip column, Charlie had advised me to stay out of sight, letting the news settle among the people in Town.

"Where the devil is Timothy?" I asked with a sigh.

Charlie and his wife exchanged a glance. "He is probably still in Somerset," Charlie said.

I took a sip of tea, glaring at the slowly dissolving cube of sugar.

I was fairly certain I had puzzled out Timothy's secrets on my own, but I was desperate to confirm my answers with him. I wanted to strike him squarely in the chest for not telling me the truth. Then, I wanted to apologize again for reading his diary. After that, I wanted to kiss him and kiss him until we both forgot why we had been angry. The problem was he was not here, and he showed no signs of returning. I had been anxious thinking that Father had somehow injured him or challenged him to a duel. I corrected my wording in my mind. *Lord Swindon*, not my father.

My suspicions about Mr. Prout hadn't been confirmed, but I couldn't deny the likelihood of the possibility that he was indeed my father. Each time I considered it, a confirming chill ran over my arms and across my shoulder blades. My mother might have been miserable in her marriage, but she also must have been a romantic like me. She had found her true love in the North. I had been a result of that.

To think that Timothy hadn't given up his search, going from village to village, year after year, brought a surge of emotion to my throat. I swallowed a gulp of hot tea to clear it. He had stopped at nothing to prove that I wasn't his half-sister. A shudder crossed over my shoulders.

Thank the heavens I wasn't.

I took a deep breath, addressing my teacup more than my companions. "Perhaps Timothy has seen sense and he doesn't want an illegitimate woman as his wife. Lady Teignmouth will have a great deal to say on the subject if he marries me." I chewed fast as I ate yet another cake. "He would be better off marrying someone else, and he must believe that too, otherwise he would have proposed by now."

"You do have a point," Charlie said in an offhand voice.

I froze, wiping crumb of cake from my lip. Tears sprung up in my eyes. I had been nothing short of a mess the past several days. "Do I?"

"Yes." Charlie took a sip of tea. "He might never come back."

I stared at him, noting a mischievous gleam in his eye. It was gone in an instant, hidden behind a frown. "It would be a great sacrifice for him to marry a woman that society doesn't approve of," he continued.

"You're right." My heart sank further. I almost picked up another cake.

A small smile broke through Charlie's facade. "But when has Timothy ever cared what society thinks?"

I looked up, a glimmer of hope jostling my optimism.

Charlie didn't say another word, though he did share a few glances with his wife. I knew a secret when I saw one. It was clear that they had one of their own; it bounced between their gazes as they sipped their tea.

I narrowed my eyes.

Henrietta sat forward with a thoughtful look. "Leonora, Anne, the weather looks delightful. Would you like to take a turn about the square with me? I know Leonora hasn't left the house in days, and the streets look quite empty at the moment."

I followed her gaze out the window. The sun shone down on the cobblestones, the nearby trees casting dappled shadows. A breath of fresh air had never sounded more divine. I gave an eager nod.

We fetched our bonnets and stepped outside. I took a deep breath, tipping my face up toward the sky. A light breeze carried the scent of flowers to my nose, and my ears filled with the soft chirping of birds and buzzing of insects. My worry over Timothy broke through the temporary peace I felt. I wanted to speculate and discuss with Anne and Henrietta again. Why didn't anyone else seem as worried as I was? They walked arm in arm beside me, whispering as they glanced in my direction.

The moment I caught them, they stopped.

I almost questioned them, but then Anne waved me

forward. "Look at these roses! They're your favorite, are they not?"

I turned toward the bush, touching the soft velvet petal of a white rose. The simple beauty captivated me. I circled my finger around each petal, the mindless motion calming the turmoil inside me. "Mr. Walker didn't think I seemed the sort of woman to like roses," I said with a hard laugh. "He advised me to like daisies instead." I looked up, my brow furrowing. Anne and Henrietta were nowhere in sight. Had they slipped behind the bush? I took a step forward, craning my neck around the leaves.

Before I could see the other side, two hands wrapped around my face, covering my eyes.

I gasped. I tried to jerk away, but then a deep voice came close to my ear. "Stand and deliver."

My heart pounded hard. My first instinct had been to writhe and scream, but the familiar voice made me freeze where I stood. I held still, a confused smile breaking over my face. "I don't have anything to give you, sir."

"I'd wager you do."

My vision was blocked, but with Timothy's voice so close to my ear, I was content not to move a muscle.

"And what if I refuse?" My voice was breathless.

"Then I shall have to kidnap you a second time." He wrapped one arm around the front of my waist, hauling me against him and lifting my feet off the ground. The other hand still covered my eyes as he spun me around and carried me several paces. I shrieked, laughing when he finally uncovered my eyes and lifted me into a carriage. I fell into the soft cushions with a thud. I blinked, disoriented, as Timothy climbed in behind me and closed the door.

His face came into focus—soft brown eyes, wide smile,

golden brown hair with a wayward strand on his forehead. He sat on the seat across from me, leaning forward. The fading afternoon sunlight cast golden hues on his skin. I couldn't look away. I gave a laugh of disbelief. Tears sprung to my eyes, as was becoming a habit of mine. "You are ridiculous." I swatted at his leg. "You frightened me!"

"I wouldn't be a proper kidnapper if I didn't." He stole my hand from my lap, pressing a kiss to the back of it. "Will you forgive me?"

I stared at his lips, then his smiling eyes, and I nearly flung myself across the carriage toward him. "Did Charlie help you plan this?"

"It was mostly Henrietta. I arrived in London this morning, and once she knew of my plans for the day, she suggested something more...theatrical."

My brows lifted in curiosity. "What were your plans for the day?"

"To knock on your door and ask you to marry me." His eyes locked on mine, and my head spun.

"That would have been less alarming," I said in a breathless voice.

"But far less entertaining." His eyes gleamed with amusement. "I also planned to explain everything to you, but Charlie told me that you had already puzzled it out on your own."

"Yes, I did." I lifted my chin. "I had to, since you showed no signs that you would ever tell me yourself. Why did you keep it a secret for so long?"

"I didn't know the right time to tell you. I didn't even find Mr. Prout until last year, just before I saw you during your visit to Bath. It was the first time I had hope for you."

"Does my fath—Lord Swindon—know about Mr. Prout?" I asked.

Timothy nodded. "He does now. Up until last week, he still suspected that my father was the one responsible for your birth. Until I found Mr. Prout, I had no way to prove that he wasn't. I planned to tell Lord Swindon sooner, so I would have a chance at obtaining his permission to marry you, but then I learned of his bargain with Mr. Verwood, and it… complicated matters. I had to come up with another solution." He exhaled slowly, raking a hand over his hair.

I stared at him, my tears still hovering on the edge of my eyes. He had done so much for me. I could hardly keep track of it all.

"Keeping you at arm's length at Foxwell House was the most difficult thing I have ever done. I couldn't tell Charlie that I wanted to marry you as soon as you came of age, not while I was acting as your guardian." He brushed his thumb across the back of my hand in slow circles as he spoke, and it was far too distracting.

I sniffed, laughing under my breath. "I don't think Charlie would have cared. He would have been overjoyed to know that I had someone willing to rescue me from the pressure of a Season. You could have made a plan to elope with me, or at least told Charlie your intentions for when I came of age. Why didn't you? I wouldn't have had to meet Mr. Walker or Sir Daniel or anyone else." My confusion had been festering, and now all the questions were spilling out.

Timothy shook his head. "I couldn't do that, not when I was unsure of your feelings. The entire point of keeping you hidden from Lord Swindon was to provide you with the opportunity to choose for yourself who you would marry. I didn't want to sway you or pressure you. I wanted you to choose the man you wanted, without any influence from anyone else. Once I knew how you felt, I could have taken you to Gretna Green, but I was afraid that your father would use your illegitimacy as a weapon against you the moment he discovered you were no longer in his control. I hoped to avoid your parentage coming to light at all, but when Lady Teignmouth published her first column, I wanted to speak with your father before he came to find you. I was afraid he would see the gossip about your attachment to me and publicize something concerning his false accusations against my father. If society thought we were siblings…that would be far worse. I wanted to explain what I knew about Mr. Prout, so that's why I rushed off to Somerset."

He wiped a tear from my cheekbone that I hadn't even noticed. "As soon as he learned the truth though, he refused accept my plea to keep the secret. He wanted to punish you somehow. Instead, he gave you the freedom you have been waiting for. He can't control you anymore. Who you spend your life with should have always been your choice. It still is."

His hand cupped my cheek, and I covered his fingers with mine, holding tight. "It's you." I grinned. "It has always been you." My eyes were wide with sincerity. The raw adoration in his gaze made my breath stick in my lungs for a long moment.

He leaned forward and pressed a fast, hard kiss to my lips, then another. He smiled against my mouth, and those two quick kisses turned into at least three more. He shifted to my side of the carriage. With one tug, he undid my bonnet ribbons and tossed it off my head. I laughed. He held my face between his hands, and he took his time kissing me, saving his words for a later moment. I felt the movement of his jaw beneath my hands, the rough stubble scratching around my lips. My heart soared. I pushed against his chest so I could look at his eyes. "I'm sorry for reading your diary…but I'm also glad I did. It gave me a reason to hope. It gave me permission to accept how madly in love with you I have always been. I never would have guessed you were such a romantic. I nearly swooned when I read that your 'heart beats for me.'"

"I still can't believe you found that old thing," he said with a groan. "How did you open the compartment in the desk? When I last placed the diary inside, the door sealed itself. I wasn't able to open it again."

"I was looking for the skull, so Chesley helped me pry the hatch open with a poker."

Timothy's face lifted with surprise. "Chesley causes nearly as much trouble as you."

I grinned, inching closer to him. "He only causes trouble at my bequest."

"You are far too persuasive," Timothy grumbled. But he was still smiling. "I would do anything for you, and you know it."

"Even elope with me to save my reputation?" I felt daring, so I pressed a kiss to the corner of his jaw.

His throat bobbed with a swallow, and he looked a warning at me. The smile on his lips made its way to my neck, and he kissed all the way up to my mouth again. I laughed. He pulled back fast to look in my eyes. "Not that. You deserve a proper wedding. Although I don't *require* your father's permission to marry, he is my friend. I would like to give the two of you a proper introduction and ask for your hand."

My father. It took me a moment to realize what he meant.

"I still can't believe Mr. Prout is my father." I shook my head, scrunching my eyes closed. It was all too strange.

"What I can't believe is that you are the daughter of a fisherman, yet you hate fish."

I shrugged. "He isn't fond of them either if he kills them for a living."

Timothy threw back his head with a laugh.

"Tell me more about him," I said.

"He loved your mother." Timothy caressed my cheek softly, pressing a kiss to my lips in the middle of his words, as if it were perfectly natural to do so. "And she loved him. She wanted to annul her marriage with Lord Swindon, but for Charlie's sake, she stayed. When she became pregnant with you, she stopped going back to the North. She was so distant with Lord Swindon by then that he knew the child wasn't his without a doubt. That's when he blamed my father. Mr. Prout didn't even know you were born until I found him."

My eyes widened. "Really?"

Timothy nodded. "Your mother had her secrets."

"Hmm. Just like you."

He sighed. "I would have told you eventually, but it was better that everyone be kept in the dark. The moment a secret like this spreads, your reputation is ruined forever. You will never be accepted here in London again."

"Thankfully I don't like London." I twisted my fingers together. "But are you certain you wish to be tied to me? Your reputation will also suffer. Surely your mother didn't intend for you to marry someone of my...situation."

"Nora—you are the only one I have ever wanted to marry." His eyes locked on mine, and butterflies fluttered through my stomach. "I don't care what anyone else thinks."

I smiled. "You're a duke, so you can do what you want?"

He laughed and took my face between his hands, pressing a kiss to my forehead, then the tip of my nose. My heart had never been more full. It was nearly bursting, and fresh happy tears stung behind my eyes.

"Precisely."

"Are we going back to the North?"

Timothy nodded.

"Do you know what else is northward?" I raised one eyebrow. "Gretna Green."

His smile grew, and he shook his head. "A proper wedding, Nora."

"No." A thrill raced across my skin. "An elopement would be far more romantic, would it not? You have already kidnapped me, so it would only be fitting if you stole me away to Gretna." I begged him with my eyes. "Imagine what Lady Teignmouth would have to say about that." I gave a wicked chuckle. "Then we might return to Somerset to see your mother, and we will already be married. She won't have the opportunity to judge your choice of wife."

He sighed. "She will be overjoyed that it's you, regardless of the circumstances. She always liked you."

I grinned. "So, are you considering it?"

His hesitant eyes traced over my face. "Is it truly what you want?"

I gave a fast nod. My cheeks ached from smiling so much. "If it means I can marry you sooner, then yes. It will be the perfect ending to the story I plan to write about my year in the North."

Timothy leaned in close, his soft eyes wrapping me up, safe and warm. "Ending? I would rather call it the beginning."

I laughed. "Very well. If we are to have a fresh beginning,

let us agree to never keep secrets from one another again," I said in a stern voice.

He smiled. "That is a good idea."

I bit my lip, remembering something that contradicted my request. "In that case, I have a confession to make."

He raised his eyebrows. "Another one?"

I grinned. It wasn't quite so embarrassing now. "When I asked for a kissing lesson, I mentioned that I had kissed one man before. Do you remember?"

His face fell. "Yes."

I hurried my words, desperate not to awaken his grumpy mood. "It was you." I slapped a hand over my mouth as I laughed. Despite all my effort not to, I still blushed. "When you were thrown from your horse, I thought you were dying. I panicked, and I kissed you. It was when I realized how much you truly meant to me. I was terrified of losing you. I swore I would never tell you."

His round eyes made me laugh again. "First Henrietta makes a habit of observing men's breeches, and now you have a habit of giving secret kisses to unconscious men?"

I swatted at his arm. "Timothy!"

He laughed, a teasing grin on his face. He intertwined his fingers with mine. "I'm relieved that it was me. I only wish I had been awake to experience it."

"I will try to only kiss you while you are awake from now on."

He was still laughing, and I had to stop myself from climbing onto his lap and kissing him senseless. He looked far too endearing with his wide smile and wayward strand of hair. Emotion struck me hard in the chest as I thought of where I would be without him. I would be trapped, lost, and alone. He had saved me time and time again, and he had given me more than I could ever repay. As I looked into his eyes, I could hardly believe that he loved *me*.

Thankfully, I had the rest of my life to be reminded. Timothy showed his love even more than he spoke it, which made it all the more true.

CHAPTER 30

EPILOGUE

N*ora's Diary*
       August 10, 1817

I often forget that I am a duchess. I find it quite humorous that I am addressed as 'your grace' when I have never once been graceful in my entire life. Thankfully the people of the North don't seem to care whether I behave like a duchess or a fisherman's daughter. Most of the time I own up to being a combination of both.

The dowager Duchess of Heywood, Timothy's mother, joined us at Foxwell House to enjoy the sea air and the benefits it may have for her health. We plan to stay in the North for the remainder of the summer months before returning to Timothy's estate. I can hardly believe I am mistress of such a grand place. Mr. Prout visits us often at Foxwell House, and I notice our similarities more each time I see him. He tells me stories of Mother. As I come to know him, I feel that I come to know her. I love every moment.

And Timothy. I love him. I have never loved anyone more.

He is my dearest friend and also my husband, which I realize should be one and the same. I cannot believe I was prepared to settle for anything less. He is my home, my sanctuary, and my greatest gift. Just yesterday I laughed until my belly ached simply because he had a streak of treacle pudding on his cheek. All he has to do is smile, and I cannot help but do the same. Waking up beside him each morning is my favorite part of the day, and I have to blink twice to confirm I'm not dreaming. He is the most noble, kind, handsome man I have ever known. I can hardly believe he is mine. There's nothing more I could ever want.

I didn't think it was possible to be so happy.

A voice from behind made me jump. "What are you writing?"

I slapped my hands over the page, smudging the wet ink. "Nothing."

"I thought I saw my name." Timothy bent over, nestling his chin onto my shoulder.

I shielded my diary with both hands, whirling to face him. He wore only his breeches, his bare torso still damp and glistening with bathwater. His hair was wet, and a few droplets rolled down his face and over the muscles in his chest, shoulders, and abdomen. It was funny how attractive I had found that one wayward strand of hair, when now I had the privilege of seeing Timothy in all his different states. The more disheveled the better, in my opinion.

I grinned up at him, pushing the diary farther away from his prying eyes. "It's private."

"Ah…is it your diary?" One dark eyebrow lifted, and I knew what I had to do.

I grabbed my diary and jumped from my chair, making a mad dash for the door.

He caught me by the waist, wrapping his arms all the way around me from behind. I laughed, kicking my legs as he lifted me off the floor. I clutched the diary to my chest. His deep laughter vibrated against me.

My feet touched the floor again, but he didn't let go. He kissed the side of my neck and my cheek in quick succession, pausing to whisper in my ear. "I think you owe me one page." I felt his smile against my skin. He smelled of fresh soap. My arms were weak, and I almost dropped the diary at his feet.

I groaned, squirming in his arms until I faced him. "It's embarrassing."

"Could it be any more embarrassing than my diary? The one you read *without* permission, might I remind you." He gave a wicked smile.

"Timothy! I thought you forgave me."

"I did, but I still think it would be an adequate sign of remorse if you handed that over." He eyed my diary again, but then his gaze shifted back to my face. "You look beautiful, by the way."

My cheeks flushed with surprise. I was still growing accustomed to the flirtatious side of him. I pushed against his chest with a laugh. He must have been lying. My hair stuck out every which way, and I still wore my night dress. "Are you trying to soften my resolve?"

"No, but if it works, I'll try again." He nudged the tip of my nose with his, then captured my lips in a slow kiss that filled my head with fog. He knew exactly how to melt me into a puddle. I gave very little resistance when he reached for the diary. It slipped right out of my hands.

He grinned with triumph, but he still sought permission in my eyes.

"Only one page," I said with a breathless laugh.

He turned to the most recent one, and I bit my fingernail as his gaze scanned over the words I had just written. I prayed that my hands had smudged the words about the treacle pudding.

His smile grew as his eyes moved down the page, and then his jaw tightened. When he looked up, his light brown eyes had turned to liquid. He blinked fast.

I cupped his face in my hands. "Timothy!" He rarely showed such obvious emotion, and it scared me. He had read my honest thoughts, the ones I hadn't meant to share with anyone. Seeing how deeply they had touched him banished my regret at allowing him to read my diary. It was the raw, unfiltered words that were never meant to be shared that told the greatest truth. He had seen my bare heart, just as I had seen his in that old diary under the desk.

"Thank you." His arms encircled me, and he pulled me against his chest.

"For what?" I laughed into his shoulder.

"You have given me everything, Nora, simply by being alive."

I laughed in my throat, tipping my head up to throw him a teasing grin. "You are such a romantic."

He gave a relenting sigh. "Only when it comes to you."

THE NOBLE CHARADES SERIES

The Earl Next Door
The Duke's Diary
The Parlor Game (Summer 2024)

Follow the author on social media to stay in the loop about release dates and news for the Noble Charades series!
Instagram - @ashtyn_newbold_author
Facebook
Newsletter

ALSO BY ASHTYN NEWBOLD

Larkhall Letters Series

Brides of Brighton Series

Standalone novels
To Marry is Madness
In Pursuit of the Painter
The Last Eligible Bachelor
An Unwelcome Suitor
Her Silent Knight
A Heart to Keep

Novellas & Anthologies
The Earl's Mistletoe Match
The Midnight Heiress
At First Sight

ABOUT THE AUTHOR

Ashtyn Newbold grew up with a love of stories. When she discovered Jane Austen books as a teen, she learned she was a sucker for romantic ones. Her first novel was published shortly after high school and she never looked back. When not indulging in sweet romantic comedies and regency period novels (and cookies), she writes romantic stories of her own. Ashtyn also dearly loves to laugh, bake, sing, and do anything that involves creativity and imagination.

Connect with Ashtyn Newbold on these platforms!
INSTAGRAM: @ashtyn_newbold_author
FACEBOOK: Author Ashtyn Newbold
TIKTOK: @ashtynnewboldauthor
ashtynnewbold.com